Something True

This is the second book in a series.

Something Tattered (Book 1)

Something True (Book 2)

SABRINA STARK

CHAPTER 1

I gave the guy at the warehouse door a desperate look. "But why *can't* I go in?"

He was huge, nearly seven feet tall and half as wide. He crossed his beefy arms and said, "Because I don't know you."

I craned my neck to stare up at him. "So?"

"So you don't get in."

Well, that was helpful.

It was nearly midnight, and I was huddled outside the nondescript warehouse with a dozen other poor slobs who'd gotten here too late to get inside without a hassle.

But in my own defense, I was three hours from home in an unfamiliar city. My GPS was on the fritz, and I'd gotten lost somewhere between Zippy's Title Loan and Marvin's Pistol and Pawn.

Behind me, I heard a female voice say, "Hey, are you gonna move aside or what?"

I turned to look. The voice belonged to a buxom brunette in a black mini-skirt and matching bustier. She was showing a lot of skin, and I gave an involuntary shiver. It was mid-November, and we were north of Detroit. It wasn't quite freezing, but it was long past bustier weather.

Where was her coat? Cripes, *I* was wearing a coat – a long one, too – and I was still freezing. Either she was immune to the cold, or she was willing to die, literally, to look like a high-class call girl.

She gave me a nasty smirk. "You see something you like?"

Embarrassed to be caught staring, I looked down, only to feel my heart leap out of my chest. *Oh, my God.* I *did*, in fact, see something – or someone, depending on how I looked at it.

The something was the slick black-and-white photo clutched in the girl's hands. The someone was the guy *in* the photo – and not just *any* guy.

My guy.

Joel.

In the photo, he was shirtless and glistening. His hair was damp, and his eyes were dark. The photo appeared to be some sort of publicity shot, like something a movie star might sign for a fan.

But Joel wasn't a movie star. He was an underground fighter – not that I'd realized it the first time we'd met. That was how long ago?

Eight weeks.

Six of those weeks had been utter bliss. I'd slept in Joel's arms. I'd kissed him a million times over. I'd felt his hands on my ass and his lips on every private inch of my suddenly warm body.

Now I could hardly breathe. My eyes were still glued to his image. It was a perfect likeness from what I could tell in the dim light of the warehouse parking lot.

His body looked amazing, practically a work of art, with all those chiseled muscles and interesting ridges in all the right places. But it wasn't primarily his body, or even his beautiful face, that I was desperately missing.

It was *him,* the incredible person I'd discovered underneath that tough exterior. He was warm and funny, and surprisingly sensitive, especially for a guy who made his money by beating the crap out of people.

My stomach sank as a terrifying realization hit home. He was probably doing that right now, inside that big gray warehouse, just a few feet away.

I *had* to see him.

And I had to stop him.

But how? Right now, I could barely move. And it was because of the photo. I couldn't bring myself to look away.

But then, suddenly, it was gone, yanked back by the girl holding it.

She made a sound of annoyance. "What's your problem, anyway?"

I looked up. "What?"

"Well, first, you're staring at *me*. And then, you're staring at *him*. What are you? Desperate or something?"

Yes. I was desperate. Stupidly, I mumbled, "I, um, know him."

"Oh yeah?" She gave me a not-so-friendly smile. "Well, I'm *gonna* know him, if you know what I mean." Her voice rose. "So back off, sister. I'm not freezing my ass off for nothing."

I could hardly think. "Huh?"

"Yeah," she said. "You think I'm dressed like this for my health?" She thrust out her chest. "I'm giving him a good eyeful of *these*."

I looked. They *were* quite nice, perfectly round and nearly overflowing from the tight bodice of her bustier. I had to wonder, would Joel really be getting an eyeful? *Oh, God*. What if it was worse? What if he'd be getting a handful? Or – my stomach gave a sudden lurch – a mouthful?

I didn't know what to say, but I *did* know that the thought of Joel ogling, touching, or kissing any other girl was a dagger straight into my own chest. I loved him. And he loved me.

I was sure of it, even now – because when it came to that kind of love, it didn't simply go away, just because everything had gone to hell in a handbasket.

The girl's annoyed voice broke into my thoughts. "Hey! I wanted *him* to look, not you."

Startled, I looked up. "What?'

"I *said*, these—" She gave her goodies a little jiggle. "–are for *him*." Her eyes narrowed to slits. "Not *you*."

My face burst into flames. It belatedly occurred to me that for who-knows-how-long, I'd been staring straight at her chest.

I was losing it, totally.

"Sorry," I mumbled. "I was, um, thinking of something else."

"Sure you were." She gave a toss of her long, dark hair. "Pervert."

Well, that was a first.

From a few feet away, the big guy blocking the door called out, "Hey! Chickies! If you're waiting for Bishop, you're in the wrong place."

I turned to look. *Bishop?* Oh. Of course, he meant Joel. That was, after all, Joel's last name. What was my problem lately? It was like my entire brain had turned to mush.

Then again, was it any wonder? Joel and I had parted on such awful terms, and I'd spent the last two weeks frantically searching for him. I couldn't eat. I couldn't sleep. I couldn't stop wondering where he'd gone or what he was doing.

I *had* to find him.

And tonight, I thought I *had* found him. But the guy at the door had just said otherwise. Was he serious?

I was just about to ask when Miss Bustier beat me to the punch by demanding, "What do you mean we're in the wrong place?"

He flicked his head toward the side of the building. "Groupies over there."

I looked to where he'd indicated. Around the side of the building, I spotted a big set of double doors. Outside those doors stood a gaggle of girls. All of them were decidedly underdressed.

The way it looked, Miss Bustier had some serious competition. As for me, I wanted no part of that scene. I bit my lip. I only prayed that Joel didn't either.

I turned back to the guy and said, "I'm not a groupie."

Miss Bustier said, "Yeah. Me neither."

The guy gave us a bored look. "Uh-huh. Do what you want, but I'm telling ya, if you wanna catch him, that's where he'll be."

And just like that, Miss Bustier was off in a flash, hustling in her high heels toward the side entrance. And heaven help me, a moment later, I was scrambling after her.

CHAPTER 2

Standing like an idiot outside those double doors, I took a subtle look around. Through the shadows, I saw long legs, high heels, exposed shoulders, and a whole lot of cleavage. I counted nine girls, including Miss Bustier.

Counting me, it was ten.

Talk about humiliating.

I felt a poke in my side and turned to look. It was Bustier, who asked, "Which one do *you* want?"

"What?"

"Which fighter?"

I didn't want to tell her, mostly because she was giving me the crazy-eye again. "I'm just waiting for a friend. That's all."

Her gaze narrowed. "A guy or a girl?"

I gave a noncommittal shrug and turned away, hoping she'd take the hint.

No such luck. She gave me another poke. "You don't mean Joel Bishop, do you? Because I already called him. Remember?"

Oh yeah. I'd called him, too, at least a hundred times. He never answered, not even once. Yesterday, I'd gotten so desperate that I'd even called one of his brothers, for all the good *that* did.

Next to me, the girl spoke again, louder now. "You heard me, right? I *said*, I called him."

Obviously, she didn't mean on the phone. "Yeah," I snapped. "I heard you." *Cripes, everyone heard you.*

"So remember," she warned, "he's mine. Got it?"

No. I *didn't* get it. And I wasn't going to get it. I'd moved heaven and earth to get here, and I wasn't about to give up, just because a stranger called dibs in a warehouse parking lot.

Behind us, a different girl said, "You're so full of it."

Bustier turned to look. "What?"

"He's not 'yours'," the girl said. "That's for *him* to decide. And besides, I was here way before *you*."

"Hey!" Bustier said, "I was here. I was just standing in a different spot, that's all."

"Sorry," the girl said, "you snooze, you lose."

Bustier glared at the girl. "I wasn't snoozing. I was waiting. Just like you are."

"Oh sure." The girl gave a snort of derision. "In the wrong place."

"Oh, whatever," Bustier muttered, turning away. She leaned closer to me and said, "Can you believe that chick?"

I gave another shrug. In truth, I couldn't believe any of this. For the life of me, I couldn't understand why a bunch of girls would be standing outside some warehouse, waiting for guys they didn't even know. What they wanted was obvious, but it still defied all logic.

Joel was amazing. He was hot as sin and tough as nails. But the thought of him having groupies had never occurred to me. Unable to stop myself, I turned to Bustier and asked, "Is it always like this?"

She looked around. "Sort of, but not *this* bad." She lowered her voice. "But you know that Joel Bishop guy I was telling you about?"

My stomach clenched. I didn't just *know* him. I *loved* him. Trying hard not to show it, I gave a casual nod.

"Well," she said, "a few months ago, he like totally disappeared. And we all thought, 'Shit, he's gone for good.'" She gave me a wolfish grin. "But now he's back, and I'm gonna welcome him home, if you know what I mean."

My gaze drifted to the photo. I *did* know. And I didn't like it.

Behind her, the other girl said, "That's what *you* think."

Bustier turned and gave the girl an irritated look. "What?"

The girl threw back her shoulders. "It won't be *you*. It'll be *me*."

Bustier rolled her eyes. "In your dreams, sister." She turned back to me and said in a low whisper, "Wanna know what I heard?"

Did I? Probably not. Still, I had to ask, "What?"

She leaned closer and said, "I heard he hooked up with some heiress, a total rich bitch."

I froze. That so-called heiress was me, except I wasn't rich. In fact, I'd used my last ten dollars for gas money to get here. Whether I had enough to get home, I wasn't so sure.

Oblivious to my inner turmoil, Bustier continued. "You know, they totally shacked up at her mansion, doing who-knows-what."

I swallowed. "A mansion?"

"Yeah. Apparently, she's got this killer place off Lake Michigan."

As Bustier prattled on, I considered my so-called mansion. The place was falling apart, and I had no money to repair it.

Some heiress.

The girl went on to say that when summer ended, Joel had ditched me to return back to fighting. None of her story was quite accurate. For one thing, summer had ended long before he left me sobbing on my front lawn. For another, I didn't have a dozen servants – or a private helicopter, for that matter.

When she finished, I gave her a long, silent look before saying, "And *where'd* you hear all this?"

"On the internet," she said. "Where else?"

I should've known.

Suddenly, the girl switched gears. "Hey, what are you wearing?"

Well, it's not a bustier. That's for darn sure. I said, "Just normal clothes."

The girl frowned. "Boy, you're not very good at this, are you?"

Under my breath, I said, "Nope. Definitely not."

She reached for the collar of my coat. "C'mon. Lemme me see."

I drew back. "No."

"Oh, come on!" Her gaze narrowed. "You got a good look at *me*."

"Yeah, well that was an accident." I reached up and pulled my coat tighter around my torso. "Besides, there's nothing to see."

"No shit?" She eyed me with new respect. "So, you're naked under there?"

Oh, for crying out loud. "No. I'm not naked. I already told you I'm wearing normal clothes."

She was still clutching my coat. "Then lemme look."

I leaned back. "No."

"Why not?" she demanded.

"Well, for one thing, because it's freezing out here."

She was still holding on. I was still leaning back. Finally, with a sound of disgust, she let go. Thrown off balance, I stumbled backward into another girl, who shrieked. "Hey! Watch it!"

I winced. "Sorry."

"You should be," she snapped.

Well, that was nice.

Ignoring the hoopla, Bustier made a sound of frustration. "Alright, fine. At least *tell* me what you're wearing."

I sighed. "A skirt and sweater, okay?"

She looked utterly horrified. "A sweater? You're shitting me, right?"

No. I wasn't "shitting" her. If anything, I felt underdressed. The sweater felt way too thin, and the skirt felt way too short. Even under the long coat, my bare legs trembled in the frigid night air.

But really, this was none of her business, and I was debating telling her so when suddenly, the double doors flew open, and a stream of people started pouring out.

In unison, we all turned to look.

They were mostly guys, and there weren't a lot of them, maybe a couple dozen at most. The way it looked, these weren't members of the general audience, but rather, people behind the scenes – fighters, friends, or whatever.

I stood on my tiptoes and searched the faces, seeking out one in particular. Finally, I spotted him, walking next to a bearded guy whose bare, muscular arms were covered in tattoos. As for Joel, he was wearing a gray hoodie with the hood pulled low over his face, almost like he didn't want to be seen.

It didn't matter. His whole face could've been covered, and I still would've recognized him, not only by his body, but also from something in the way he moved, like bad-ass poetry in motion.

Suddenly, I could hardly breathe, much less think. I loved him so much, it hurt.

But did he still love me?

Next to me, Bustier called out, "Joel! Over here!" She scrambled forward, heading straight toward him. With the spell broken, I followed after her, only to stop in mid-stride when Joel turned in our direction. Finally, I could see his whole face. His gaze passed quickly over Bustier and landed, hard, on me.

When our eyes met, he stopped moving, and so did I. His mouth was tight, and his eyes were hard. The way it looked, he wasn't happy to see me.

Not even a little.

☐

CHAPTER 3

As I watched, Bustier plowed into him and threw her arms tight around his neck. "Welcome back!" she squealed.

A split-second later, another girl – the one who'd been standing directly behind us – barreled into him from the other side. "Yeah, where have you been?" She wrapped her arms tight around his waist and didn't let go, even when he made to move to acknowledge her.

Watching through the milling crowd, I had no idea what to do. Unless I was willing to dive for his legs, there really wasn't an open spot.

And it wasn't like Joel was shaking them off or anything.

In fact, he wasn't doing anything at all. He didn't move, and his face didn't change expression as he stared at me from across the distance. His eyes – dark and brooding – held me in that familiar spell. I could've move, and I couldn't look away.

As if sensing Joel's inattention, both girls turned to follow his gaze. When they saw me staring, both of them frowned.

Like in a trance, I started moving forward. But I'd barely gotten two steps when Joel wrapped an arm around each girl and deliberately turned away, leaving me staring after them.

Was he leaving? With them? Panic surged through me, and I called out, "Wait!"

But he didn't wait. He didn't even look. He just kept on going, heading toward a small, dimly lit parking area on the far side of the building. As the three of them walked, Joel's scantily-clad companions gazed, star-struck, up at him, their earlier animosity apparently forgotten.

Ignoring the small crowd milling around me, I stood for a long, awful moment, watching their receding backs.

From a few feet away, a male voice said, "Looking for company?"

I didn't even look. *Yes. But not from you.*

I shook my head and kept my eyes trained on Joel and the two girls. Already, they were nearing that other parking lot. In the distance, I spotted Joel's car, parked next to a big dark pickup.

My mind – not to mention my stomach – was churning like crazy. What should I do? What *could* I do?

"Aw c'mon," the guy said. "So you didn't get your first choice. Big deal." He gave a low chuckle. "If you're nice to *me*, I'll put in a good word for ya."

Ick.

Reluctantly, I turned to look. He was a big, thick-necked guy in a shiny running suit. His hair was pale, nearly white, but shaved along the sides. Was he a fighter? He looked like a fighter. But I didn't care. He wasn't *my* fighter.

I wanted nothing to do with him – or any other stranger, for that matter. "I'm not interested," I said, turning, once again, to look at Joel. Obviously, they were heading to his car. If I didn't do something now, they'd probably soon be driving away.

To where? And to what?

The possibilities were too horrible to contemplate.

Before I knew it, I was scrambling after them, weaving my way through the small crowd until I was walking on my own, heading straight in their direction.

By the time I caught up, they'd almost reached Joel's car. Unlike the huge parking lot on the building's other side, this parking area was small and dark, with only a few vehicles.

Behind me, in the distance, I could hear people pouring out from the main entrance, laughing and talking as they made their way toward their cars, trucks or whatever.

But over here, it was just us.

From a few paces away, I stopped and called out, "Joel, wait!

Please?"

He stopped, but didn't turn around. Unfortunately for me, the girls weren't so reluctant. Bustier looked over her shoulder and said, "What's your deal, anyway?"

"Yeah," the second girl chimed in. "Take a hint, will ya?"

Ignoring them, I focused all of my attention on the guy I loved. He still hadn't turned around, but he *was* listening, right?

"Joel, seriously," I said, "there's something I need to tell you, and it can't wait."

Finally, after a long, awkward moment, he let go of the girls and turned slowly to face me. His posture was stiff, and his eyes were so cold, they gave me a shiver. In a tight voice, he said, "Alright. Go ahead."

I swallowed. "What?"

"Go ahead," he repeated. "Tell me and be done with it."

I almost flinched. Where was the guy I loved? He had to be in there somewhere, right? I gave his companions a nervous glance. "Can't we talk alone?"

Bustier gave a snort of disbelief. "You've got to be kidding me." She looked to the other girl and said, "Can you believe this chick?"

If it weren't so pathetic, I might've laughed. It was, after all, the same exact same thing she'd said to me earlier about her new best friend.

Ignoring them, I inched forward, walking slowly until I was standing within arm's reach. I gave Joel a pleading look. "Just five minutes, okay?"

He watched me in stony silence, but said nothing.

I tried to smile. "Please? I drove all this way just to talk to you."

He gave a tight shrug. "Not my problem."

"Yeah," Bustier chimed in, "like he'd care."

I looked to Joel, waiting for him to contradict her.

He didn't.

The other girl snickered. She looked to me and said, "So *now*, you need to drive all the way home." She made a fake pouty face. "Bummer for you, huh?"

Yes. It was a bummer and then some, but I wasn't going anywhere yet. I returned my attention to Joel. The way it looked, he *didn't* care. But that *couldn't* be true.

Somewhere, under that cold, hard façade was the guy I loved. I just needed to reach him. But how? I was still searching for the perfect thing to say when Bustier suddenly blurted out, "Oh, my God, you're *her.*"

I froze. *Oh, crap.*

CHAPTER 4

Bustier laughed like I was the funniest thing she'd seen in forever. Through her continued laughter, she said, "No freaking way! No wonder you were so funny about it." She turned to the other girl and said, "You know who she is, don't you?"

The other girl frowned. "A stalker?"

"Yeah, totally," Bustier said. "But she's also Melanie Blaire."

Melody. Not Melanie. But that was hardly the point.

The other girl scrunched up her face and said, "Melanie who?"

"*You* know," Bustier said. "She's that rich bitch he hooked up with over the summer."

The other girl turned and gave me a dubious look. "I dunno," she said. "She doesn't *look* rich. I mean, look at her coat. It's like, older than me."

Stupid or not, heat flooded my face. The coat *was* old. It had been my mom's. I wasn't a huge follower of fashion, but I did know that the coat was several seasons out of style. This was no surprise, given the fact that my mom, along with my dad, had died over five years earlier in a private plane crash.

On instinct, I wrapped the coat tighter around my torso and tried to act like I didn't give a flying flip that it was old and didn't fit so great.

I couldn't afford to care. It was the only long coat I had, and I couldn't justify a new one. Whenever I had any money, which was nearly never, I sunk it straight into the house – because let's face it, keeping the furnace running was a lot more important than wearing the latest fashions.

Still, the remark stung, not because I wanted to impress some random hoochie, but because Joel was just standing there, letting them make fun of me.

Didn't he care? Not even a little?

I searched his face, looking for some sign of the guy I used to know. Almost from the first, he'd been the only person in forever to actually stick up for me, to take my side when I was terribly outnumbered.

I almost wanted to cry. I was outnumbered *now*. Two against one. My stomach sank. Or was it three against one? From the look in Joel's eyes, I knew one thing for sure. It definitely wasn't two against two.

Bustier gave me a dismissive look. "Seriously, take a hint, okay? He's done with you." She gave a mean little laugh. "I mean, you've got loads of money. Go buy yourself a pool boy or something."

My mouth tightened. "I don't *have* a pool."

She smirked. "You don't need a pool to have a pool boy." She laughed. "Dumb-ass."

Finally, Joel spoke up. "Look, if you've got something to say, just say it."

My gaze snapped in his direction. *Oh, God.* That sharp tone had been for me. Not her. My mouth opened, but all that came out was a jumbled mess of nonsense. "I, um, well, you see…"

Bustier laughed. "You know what? I think she's high."

I wasn't high. I was low. Really, *really* low. And just when I thought I couldn't feel any lower, Joel's voice cut across the short distance. "Is that it? You done?"

"No," I said, feeling the first sting of tears. "I'm not done. I haven't even started."

Joel lifted his wrist and glanced at his watch. "Yeah? Well, you've got one minute."

Was he serious? He looked serious. I gazed up at him, wondering how on Earth I could pack everything I needed to say in one measly minute.

The other girl gave me a sarcastic smile. "Tick tock."

There were so many things I wanted to say.

I love you.

It wasn't my fault.

Don't give up on us. Please?

But from the look in Joel's eyes, he didn't want to hear any of these things, and heaven help me, I couldn't bring myself to say them – not here, not in front of an audience, and especially not to the snickers of Bustier, who looked to the other girl and said, "See? She *is* high."

The other girl nodded. "Oh yeah. For sure. I mean, she can afford the good stuff, you know?"

I couldn't help it. I gave a bitter laugh, or at least, that was my intention. But it came out as a choked sob, devoid of any humor, bitter or otherwise.

Desperate now to end this already, I looked to Joel and said, "Fine. I wanted to tell you that you shouldn't be fighting."

At this, both girls burst out laughing. Bustier said, "Oh sure. And suckers shouldn't be sucking."

I gave her an annoyed look. *Who sounded high now?*

I turned back to Joel, who gazed at me with cold, dark eyes. Well, at least, *he* wasn't laughing. That was something, right?

Ignoring the snickers of his companions, I bumbled on. "You know, because of the suspended sentence. Derek knows about it, and I'm pretty sure he means to cause trouble." I winced. "He knows the prosecutor or something. And anyway, I don't think it's safe."

Bustier gave another bark of laughter. "Safe? You're shitting him, right?" She looked to Joel and said in a tone of mock-concern, "Ooh, I bet you're really scared, huh?"

Joel had no reaction – not to me, and not to her. Desperately, I searched his face. When he said nothing, I said in a voice that sounded way too small, "You heard me, right?"

As an answer, he lifted his wrist and looked at his watch. "Time's up." And with that, he turned away, guiding the two girls toward the passenger's side of his vehicle.

I watched in silent dismay as he opened the passenger's side door and held it open while Bustier and the other girl jostled against each other, trying to claim the front seat.

In the end, Bustier won by elbowing the other girl out of the way and launching herself, sideways, into the car. After a few choice words, the other girl gave it up and climbed awkwardly into the back.

Joel closed the car door behind them and circled around to the driver's side. A moment later, he slid into the driver's seat and slammed the door behind him.

Standing alone, I watched in stunned misery as he fired up the engine and peeled out of the lot, leaving me staring after him.

CHAPTER 5

It took me a moment to realize I was crying – not the loud, sobbing kind, but the quiet pathetic kind, with a lot of tears and sniffling. I stood there for the longest time, staring at his empty parking spot.

He'd left. He'd actually left. And with those other girls, too.

I was so lost in my own wretchedness that it took me a moment to realize that someone was talking to me. Startled out of my trance, I whirled around to look.

It was the same guy as before. He said, "Man, you took it hard."

I gave a confused shake of my head. "What?"

"I mean, I've seen girls disappointed before, but you're the first one to cry about it."

I swiped at my damp eyes. "I'm not crying."

"Uh-huh. If you say so."

"Well, I'm not crying anymore. I just, uh, stubbed my toe."

I stubbed my toe? Seriously, couldn't I do any better than that? Still, it wasn't *quite* a lie. I *had* stubbed my toe, but that was three days ago, and I hadn't cried about it.

The guy gave me a wolfish grin. "Want me to kiss it and make it better?"

I drew back. "No."

"Good thing." He shrugged. "I'm not a foot person, if you know what I mean."

I *didn't* know. And I didn't want to know. I glanced around. It suddenly struck me that I was outside in a crappy part of town, alone with a stranger, after midnight.

On the other side of the building, the hum of voices and cars had grown eerily silent. Just as I noticed this, the big overhead lights flickered off, making everything go suddenly dark.

Well, that wasn't ominous or anything.

I bit my lip. Where was everyone? Gone? Already? The way it looked, I'd been standing out here longer than I realized.

At something in my expression, the guy said, "Yeah, no shit."

"What do you mean?"

"You know what I mean." He flicked his chin toward the other the parking lot. "You got a car over there? C'mon, I'll walk you over."

I hesitated. I'd be an idiot to trust him. But I'd be an even bigger idiot to keep standing out here by myself.

So reluctantly, I moved forward, keeping what I hoped was a safe distance between me and the stranger. Following my lead, he turned and began walking alongside me toward the other parking lot.

We were halfway to my car when he said, "Ten bucks he'll be back."

I reached up to rub at my still-damp eyes. They felt warm and swollen, like I'd been crying for hours. Lost in thought, I mumbled, "What?"

"Joel," he said. "Ten bucks he ditches them and circles back."

It was a nice story, but I didn't believe it for one minute. I kept on walking. "Why *would* he?"

"My guess? To find *you.*"

I gave a bitter scoff. "Yeah, sure." There was no way on Earth that I'd be taking such a bet. Not only did it seem incredibly far-fetched, I didn't even *have* ten dollars.

"Alright, how about this?" the guy said, "I'll give you two-to-one odds. Your ten to my twenty."

"I don't *have* a ten."

With annoying optimism, he said, "Hey, I can break a hundred."

I sighed. Maybe *he* could, but *I* couldn't. In fact, if I searched every inch of my car, I *might* find two bucks in spare change. But there was no way I'd be sharing *that* sad fact with a stranger, so all I said was, "I'm not a betting person."

"Good thing for you," he said. "I would've cleaned you out."

I wanted to roll my eyes. Was he joking? I had no idea. But I *did* know that the odds of Joel returning any time soon weren't looking nearly as good as the guy seemed to think.

As I trudged along beside him, I couldn't help but wonder why he was being so nice to me. Was it because he knew Joel? Like maybe they were friends or something? Or maybe, he was just a decent guy.

Of course, there was always the chance that he'd toss me into my own trunk and steal the car with me inside it. But somehow, I didn't think so, so I tried to be thankful, even if I was too depressed to be decent company.

As we headed toward my car, I considered all of the things that I *didn't* get to say. For one thing, I'd been meaning to tell Joel that I still had his money – over fifty-three thousand dollars in cash.

He'd left it, stashed up in my guest house. I'd found it only hours after he left. And yet, I hadn't touched a single one of those dollars, not even tonight, when I'd been facing a three-hour drive on a nearly empty tank.

I also had Joel's paintings, a bunch of his clothes, and a slew of memories that broke my heart. Did he know that I still loved him? And if so, did he even care?

The stranger's voice interrupted my thoughts. "If it makes you feel any better, the guy's been a total asshole since he got back."

"Joel?" I stopped in my tracks. "He has?"

"Yeah. And I'm guessing you're the reason."

"What makes you say that?"

"Not hard to figure out," the guy said. "The way he peeled out of here? He was pissed."

"So?"

"So you don't get *that* angry over some girl you don't care about."

"Oh." I started walking again. "Yeah, well, I wouldn't be so sure."

In spite of my lackluster response, I'd be lying if I didn't admit that the guy's words had sparked an embarrassing leap of hope in my heart. *Did* Joel still care? It would be nice to think so.

And yet, now that I'd passed the crying phase, a different emotion was creeping up with a vengeance. That emotion was anger. *My* anger. He'd treated me like garbage. He'd stood aside, saying nothing, as those two other girls ridiculed me right to my face.

And then, he'd left me standing there, alone, in a dimly lit parking lot. True, maybe I'd brought most of this on myself, but if Joel cared at all, he sure had a funny way of showing it.

I was still mulling all of this over when we finally reached my car. Around us, the parking lot was now almost completely empty and utterly dark. Aside from a big grey van, parked tight against the driver's side of my car, there wasn't a single vehicle in sight.

I gave the van a closer look. It had two flat tires and a bunch of flyers tucked underneath the front windshield wipers. Obviously, the van had been there a while, and wouldn't be leaving anytime soon.

Pushing aside the distraction, I reached into my jacket pocket and pulled out my keys. And then, I turned to the stranger and said, "Thanks."

"You're welcome." He grinned. "And you owe me."

I wasn't following. "What?"

"The bet."

"But we didn't bet," I pointed out. "And besides, I still wouldn't owe you. It's not like he came back or anything."

He was still grinning. "You sure about that?"

I listened. Somewhere in the distance, I heard the squeal of tires, like a speed-demon driver had taken a corner way too fast. I froze, trying to listen more closely. Soon, I heard it again.

But it couldn't be Joel.

Could it?

CHAPTER 6

In front of me, the stranger said, "See?"

I *didn't* see. But I could hear. The sound was getting closer with every passing second. And yet, there was no guarantee that the sound was coming from *Joel's* car.

I gave a small shrug. "That's probably someone else."

"Nah. It's him."

"How can you be sure?"

"I know the car."

I frowned. "But they all sound alike."

"To *you*, maybe. Not to me." His eyes filled with mischief. "Now c'mon. Let's have some fun with it."

I stared up at him. "Fun? What kind of fun?"

"You wanna see Joel flip out?"

I drew back. "No."

"Aw c'mon. Sure you do."

I shook my head. "No. I don't."

"What about payback?" he said. "The guy was an asshole. Don't you wanna give as good as you got?"

I wasn't even sure what he meant, but I did know that I wasn't the type to play games. Whatever this guy had in mind – regardless of how nice he'd been about walking me back – I wanted no part of it.

I gave another shake of my head.

He looked far from discouraged. "Trust me. You'll thank me later."

"Thank you? For what?"

He flashed me a sudden grin. "For this."

Before I knew it, he'd moved forward. On instinct, I backed up until my butt hit the front bumper of my car. I gave a little gasp. "What are you doing?"

He loomed over me, large and imposing, until our lips were almost within kissing distance. "Nothing."

I leaned my head back, trying to get some space. "Then stop it."

"Stop what?" He sounded perfectly reasonable. "I'm not doing anything."

"Yes, you are."

He gave a cheerful laugh. "I'm not even touching you."

It was true. He wasn't. And yet, I found myself reaching back with both hands, searching out the hood of my car, if only to make sure that I didn't topple over. Briefly, I considered the opposite approach – reaching out to push him away – but I wasn't sure I could do that and still maintain my balance.

And yet, for some odd reason, I wasn't afraid. Maybe I should've been, but the guy's eyes were filled with so much good-humor that it caught me off-guard.

As if making casual conversation, he said, "You see any good movies lately?"

Movies? What the hell? Enough was enough. I gave him a serious look. "I'll scream," I warned.

He nodded. "Good idea. That'll *really* make him nuts."

I stared up at the guy. *Speaking of nuts.* What on Earth was he up to?

Unfortunately, I had no time to figure it out, because a moment later, amidst the sound of squealing tires, I was nearly blinded by the sudden glare of headlights coming up, hard and fast, toward the passenger's side of my vehicle.

I turned to look and felt my eyes widen. Sure enough, it was Joel's car. Or at least it looked like Joel's car, as much as I could tell in the blinding light. But soon, I didn't have to wonder, because the car squealed to a sudden stop a few feet away, and Joel practically jumped out, leaving the driver's side door open and the car running as the headlights blazed on.

The hoodie he'd been wearing earlier was gone, revealing a dark gray T-shirt that did little to hide his powerful physique. He strode forward, calling out as he moved, "What the fuck are you doing?"

In front of me, the guy took a casual step back, finally giving me some space. Looking oddly unconcerned, he said, "Who? Me?" He flicked his head in my direction. "Or the hottie?"

Joel's gaze zoomed in on me. "You okay?"

At this, the stranger gave a low chuckle. In a tone laced with sin, he said, "She's more than okay. You get a look at those legs?"

I stared at him. My coat was long. As far as my legs, I was barely showing ankle, much less thigh or calf. I could have chicken-legs for all he knew.

It suddenly hit me that I was still leaning back against my car. Forget my legs. My hands were freezing on the cold, metal hood. I pushed away and turned to face Joel. I said, "What are you doing here?"

His gaze narrowed. "I should ask you the same thing." He looked back to the guy and said, "So tell me." He took a step forward. "What the fuck were you doing?"

The guy grinned. "Me? I was making a new friend." Sounding annoyingly cheerful, he asked, "What the fuck were *you* doing?"

Joel's gaze was dark, and his body was rigid. As he stared at the stranger, his biceps bulged, and his forearms looked ready to mangle something – or more accurately, *someone* right here in this parking lot.

I wanted to say something to diffuse the tension, but I still wasn't quite sure if the stranger was messing with Joel because they were friends, or because they weren't.

Their reactions were so completely different that I couldn't be certain either way.

Joel took another step forward. "You were all over her."

I spoke up. "No, he wasn't."

Both guys turned to look. In the stranger's eyes, I saw a flash of humor, like he was loving every minute of this.

As for me, I wasn't. And obviously, neither was Joel. If anything, he looked angrier than ever. *So much for reassuring him.*

Joel gave me a hard look. "I'll talk to *you* later."

My jaw dropped. "Oh, really? Well, that's rich."

In a tight voice, he said, "What?"

"I *tried* to talk to you. Remember?"

His mouth thinned, but he said nothing.

Into his silence, I continued, "And now, you're acting all mad? Like you caught me making out in the back seat or something?" Recalling those girls, I gave him a hard look of my own. "What were *you* doing in *your* back seat?"

Maybe it was a stupid thing to say. Obviously, Joel hadn't had been gone long enough to engage in any serious backseat action. And yet, my stomach clenched at the memory of him ditching me for those two groupies, or whoever they were.

When he *still* made no response, I said, "And where *are* your friends, anyway?"

Looking more irritated than ever, he said, "What friends?"

"Oh, you know," I said. "Bustier and whoever."

He frowned. "Bustier?"

The stranger laughed. "I think she means Rhonda."

Joel turned to glare at the guy. "I wasn't asking *you*."

The stranger looked undaunted. "Hey, where'd you leave them, by the way?"

"Does it matter?"

"Hell yeah," the guy said. "They're probably hot and bothered. They might need cheering up."

Joel's gaze flicked briefly in my direction. Through clenched teeth, he said, "Like you were cheering *her* up?"

The guy held up his hands, palm-out. "Hey, you're the one who left. Finders keepers, right?"

"Just try it," Joel said. "You find her again, you keep on walking."

Listening to this, I gave a snort of disbelief. "Oh, that's nice."

In that same tight voice, Joel said, "What?"

"Keep walking?" I repeated. "You know what? I was lucky he *didn't* keep walking, so stop giving him grief, okay?" I lifted my chin. "He was a perfect gentleman."

At this, the stranger burst out laughing. "Oh shit. There goes my reputation."

I didn't see the humor, and from the looks of it, neither did Joel. He gave the guy an annoyed look. "Don't you have someplace to be?"

"Sure," the guy said. "Just tell me where you dropped them."

I felt my brow wrinkle. *Them?* Meaning those two girls?

Joel gave me a sideways glance before muttering, "Denny's."

"Which one?" the guy asked. "The one on the Parkway?"

"Uh, yeah." Joel slid another glance in my direction. "I gave them a fifty. You know, for pancakes or whatever."

"Dude," the stranger said, "it wasn't pancakes they wanted. Sausage maybe. But pancakes? Nah, I don't think so." He was grinning again. "Lucky for them, I've got just the thing they need." He turned to me and said, "You gonna be alright?"

Joel's voice cut through the short distance. "If you wanna worry, worry about yourself."

"Yeah, yeah," the guy said. He turned and walked to the driver's side of Joel's car. He reached in past the open door, cut the engine, and turned off the headlights. When he finished, he turned back, tossed the car keys to Joel, and kept on walking, heading toward the other parking area.

Over his shoulder, he called back, "I wasn't kidding about the legs."

CHAPTER 7

The guy's words echoed across the darkened parking lot. I looked down toward my feet. Unless the guy was an ankle person, he *had* to be kidding. Even my shoes weren't terribly sexy – just basic black heels.

I turned and gave Joel a perplexed look. "Where's he going?"

"Why?" Joel said. "You wanna go with him?"

God, did he have to be so awful? "No. I'm just wondering. Like, does he have a ride?"

"Forget him. He can take care of himself."

Well, obviously.

But driving here, I'd passed the Denny's along the way. It was at least five miles down the road. I glanced at the guy's receding back. "But is he walking?"

"Yeah," Joel said, sounding irritated by the question. "To his truck."

I recalled the pickup that I'd seen near Joel's car in the other lot. Suddenly, everything made a lot more sense. The guy hadn't been following me. He'd been heading out to his own vehicle. And yet, he'd made a special effort to turn around and walk me back.

I heard myself say, "He's nice."

Joel made a scoffing sound. "Nice, huh?"

I recalled what an ass Joel had been earlier. "Nicer than you." I glanced away and murmured, "Tonight, anyway."

He stalked forward, closing the short distance between us. "Why are you here?"

I glared up at him. "I already told you, not that you wanted to listen. I came to tell you about Derek." I gave a small shrug. "And other things."

"Like what?"

Oh, so *now* he wanted to know? Funny, there were things that *I* wanted to know, too. I said, "So why'd you come back, anyway?"

"You don't know?"

"No," I snapped. "I *don't* know."

He moved a fraction closer. "I came back because I shouldn't've left you here." He shoved a hand through his hair. "Fuck. If something had happened…"

"But it didn't." *No thanks to you.*

But I didn't say it, because I wasn't blind to the fact that I'd come out here on my own. If anything bad had happened, I had mostly myself to blame.

Joel's gaze hardened. "Yeah. And you've Cal to thank for *that*, huh?"

Yes. I did. That was, of course, assuming that he meant the guy who just left. But Cal wasn't the guy I loved. Joel was, even if he was being a total jerk at the moment.

Looking to move past this, I said, "So what is he? A friend of yours or something?"

"Why? You interested?"

"You know what?" I said. "Never mind. Forget I asked."

Joel made a scoffing sound. "What? You want his number?"

"You mean his phone number?" I stared up at him. "Is that a serious question?"

He looked away, staring off at who-knows-what. After a long, tense moment, he gave a tight shrug that told me exactly nothing.

I studied his face in profile. He wasn't seriously offering me another guy's phone number, was he? Even now, I just couldn't see that happening. But what if I was wrong?

What if he truly didn't care? If that was the case, I *had* to know. In a quiet voice, I asked, "If I did want his number, would you give it to me?"

He turned and gave me a long, cold look. "Hell, if that's what you want, I'll call him now." His lips formed a nasty smirk. "Maybe there's room for you at Denny's."

I rocked backward, almost like I'd been slapped. "You don't mean that."

"Hey, you do what you want. I'm not the boss of you."

No. He wasn't. But he'd never been such an asshole before. I almost didn't know what to say. A sound – a half-sob, half-scoff – escaped my lips. "Yeah. I guess you're not."

Under his hard gaze, I took a deep breath and stiffened my resolve. I did love him. Or at least, I loved the guy I *thought* he was. But the person in front of me was a stranger – a cold, hard stranger who obviously cared nothing for me or my feelings.

I looked to my car. I was still standing in front of it. But with just a few short strides, I could yank open the driver's side door – well as much as it *could* be yanked, with the van parked so close – and then, I could climb into the driver's seat and drive off, leaving all of this behind me.

My stomach clenched.

Leaving Joel behind me.

Forever?

It sure felt that way.

I was still looking toward my car door when Joel said, "You wanna go? *I'm* not stopping you."

His words sliced through me. If that wasn't a hint, I didn't know what was.

The way it looked, he'd only returned to make sure I wasn't dead in the parking lot. Maybe I should've been grateful, but I wasn't. Probably, all he wanted now was to get back to Rhonda and what's-her-name.

Screw this. Screw everything. I looked back to Joel and said, "You know what? Maybe there's room for *you* at Denny's."

His jaw tightened. "What?"

"Yeah. Because I'm not stopping *you* either."

"Yeah?" he said. "Well, good."

"Yeah, good. I hope you *do* go. And I hope you screw them silly." I was practically choking on my own words, but I kept on going. "And, I hope…" *Damn it. What?* "…I hope your privates fall off from whatever social disease they wanna give you." I wanted to cry. Maybe I *was* crying. I mumbled, "Assuming they haven't already."

And with that, I turned and stumbled into the narrow gap that separated my car from the van. He wanted me to go, huh? Well, I'd go, alright. And this time, I wouldn't be looking back.

But just as I reached my car door, I felt a hand on my elbow. I whirled to see Joel staring down at me.

He said, "Is that what you really want?"

"Why?" I was shaking now. "Do you care?"

He looked at me for a long, awful moment before whispering a single word that changed everything. "Yes."

CHAPTER 8

Suddenly, I could hardly breathe. "What?"

We were standing so close, I swear I could feel the heat of his anger – or whatever it was – radiating off him like a physical force.

He moved his head closer to mine until our lips were almost touching. In a low, ragged voice, he said, "I care." His gaze grew intense. "Too fucking much."

The mental whiplash was almost impossible to bear. Against all logic, I had a sudden, stupid urge to throw myself into his arms and bury my face against his chest.

But why would I do that? He was the reason I was upset. Somehow, I managed to say, "But you were so awful."

"I know."

"But why?"

He gave me a look of pure anguish. "Because you shouldn't be here."

"Why not?"

"You *know* why."

I shook my head. "No. I don't." I took a deep, shuddering breath. "I mean, I know that everything ended so terribly, but I never had the chance to explain."

In the back of my mind, I realized that technically, Joel was right. I *shouldn't* be here. Derek, my ass-hat of a lawyer, had issued the ultimate threat. If I didn't get rid of Joel, he was going to make sure that Joel ended up in trouble one way or another.

But then, the day after Joel had left in such a horrible rush, I'd discovered something new, something that had propelled me on this desperate search.

Derek was determined to destroy Joel regardless. I knew this, because Derek had been dumb enough to brag about it all over town.

So now, here I was, hoping to explain and somehow, make it right. I'd also been hoping that together, Joel and I could come up with some sort of solution, and if there was any justice in this world, make a fresh start.

Or, at least, that had been my original plan, right up until Joel had ditched me for a couple of random hoochies. Even now, just thinking about it sent a fresh wave of pain straight through my heart. I had to be honest. "You hurt me."

"I know." His voice was almost too low to hear. "I was an asshole."

I waited for him to say he was sorry. And when he didn't, I asked, "Was that supposed to be an apology?"

"No."

"So you're not sorry?"

"I am. But I'm not gonna say it."

"I don't get it," I said. "Why?"

"Because I don't *want* you to forgive me."

"Why not?"

"I already told you." His eyes were filled with regret. "Because you shouldn't be here."

I gave a confused shake of my head. "So, you were *trying* to drive me away?"

He was quiet for a long moment before saying, "It's better than what I wanted to do."

"Which was...?"

His gaze dipped to my lips. "You don't wanna know."

Something about that look sent a bolt of heat straight to my core. He was so near, and yet so far off in the ways that counted. I wanted to be closer, but just in time, I recalled those girls.

I had to ask, "If I hadn't shown up tonight..." I paused and looked away. I almost couldn't say it.

His voice was softer now. "What?"

"Would've you left with them. I mean, *really* left with them?"

Slowly, he shook his head. "No. And you wanna know why?"

"Why?"

"Because they weren't you."

The words were exactly what I wanted to hear. And yet, I couldn't help but wonder how far that claim went. "But like in the past two weeks," I persisted, "what have you been doing?"

"Nothing."

I bit my lip. "Do I need to ask the other question?"

Again, he moved a fraction closer. "*Who* have I being doing? Is that what you wanna know?"

Suddenly, my lips felt very dry. "Maybe."

"You think you're that easy to forget?"

"I don't know," I admitted. "People have different ways of forgetting."

"Not me. Not since you. Now, you want an answer to that question?"

Silently, I nodded.

"Alright." His gaze locked onto mine. "No one."

Relief coursed through me, and I let out a long, unsteady breath.

Joel moved a fraction closer, and his voice became nearly a caress. "I wanna kiss you."

And just like that, my knees went almost too wobbly to stand. "What?"

His eyes searched mine. "But if you want me to leave, just say the word."

I blinked. "And you would?"

"The truth?" He hesitated. "I dunno."

It was funny. I felt the same way. Already, tonight had been roller coaster ride of emotions. Even now, not a single thing had been resolved. But he was so achingly close. And I did want that kiss.

Standing there, in that desolate parking lot, I realized something. A kiss wasn't the only thing I wanted. Against any sense of self-preservation, I wanted to feel him inside me, right here, right now. I wanted proof that he still cared. And I wanted to believe that by some miracle, he was still mine and only mine.

In a breathless whisper, I confessed, "I don't want you to leave."

"Good." And with that, he lowered his head and gave me a kiss so intense, it sent my pulse jumping. As his mouth claimed my own, I sagged against him and gave a muffled moan of pure bliss as he wrapped me in his arms and pressed his body tight and hard against mine.

Through the haze of love and lust, I vaguely realized that my back was now pressed against my car door. I should've been cold. I should've been uncomfortable. I should've cared that we were outside, and that I was in a strange town with a guy who'd made me cry not too long ago.

But suddenly, none of that mattered. When his lips left mine, I couldn't stop myself from whispering, "I missed you."

His hands were in my hair, and his lips were trailing tender kisses down my neck. "I missed you, too." His breathing was ragged, just like my own, even as he said, "I've been so fucking miserable. You have no idea."

Actually, I did. I'd been miserable, too. I'd been lost in sleepless nights and empty days. I'd been wandering the places we used to go, searching for some sign of him – or at the very least, a memory to keep me going for another day.

I was trembling, now. And maybe he was trembling, too. Into my hair, he whispered, "I love you." He clutched me tighter. "God, I love you so fucking much."

My breath caught. "You do? Still?"

"You've gotta ask?"

No. I didn't. I could hear it in his voice. I could feel it in his touch. And I swear, I could sense it crackling in the air around us, like a fire, refusing to be put out.

I almost wanted to cry, but this time, it wasn't with sadness. "I love you, too. I never stopped." I drew a nervous breath. "And Joel?"

"Yeah?"

"I want you." I swallowed. "And I mean right now."

CHAPTER 9

Suddenly, he became very still. He didn't breathe, and he didn't move. After a long, tense moment, he said, "No."

I was so lost I could hardly think. "What?"

"You don't." His arms grew rigid around my back. "Not here."

That's what *he* thought. With both hands, I reached out and pulled his hips tighter against mine. "You're wrong," I told him.

As if unable to stop himself, he surged forward, capturing me tighter against my car. Our bodies were pressed so perfectly close that I could feel almost everything that I'd been missing – the defined muscles of his chest, the tight hardness of his abs, and lower, the telltale proof that I wasn't the only one who wanted this.

I heard his breath in my ear and felt his heart beating, too fast and too hard, just like mine. His grip tightened, and his hardness surged. For one breathless moment, I thought he'd take me right then and there, in spite of his earlier refusal.

But he didn't.

To my infinite frustration, he held himself in check, as if he didn't know whether to move forward or back away. As for me, I knew exactly what I wanted. I pressed my hips tight against his pelvis and almost smiled when he gave a low, muffled moan just before lowering his head and murmuring into my hair, "No fucking way."

His words said one thing, but his body said another.

As for myself, every inch of me – inside and out – coalesced into one raw, aching need. I felt like if I didn't have him, like now, I'd be lost and alone forever.

In a silent plea, I pressed myself tighter against him. At the feel of his hardness, ready, if not yet willing, I caught my breath. Already, I could feel the slick warmth of my own readiness, deep inside me, like an ache that had to be answered by him, and only him.

More desperate now, I pulled him tighter against me. I was wet. He was hard. And I'd missed him more than simple words could express. When I ground against him, his voice became a ragged whisper, "Baby, you've gotta stop."

I was almost too breathless to speak. "Why?"

"Because you're making me too dumb to say no."

"So don't."

Again, I pressed my hips forward, begging him with my body, if not with my words. All my life, I'd played it safe. I'd been the good girl, the kind of person who never broke any rules or heaven forbid, risked a public spectacle.

But out here, we were utterly alone and hidden, not only by darkness, but by a vehicle on either side. Both of us were ready, and the thought of parting in any way, without consummating whatever this was, well, it was impossible to consider. The last two weeks had driven me crazy, and finally, I knew that I wasn't the only one. I heard myself say, "I know you want me."

"You think I'm gonna deny it?"

"No." I lifted my face and brushed my lips softly against his ear. In a low whisper, I said, "What I *think* is you're gonna lift up my skirt, move aside my panties, and take me, hard, right here, right now."

His hardness surged, and a muffled moan escaped his lips. His reaction told me all I needed to know. I didn't need to stop, and I wasn't going to stop. Whether he'd admit it or not, he wanted me just as badly as I wanted him.

I ran my hands along the side of his waist, and then up underneath the back of his shirt. I felt the muscles of his lower back, warm and hard, shifting against my trembling fingers. My touch, at least so far, had been innocent enough, and yet, I heard his breath hitch and felt his hardness respond, surging against my pelvis.

I slid my hands down to his hips and paused only a moment before zeroing in on what I desperately wanted. Savoring the feel of his rock-hard abs, I slid my fingertips into the waistband of his jeans. When my fingers brushed the tip of his erection, he gave another muffled moan. "Baby, seriously, you're killing me."

That's what he *said*, but I couldn't help but notice that he wasn't pulling away, so with both hands, I frantically worked at the button of his jeans, and finally managed to pop it open. And then, I went for the zipper.

I almost couldn't believe I was doing this. This wasn't me. But maybe that was a good thing. Maybe if I'd been more daring all along, I would've spent less time worrying, and more time living life to its fullest. The last two weeks had taught me something – a lesson I'd never forget. In the big scheme of things, a public spectacle was nothing compared to giving up the guy I loved.

And besides, no one could see us, not really, so with eager hands, I stroked his length, loving the feel of his erection surging warm and ready in my loving grip.

He felt amazing, just like I remembered, but it wasn't enough. I wanted to grip him with more than my hands. I wanted him inside me. Desperately, I shoved down his jeans, pushing them down past his hips.

Finally, as if he couldn't resist any longer, he reached out and tore open my coat. I heard a button pop and roll somewhere along the pavement, but I couldn't bring myself to care.

With both hands, he hiked up my skirt and moved aside the crotch of my panties. His fingers found my wetness, and he sucked in a breath.

I was breathing harder now, too. I had to have him. Desperately, I guided his hardness toward the intersection of my thighs. He said my name, low and ragged. And then, reached behind me and gripped my ass with both hands, lifting me tight against the car as he finally gave me exactly what I wanted – every inch of him, surging hard into my hot wetness.

I moaned into his shoulder. It was everything I'd wanted and then some. I tried to be quiet, and from what I could tell, so did he, even as he claimed me right there, in the darkened parking lot. I wrapped my legs around his hips, wanting to be closer in every possible way. As he moved, he kissed me, hard and hungry, like he, too, couldn't get enough.

And then, almost before I knew it, I was convulsing against him, wrapping my arms tighter, my legs tighter, and even my insides tighter, wanting to hold onto him, to hold onto this moment, for as long as humanly possible. And then, he was shuddering against me, driving into me harder and faster, until with a final shudder, he buried his face in my hair and whispered, "God, I missed you."

I smiled against his shoulder. "I missed you, too."

After a long, intense moment, he pulled back just far enough to give me one final kiss, this one more tender than the ones before. When the kiss ended, he rested his forehead against mine and whispered a curse so low, I could hardly hear it.

I almost wanted to giggle. Smiling, I pulled back to tease, "That's *one* way to put it."

He was still holding me, like I weighed nearly nothing. I leaned my head on his shoulder for a long blissful moment before pulling back and unwrapping my legs from his waist. Gently, he set me back down and leaned over me just enough to whisper in my ear, "You're my drug. You know that?"

Feeling flirtatious now, I said, "Is that a bad thing?"

He gave a rueful laugh. "Probably." He pulled back and looked at my coat. He frowned. "I ruined it."

I looked down. He was right. The buttons hadn't just popped off. They'd popped off and taken some of the fabric with them – or maybe he'd torn it. I didn't know, and I couldn't bring myself to care.

Maybe I should've. It was, after all, the only long coat I had. But suddenly, winter wasn't looming endless and cold. Who needed a coat when I had Joel, the guy who warmed my heart and soul like nobody else?

Together, we managed to reassemble ourselves into something that wasn't quite so X-rated. My panties were soaked, so slid them off and wadded them into a tight ball that laughingly, I tucked into the pocket of my now-ruined coat.

As for Joel, he finished zipping his jeans and fastening the button. And then, he moved forward and gathered me in his arms. We stood like that, pressed against my car, for a long, quiet moment. I wasn't sure where we went from here, but I knew that things were a million times better than they had been this time yesterday.

I pulled back to gaze up at him through the darkness. "See? Aren't you glad you didn't say no?"

He gave me the ghost of a smile. "I *did* say no."

"Yeah, but you didn't mean it."

"The hell I didn't." He gave our surroundings a long look. "Shit, if something had happened…"

I smiled up at him. "But it didn't."

I waited for him to smile back. But he didn't. Instead, he flicked his head toward the other parking lot and said, "You wanna talk? We can sit in my car."

I *did* want to talk. But from the look in his eyes, I wasn't quite sure that he and I wanted to discuss the same thing. As for me, I wanted to discuss patching things up. But what *he* wanted, I suddenly wasn't so sure.

And yet, I nodded anyway, because after all, how bad could it be?

Unfortunately, it didn't take long for me to find out.

CHAPTER 10

Sitting in Joel's car, I told him everything that had happened. I began with Derek's threat to have Joel thrown in jail for violating the terms of his suspended sentence, and I ended with me coming out here tonight, not only to warn Joel, but to tell him all of the other things that I couldn't two weeks earlier.

All of it, I explained, was just one big, crazy mess. Even as I talked, I considered all of the damage that had been done, mostly on the day of Joel's heart-wrenching departure.

He'd gotten that terrible letter, claiming that he had no talent. He'd had movers show up to transport all of his stuff to who-knows-where. He'd gone from having the world at his fingertips to losing almost everything in an instant – including me.

As I spoke, he said nearly nothing. Mostly, he watched me from the driver's seat, listening with an expression that I couldn't quite decipher. Long before I finished, I started to wonder if his unnatural silence was a good sign or a sign of something more ominous. Either way, it was making me uneasy.

"So anyway," I concluded, "when I learned that Derek wasn't going to leave you alone regardless, I thought, 'Forget waiting six months. I've got to find him *now*.'" I gave a shaky laugh. "So here I am."

In the driver's seat, Joel wasn't laughing, not even a little. Abruptly, he said, "How'd you find me?"

I gave him a perplexed look. Of all the things to say, why'd he pick that? Still, I replied, "You remember Chester, right?"

"Yeah." Joel frowned. "The shirtless guy."

"Well, he's not *always* shirtless," I said. "But anyway, you remember his friend, Mike? I got ahold of him, and he pointed me in the right direction. He's a huge fan, by the way." I couldn't help but smile. "To help me find you, guess what he wanted."

"What?"

"Your autograph."

"Yeah? Well, tell him to shove it."

I felt my eyebrows furrow. "Why?"

Ignoring my question, he said, "Or, if you don't wanna tell him, *I* will."

From the look on Joel's face, the conversation wouldn't be a friendly one. Obviously, I was missing something. "But he's the reason I found you."

Joel's expression darkened. "If I wanted to be found, I would've answered my phone."

I drew back. I almost didn't know what to say. "So you knew I was calling?"

"What do *you* think?"

At this point, I didn't know what to think. Even at the time, I realized that he was probably giving me the silent treatment, but to have him toss it in my face like this, well, it wasn't what I'd expected. "I left a bunch of messages," I said. "Did you get them?"

"Yeah. I got them."

"And did you listen?"

When Joel gave a tight nod, I asked, "So why didn't you call me back?"

"Because I figured you'd get the hint."

I was staring at him now. "What are you saying?"

With every passing moment, that queasy feeling was growing again. Ever since we'd gotten into Joel's car, he'd been acting like a different person. Where was the guy who'd been kissing me – and more – not too long ago?

When Joel said nothing, I persisted, "Are you still angry? Is that it?"

He turned to stare silently out the front windshield. More confused than ever, I turned my head to follow his gaze. Outside, there was nothing to see, just my car and the van parked beside it, with all those flyers tucked under the windshield wipers. As I watched, a sudden gust of wind carried one of the flyers away, sending it fluttering across the dark pavement.

In my seat, I gave a little shiver. Even with the car running, I felt a slow chill, creeping up my spine. In the driver's seat, Joel still hadn't answered my question.

I turned to study his face, well, the half I could see, anyway. Bracing myself, I said, "Just tell me."

He didn't even look. "Tell you what?"

"Well for starters, why you're acting so funny."

He gave a humorless laugh. "Funny, huh?"

If there was a joke in all this, I sure as heck wasn't getting it.

Finally, he turned to face me. "I heard about your trip."

I gave him a perplexed look. "What trip?"

"To my dad's place."

Oh. That. It wasn't so much a trip as a daylong effort in futility. Joel's hometown was a four-hour drive from mine, which meant I'd spent eight hours on the road for absolutely nothing.

His dad hadn't even answered the door. But he *had* been home. I'd been almost sure of it, thanks to a blaring television and the sounds of movement behind the front door.

I said, "I was hoping to find you there." I tried to think. "Is that why you're mad?"

He gave a tight shrug. "I'm not mad."

"Oh, come on," I said. "Obviously, something's wrong. What is it?"

Once again, he ignored my question. "And you called Jake."

"Well, yeah. Because I was worried."

"About what?"

"You, actually."

"Yeah? Well, don't."

"Don't what? Worry? You *did* hear everything I just told you, right? About Derek? And his threats to get you thrown in jail?"

"I heard."

"So, you could see where I'd be concerned, especially when you didn't return my calls." My voice was calm, but beneath the surface, a storm was brewing. Trying not to show it, I continued. "I mean, look at it from my point of view. Derek shows up, he tells me about the suspended sentence – something *you* never mentioned, by the way – and I'm stuck dealing with it all by myself."

"That was *your* choice," Joel said. "Not mine."

"Yeah," I said. "Like it was *your* choice to not tell me you were in some sort of trouble."

"I wasn't worried. Why should *you* be?"

He was totally missing the point. I tried again. "You should've told me." I gave him a pleading look. "Seriously Joel, all those nights we spent together? All those days? And you never thought to mention it? Not even once?"

He gave another shrug, but said nothing.

I made a sound of frustration. "Okay, I get it. You're mad at me for not telling you earlier. But in my own defense, I had just a few short hours to figure things out. You had weeks, almost months, to tell me what was going on. Why didn't you?"

"Because it wasn't a big deal."

I felt my gaze narrow. "I don't believe you."

"Alright."

Alright? That's it?

With a weary sigh, I leaned back in my seat and closed my eyes. This was going nowhere, or maybe it *was* going somewhere, and I didn't want to accept it.

Joel's voice, softer now, broke into my thoughts. "Lemme ask you something."

I turned to look. "What?"

"What's changed?"

I gave a confused shake of my head. "What do you mean?"

"I left what, two weeks ago?"

Yes, but it felt like longer. The day of Joel's departure had been one of the worst days of my adult life. Within just a few hours, I'd gone from hearing Derek's threat to watching in shock as an unexpected moving truck rumbled into my driveway, causing Joel to assume the worst. From start to finish, it had been a total nightmare.

I gave a silent nod.

"Between then and now," Joel said, "what's different?"

The question caught me off-guard, and I wasn't sure how to answer. Still, I gave it my best shot. "Well, two weeks ago, I thought that if we gave each other up for six months, everything would be okay. But now that I know that Derek isn't going to let up regardless, I figure we might as well face the problem together."

"What you mean," Joel said, "is you're gonna let me drag you down in the mud."

"No." I gave a decisive shake of my head. "That's not it at all."

He gave me a smile that didn't reach his eyes. "Isn't it?"

I felt a sudden twinge of panic. "No. Definitely not."

Abruptly, Joel said, "Wanna know why I won't give that fucker an autograph?"

Startled, I said, "Uh, sure. Why?"

"Because the dumb-ass sent you here." His jaw tightened. "Alone."

I didn't want to talk about Mike. I wanted to talk about Joel. Hoping to move past this, I said, "He didn't *send* me. I came on my own. He did me a favor, remember?"

"You think so, huh?"

"I *know* so. I had to beg him, actually. He acted like it was all a big secret or something."

"Yeah? You wanna hear another secret?"

From the tone of his voice, I wasn't so sure. Still, I nodded.

"He's lucky I don't track him down and kick his ass."

I didn't like the sounds of that. "Why?"

"Because begging or not, he should've said no." Joel did a quick scan of our surroundings. "Take a good look. You're in a shitty part of town. And you had to drive through a shittier part to get here."

I knew which part he meant – a stretch of burnt-out buildings, covered in graffiti. It made this desolate parking lot look like a fine slice of heaven. Still, I said, "It wasn't *so* bad."

"Right." He turned and gave my car a quick glance. "And *that* thing? Fucker breaks down every two weeks."

I wasn't used to him swearing so much. And I loved my car, even if it *was* mostly for sentimental reasons. It had, after all, been my mom's. I said, "It's not *that* often."

Ignoring me, Joel kept on going. "And you end up *here*. In a place you don't know, with the worst kind of people."

"That's not true," I said. "At least not now." My voice softened. "I'm with you."

Joel made a scoffing sound. "Yeah. You're with me. A royal fuckup."

"You are *not* a fuckup."

"Uh-huh. But forget me for a minute. Let's get back to your dumb-ass friend. I don't care if you were begging on your knees, he should've said no. Or shit, if he couldn't do that, the fucker should've manned up and brought you here himself."

Why did this matter? I sighed. "Oh, stop it. Even if he wanted to, he couldn't've."

"Yeah? Why not?"

"Because he's at a wrestling meet in Ohio."

"Fuck Ohio."

I took a deep breath. "Look, I don't want to be rude, but can you calm down? Please? It's not a big deal. Everything was fine. I mean, seriously, *you* don't always play it safe."

"Yeah? And you're not me."

Well, there was that.

Joel continued. "And neither is your friend."

"Forget Mike," I said. "Let's talk about something else, okay?"

Looking anything but eager, Joel said, "Like what?"

"Well for starters, about your stuff. Do you know, I wouldn't let the movers take it?"

If Joel was relieved, he didn't show it. "Oh, yeah?"

"Yeah, so it's still there." I gave a nervous laugh. "And of course, I still have your money. And just so you know, it's all still there. I mean, like I haven't touched it or anything." I gave a playful eye-roll. "Well, other than to put it in my safety deposit box."

The longer I talked, the more unhappy Joel was looking.

Into his silence, I rattled on, "So, if you want, we could go get it. I mean, not tonight, because the bank doesn't open until tomorrow. But we could *leave* tonight. It's a three-hour drive, but—"

"Melody."

I froze. Even as I'd been talking, I'd known that something wasn't quite right. The look in Joel's eyes only confirmed it. With growing fear, I asked, "What?"

"I'm not coming back."

CHAPTER 11

Joel's words echoed in the quiet car. I gave a small shake of my head. "What?"

Somewhere behind me, I heard a vehicle rumbling up toward us. I didn't even turn to look. My eyes were still trained on Joel's face. Somehow, I managed to say, "You don't mean that."

"I'm sorry." His voice grew very quiet. "I should've told you."

I gave him a confused look. "What do you mean? When?"

Slowly, his gaze shifted to my car, wedged next to that dark van. I looked, but saw nothing. And then it hit me. "You mean before…?" I didn't even know how to say it.

But soon, I didn't need to, because Joel saved me the trouble by saying, "Before fucking you in the parking lot?"

I sucked in a breath. I wouldn't have put it *that* way. In fact, I probably wouldn't have said it at all. Even now, I could hardly speak. "You're not serious? You *knew* before—"

"Yeah," he said. "I knew."

I was still staring at him. Our lovemaking – or whatever he wanted to call it – had meant something to me. It had meant something to him, too. Or at least, I'd thought so at the time.

Shadows cast by the approaching headlights crept across his face. It was the face of someone heading for the gallows. He said, "You should go."

My jaw dropped. "You're kidding, right? Like what, you're dismissing me?"

Maybe I should've been nicer. If anything, Joel looked more

miserable than *I* felt. And that was saying something. "Well?" I demanded. "Are you?"

He gave me an anguished look. "It's not like that."

My tone grew sarcastic. "Oh, isn't it?"

Behind me, I heard the unknown vehicle pulling up beside us on the passenger's side. I still didn't turn to look. I didn't care who it was or what they were doing. All I knew was, I wasn't going anywhere, not yet.

I met Joel's troubled gaze. "Just tell me what's going on." My heart was pounding now. "I mean, how could you act like you care—"

"I care." He took a ragged breath. "It was no lie."

My voice rose. "And what about you still loving me? Was *that* a lie?"

His voice was just above a whisper. "No."

"So?" I made a sound of frustration. "What is it then?"

A tap on my car window made me jump in my seat. I whirled to look and saw Cal standing just outside my car door. Behind him was his truck, with the engine no longer running.

Funny, I hadn't even heard it turn off.

Cal grinned at me through the glass. "See?"

See what? My hopes shattered into a million pieces? I gave a stunned shake of my head.

He motioned for me to roll down the window, but I was too numb to move. Part of me wanted to scream at Cal to go away. But I didn't. In spite of everything, I couldn't help but recall how nice he'd been to me earlier.

And plus – a wild thought suddenly hit me – maybe this little visit, or whatever it was, would give Joel some time to cool off, and maybe rethink what he was saying.

With a trembling hand, I reached out and pressed the window-control button. When the glass slid down, Cal said in a tone filled with mischief, "So what were *you* kids doing?"

Joel's voice sliced past me. "Talking. Now get the fuck out of here."

I winced. *So much for cooling off.* I gave Cal a worried look. Silently, I mouthed, "Sorry."

Looking utterly unfazed, Cal lowered his head to look at Joel. "Damn," Cal said. "I thought you'd be in a better mood." He looked back to me and said, "You know, he's been a total dick for two weeks now."

Cal had mentioned something similar during our walk through the parking lot. And just like before, I felt a spark of pathetic hope kindle in my chest. The last two weeks had been miserable for me, too. That had to mean *something*, right?

From the driver's seat, Joel said, "Is there a reason you're here?"

"Yeah," Cal said. "You locked me out again." He laughed. "And get this. Your two little friends? They were gone by the time I got there. So thanks for nothing, you prick."

Yes. Joel *was* a prick, at least right now. But that wasn't *really* him. Somewhere, underneath all that, was the amazing guy I still loved.

Hoping to keep Cal talking, I forced a smile. "So it was waste, huh?"

"Not a total waste." He gave a casual shrug. "Had some pancakes, a bunch of bacon, some orange juice. Still, it was pretty damn disappointing."

He flashed me a sudden grin. "But get this. Wanna know why they weren't there?"

I gave a hesitant nod. Anything to keep him talking.

He laughed. "They got kicked out."

I heard myself murmur, "Kicked out? For what?"

"Fighting." He made a scoffing sound. "And the worst thing? Happened like five minutes before I got there."

I could hardly think, but the story sounded like it might be funny. Funny was good, right? Something to break the tension? Hoping for one heck of a punchline, I said, "You mean, like with other customers?"

"Hell no. I mean with each other." Cal was grinning again. "And I mean a big ol' cat-fight, with slapping and hair pulling." His smile faded. "Sucks that I missed it." He looked to Joel and said, "You owe me, by the way."

In a tight voice, Joel said, "For what?"

"For keeping your girl safe while you pulled your head out of your ass."

Hoping to see Joel's reaction, I turned to look.

His expression was stony, even as he told Cal, "And I'm gonna owe you again."

Behind me, Cal asked, "For what?"

"For keeping her safe now."

I felt my brow wrinkle. "What?"

Cal said, "Yeah. What the hell are you talking about?"

Joel visibly swallowed. "Follow her to the highway, okay?"

I felt a new surge of panic, "But I'm not leaving."

Joel gave a slow shake of his head. "You can't stick around here."

"Why not?" I demanded.

"Because it's not safe." His gaze shifted back to Cal. "You got this?"

I spoke up. "No. He doesn't." I turned to Cal and said, "Could you excuse us for a minute?"

Cal's gaze shifted from me to Joel. With no trace of humor, he said, "Uh, yeah. I'll be in the truck."

I was so distracted, I forgot to thank him. Instead, I pressed the button to roll up the window and whirled back to Joel. "What was that about?"

"It's the middle of the night."

"So?"

"So the town's shitty, and your car sucks."

"Oh, is that so?"

"You know it is." His voice grew quieter. "He'll watch out for you."

"Oh," I said, my tone growing snotty. "Thanks ever so much." My stomach was in knots again, and why wouldn't it be? The last couple of hours had been a roller-coaster ride of epic proportions.

Now, I was rocketing downward with no bottom in sight. I wanted to scream and not in the fun way. "What's your deal, anyway?"

"I already told you."

"No," I said. "You haven't. Not really. So just go ahead. Spell it out, alright?"

"Alright, you wanna know?" Without waiting for my answer, he plunged on. "In my life? There's no place for someone like you."

The statement was a dagger straight into my heart. "Someone like me? What do you mean?"

"You think I'm in trouble? Well, maybe I am. And maybe it's gonna suck. And maybe I don't want you to be part of that."

What a crock. "Oh," I said, my tone growing snotty again, "so you're doing it for me? Is that what you're saying?"

"No. I'm doing it for me." His eyes were anguished. "If anything ever happened to you—"

I gave a snort of derision. "That's funny. Something's 'happening to me' now." It was true. My heart was breaking, but I was almost too angry to care.

He glanced away. "It could be worse."

I knew firsthand, it could *always* be worse. But that wasn't the point. Obviously, Joel had made his decision. And short of begging, there wasn't much I could do.

Funny to think, I *had* begged. On the day he left, I'd begged him to wait. And then, after he'd gone, I'd left countless messages, begging for him to call me back. And even tonight, I'd practically begged him for whatever that was outside my car.

I was such an idiot. Even now, after everything, I was like two seconds away from begging him to reconsider.

Suddenly, I was tired of begging. What was the point, anyway? Even if I convinced Joel to change his mind, what then? He'd just change it back tomorrow.

Oh sure, maybe tonight, he'd hold me and kiss me and tell me that he loved me. But it wouldn't be a forever thing. That much was obvious.

When it came to Joel, I didn't want something temporary. I wanted him forever – or at least I had. But now, I wasn't so sure. If he could give me up so easily, what did that really say? Did I love him more than he loved me?

Who knows? Maybe he didn't love me at all, at least not in the way that mattered.

I took a shaky breath and said in the coldest voice I could muster. "Alright. If that's what you want."

"It's not what I want. It's—"

"You know what?" I held up a hand. "Just spare me, okay? What are you gonna say? That you're doing this for me? That you're gonna save me from pain or danger, or cripes, even public disgrace? Well, let me tell you something, I don't want to hear it."

I forced something like a laugh. "And now, you're gonna make your friend follow me to the highway? Well, thanks for nothing."

Joel's gaze blazed into mine. "Wanna know why I won't do it?"

I gave a half-shrug.

He said, "Because I'm not sure I'd stop."

I gave him a thin smile. "Don't worry. I'm sure you'd find a way." And with that, I opened the car door and got out. A second later, I slammed the door so hard, I swear, I could hear the widows rattle.

Afterward, I didn't even look back, even though I sorely wanted to.

CHAPTER 12

The next couple of weeks passed in a slow, dreary procession of empty cloudy days. I thought of him every day and dreamed of him every night.

Even when I didn't remember those dreams, I knew exactly who'd been starring in them, whether from the tears on my pillow or from the sweet blissful feeling that faded the instant I realized that none of those dreams had been real, whether figuratively *or* literally.

All the while, I did nothing to try to contact him. I still had his money, and it wasn't the only thing I had. I had his clothes. I had his tools. I had his paint brushes and canvases, along with the few completed paintings that he'd been storing for who-knows-how-long.

Everything was exactly as he'd left it, whether in the guest house or in the studio above. It wasn't just sappy sentimentality that kept me from moving it to someplace else. Storage was expensive, and I could barely pay my gas bill.

With summer long-gone, I'd lost even my seasonal job at the cookie shop, along with the pittance I received for mowing the lawn and weeding the flower beds. No matter where I looked, everything felt dead and empty. The tourists were gone, the grass had gone dormant, and all of the flowers were long-dead.

With Aunt Gina in France, learning to be a chef, and Cassie visiting her parents in Indiana, I'd spent Thanksgiving alone, watching old movies and pretending that it was just another day.

In just a few short weeks, it would be Christmas, not that I cared.

In fact, I was having a hard time caring about anything, no matter how much I tried to fake it.

I was also looking for work, not that I'd found any, which totally sucked, because I needed money now more than ever. Just before Thanksgiving, I'd developed a weird drainage problem in all of the bathrooms.

Every single sink, tub, or shower was draining so slowly, it took forever for the water to go down. After days of hoping things would magically improve on their own, I'd given up and done the unthinkable.

I'd called a plumber.

It was mid-morning, and I was expecting him any minute when the doorbell rang. But when I answered, it wasn't the plumber. It was Derek, dressed in a suit and tie.

He gave me a big salesman-like smile. "How's it going?"

I didn't smile back. "What do you want?"

"Oh come on," he said. "You can't *still* be mad?"

Mad didn't even begin to describe it. While standing in the open doorway, I thought of everything Derek had done. He'd blackmailed me with threats. He'd sent a fake letter that convinced Joel to give up any artistic aspirations. He'd hired a giant moving truck – *without* my permission, no less – to haul away Joel's stuff.

And now, on top of everything else, he kept stopping by, even though I'd made it perfectly clear that he wasn't welcome. Ignoring his question, I said, "You're supposed to call first, remember?"

"I did call." He frowned. "Twice."

"Yeah. I know. And I didn't answer, so you should've stayed home."

"I wasn't *at* home," he said. "I was at the office."

"Well, goodie for you."

Derek's jaw tightened. "I know you don't believe this, but I'm here as a friend."

Sure, he was. I muttered, "Some friend."

He gave me a pleading look. "Has it ever occurred to you that we had your best interests at heart?"

I wanted to slap him. "Look, we've been through this. For the millionth time, no. It has not occurred to me. Wanna know what I think?"

"What?"

"It's not *my* interests that you care about."

His eyebrows furrowed. "What's that supposed to mean?"

"You know what it means. Between you and your dad, you're determined to keep me under your thumb." I lifted my chin. "Well, I'm tired of it."

"Yeah," Derek said. "I heard."

I froze. In a carefully neutral voice, I said, "You heard what?"

"That you're looking for another law firm."

Damn it. I didn't want him to know. Not yet. I tried for a casual shrug. "Where'd you hear that?"

"It's a small town. Word travels."

He was right about the town, and yet, I found his story hard to believe. It was true that I'd been seeking out other law firms, but I'd purposely avoided talking to anyone within a hundred miles of here.

I said, "I don't care what you heard. Is that it? Are we done?"

"No. Not by a long shot. I also heard you're looking for a job."

I sighed. Now, this I *could* blame on the size of the town. I'd been applying all over the place, with no luck. When it came to potential employers, everyone was oh-so-nice, but every single one of them had fallen into one of two categories – those who thought I was looking for kicks, and those who thought I was looking to do unpaid charity work.

Either way, it wasn't helping me pay my bills *or* to complete my art history degree. It was all so incredibly frustrating. I'd been just a few semesters away from graduating when I'd been derailed by a sudden lack of funds, along with the need to keep a better eye on the estate.

So, of course, I was looking for a job. What else *could* I do? I gave Derek an annoyed look. "So?"

"So I'm here to offer you one."

I crossed my arms. "Oh yeah? Where?"

"At the law firm. You could clerk or something."

I wasn't stupid. I saw the job offer for what it was – just another way to keep me under their control. I gave him a thin smile. "Don't you need a law background for that?"

"Normally. But you're practically family. We'd work it out."

I felt my jaw clench. "Let's get one thing straight," I said. "You're nothing like family."

In hindsight, it was hilarious to think that I'd once felt otherwise. Until just a few months ago, Derek had been like the brother I never had. Now, he was a thorn in my side that kept coming back, no matter how many times I plucked it out.

"Oh come on," Derek said. "Don't be like that. We *are* like family." He gave me a hopeful smile. "We've always been, right?"

"Oh, sure." My tone grew sarcastic. "Just like Aunt Vivian is family."

His smile disappeared. "What's that supposed to mean?"

But from the look on his face, he knew exactly what it meant. Aunt Vivian was married to my dad's brother. And just like Derek, she took a keen interest in my affairs. But where *she* was content with merely swiping my stuff, Derek seemed determined to ruin my life – and, the way it looked, steal a lot more than a few wine glasses.

When it came to estate-management, he and his dad were either crooked beyond belief or incredibly incompetent. Either way, they weren't doing me any favors.

"Look," I said, "I don't know what you mean to accomplish with these little visits, but let me tell you again. I will *never* forgive you for what you did."

He practically groaned, "But I'm *trying* to make it up to you."

"By what?" I snapped. "Looking to get Joel arrested?"

He tensed. "What do you mean?"

His reaction only confirmed what I'd heard through the grapevine. "Oh, just stop it," I said. "Like you said, it's a small town, so don't pretend that you care one bit about me, when you're going after him anyway."

Just thinking about it, I wanted to scream. On that godawful day, I'd done everything they asked. And for what? I hadn't saved anyone –

not me *or* Joel.

Derek stood there for a long silent moment before looking down to mumble, "Well, if he's doing something illegal, it's not *my* fault."

"Oh yeah? Well, he wouldn't *be* fighting anymore if you hadn't interfered." I was shaking now with long-suppressed rage. "How could you?"

Slowly, Derek lifted his gaze to mine. In a quiet voice, he said, "Hey, it's not *me*. It's my dad. He's concerned about you. That's all."

More likely, he was concerned about my money, assuming there was any left. I made a scoffing sound. "Sure he is."

"He is," Derek insisted. "And I am, too. Can't we just put it behind us?"

I stared at him. "Put it behind us? Are you kidding me? When you're *still* threatening him?" My voice rose. "Listen, you jackass. I don't care how many 'jobs' you offer me, or how many times you stop by, you're *not* my friend and you're *not* my family." I could hardly breathe. "So fuck off!"

And this, of course, is when I spotted the white service van rumbling into the driveway. *Damn it.* It was the plumber, and I was on the verge of losing it.

Or maybe I *had* lost it. I looked back to Derek, who just stood there, staring at me in stunned silence.

He looked almost ready to cry. And awful or not, it made me feel just a little bit better. I summoned up a stiff smile. "And while you're at it, get the hell off my porch."

Finally, looking like a survivor of some natural disaster, he turned and practically staggered down the front steps and toward his car. With slow, jerky movements, he opened his car door, climbed inside, and shut the door behind him. And then, he sat, not driving away, but not getting back out either.

I was still shaking and couldn't seem to make myself stop, even as the plumber pulled up and parked beside Derek's car.

I felt like crying, but somehow, I kept the tears at bay, even a half-hour later when I received a double dose of bad news.

One had to do with my plumbing, and the other had to do with Joel.

CHAPTER 13

I gave the plumber a worried look. "So it's not just a clogged pipe or something?"

He shook his head. "Sorry. More like a clogged house."

"But how?" I asked.

"My guess? You've got a crushed sewer line. And just to be clear, I'm talking the main one." At my confused look, he added, "It's a big, underground pipe that runs from here to the road."

I didn't know a thing about sewers, but I *did* know that my front yard was huge, which meant that my sewer line was probably a lot longer than most. I winced. "That sounds expensive."

"Well, it's not cheap. You'll need to call in a specialist."

My stomach sank. And here, I thought a plumber *was* a specialist. "Like who?"

"A sewer contractor." He glanced toward the front of the house. "They'll need to dig up the front yard, see if they can find the damage. And then, they've gotta fix it."

The more he talked, the more expensive this sounded. I wanted to cry. I asked, "I don't suppose it's something I can do myself?"

He gave me a look. "I dunno. You got a backhoe?"

I wasn't exactly sure what a backhoe was, but I *did* know that I didn't have one. "No." I tried to laugh. "Not that I know of."

"Yeah, me neither."

Inside my pocket, my cell phone buzzed. With a quick apology, I pulled it out and looked at the display, only to feel my heart-rate quicken. There was no way I'd let this go to voicemail.

Excusing myself, I stepped away and answered with a quiet, "Hello?"

On the other end, Mike skipped the hello-thing and said only two words. "Tomorrow night."

I froze. For two harmless words, they struck fear straight into my heart. "You don't mean Joel's fighting tomorrow night?"

"Sure, I do. That's what you wanted to know, right?"

I *did* want to know, but I wasn't happy to hear it. Sooner or later, he'd be caught, and if Derek had *his* way, Joel would be in serious trouble.

As my thoughts churned with the awful possibilities, Mike promised to text me the location of the fight. And then, just as I was ready to say goodbye, he said, "So, you got that autograph?"

I cringed. This was another problem. When I'd promised Mike that autograph, I never imagined it would be difficult to get. Even if Joel and I weren't officially together, I figured he'd at least be willing to scribble his name on something – if not for me, then definitely for a fan.

Turns out, I'd figured wrong, but I hated the thought of not living up to my end of the bargain.

"Sorry," I said, "not yet." Hoping to sound more optimistic than I felt, I added, "But I'm still working on it."

I tried to think. I still had Joel's money. He had to pick it up eventually, right? Maybe, when he did, I could have him sign a receipt or something. And maybe, if I used fancy paper, I could frame the thing so it didn't look so pathetic.

On the phone, Mike gave a cheerful laugh. "You know what? Forget that. I don't know what the hell I was thinking."

My shoulders sagged in relief. "Really?"

"Sure," he said. "I'll just ask him myself when I meet him."

I swallowed. "What?"

"Yeah." He hesitated. "You said I could meet him, right?"

Had I said that? I couldn't remember, but I couldn't rule it out either. At the time, I'd been incredibly distracted.

Regardless, there was no way on Earth that I wanted to encourage any such meeting – not unless Mike *wanted* an ass-kicking. *Damn it.* This was all my fault.

I gave a nervous laugh. "But you've already met him."

At the memory, my heart ached like it always did. It had been the night of my birthday. I'd been standing along the roadside, talking with Mike and Chester outside Mike's pickup, when Joel had roared up – in a stolen car, no less – to give me a ride.

On the phone, Mike said, "You mean that night on the road? That doesn't count."

"Why not?"

"Because I wasn't even sure it was him."

"Oh, well—"

"So, does he like burgers?"

"What?"

"Burgers," Mike repeated. "I was thinking I'd take him out for a burger and beer."

Funny, I could use a beer right now, and I didn't even like the stuff.

Behind me, I heard the plumber say, "Sorry to interrupt, but I've gotta get going."

I turned and gave him an apologetic smile. I held up a finger to indicate that I'd be just another minute. Into the phone, I said, "Hey Mike, I've gotta go, but I'll keep you posted, okay?"

After disconnecting the call, I turned back to the plumber and said, "Sorry about that."

"Hey, I bill by the hour," he said. "Normally, I'd let you talk all you want, but I'm late for another stop." He ripped the top paper off his clipboard and handed it over. "By the way, I take cash or check."

I looked down at the bill and tried not to cringe. The amount was pretty much what I'd been expecting, but it still hurt to see, especially when the problem wasn't even solved.

As I dug out my checkbook, I asked, "For that sewer work, what kind of money do you think I'm looking at?"

He shrugged. "A few thousand at least."

I swallowed. "Dollars?"

"Well, it sure ain't pennies."

"Why so much?" I asked.

He gave me a look. "You ever price a backhoe?"

It was kind of hard to price one, when I didn't know what it was. "No," I admitted.

"Well, *I* have. And let's just say, there's a reason I don't have one."

My mind was going a million miles a minute. There was no way I could afford such a major repair, at least not now. "Just out of curiosity," I said, "what happens if I don't get it fixed?"

"That depends," he said. "You like raw sewage?"

"Not particularly."

"Then I'd get it fixed. And I wouldn't put it off either."

As I wrote out the check, I wanted to cry. Funny, everything today made me want to cry. It had been one of those days, and now I had a scarier decision on my hands.

But this one didn't have to do with the plumbing. It had to do with Joel. I had to stop him from fighting – which was why, five hours later, I was in downtown Detroit, seeking out Joel's least-favorite brother.

CHAPTER 14

Standing on the busy sidewalk, I stared up at the tall, upscale building. The building was so upscale, in fact, that when I approached the glass double-doors out front, I was greeted by a uniformed doorman, who said with an easy smile, "Can I help you?"

I nodded. "I'm here to see Jake Bishop."

And just like that, his smile was gone. "About what?"

Startled by his sudden change in demeanor, I said, "Well, actually, it's private."

He gave me the squinty-eye. "You got an appointment?"

"No," I admitted. "Do I need one?"

In truth, there was a reason I didn't have an appointment. I hadn't called ahead, because I didn't want Jake to know that I was coming. I'd never met him in person, but I *had* talked to him on the phone for like thirty whole seconds.

It hadn't gone well.

In front of me, the doorman gave a weary sigh. "Look, he's engaged, alright?"

I drew back. *Talk about insulting.* "You think I'm here to hit on him?"

"I don't know. Are you?"

"No."

He gave me a dubious look. "If you say so."

He turned away, heading toward a tall desk in the center of the lobby. Unsure what else to do, I followed after him. After reaching the desk, he opened the top drawer and pulled a thick, black appointment book. He flipped it open to someplace in the middle and turned it around to face me.

He handed me a pen and said in a bored tone, "Sign your name. I'll add you to the list."

"What list?"

"Of people who stopped by."

I felt my gaze narrow. I didn't drive five hours to be given an obvious brush-off. "Does he ever *look* at the list?"

The doorman gave a non-committal shrug that didn't inspire a whole lot of confidence.

It felt like a kick in the stomach. Then again, everything felt like a kick in the stomach. On top of everything else, I wasn't feeling so great. A couple of hours east of here, I'd made the unfortunate decision to partake in gas station nachos, and I'd been queasy ever since.

Or maybe it was just nerves. Either way, the doorman wasn't helping.

"Look," I said, "I'm here about his brother."

"Uh-huh. Nice try."

"What's that supposed to mean?"

"Sorry, but I've heard them all."

Desperately, I tried to think. "How about Luna? Is *she* here?" I'd never met Jake's fiancée, but that *was* her name, wasn't it?

Before the doorman could answer, a loud commotion made us both turn to look. Near the small bank of elevators, a couple of college-aged guys had emerged from the nearest elevator and were arguing up a storm.

One was blond, and the other had hair so dark, it might've been black.

"Your ass," the blond one was saying. "Bruce Lee would've mopped the floor with that guy."

The dark-haired one gave a snort of derision. "No way, dude. Compared to him? Bruce Lee's a pussy."

The blond froze. "You wanna say that again?"

"Hell yeah," the dark-haired one said. "Pussy, pussy, pussy…"

Suddenly, the blond took a flying leap straight for the dark-haired guy. A moment later, they were rolling around on the ornate carpet with a whole lot of scuffling and swearing. Somewhere behind them, an attractive girl around my own age stepped out of the same elevator.

She stared down at them and groaned, "Oh, crap. Not again." She looked to the doorman and called out, "Pete, get the hose, will ya?"

Immediately, the guys stopped fighting. The blond sat up and said, "Nice try. He don't got no hose."

"Yeah," the dark-haired guy said. "Like we're gonna fall for *that* again." He pushed himself up and looked to the blond. "We should give *her* the hose. See how *she* likes it."

The blond grimaced. "Dude, you hear how that sounds?"

Now, they were both looking disturbed. In unison, they shifted their gaze to the girl.

She held up her hands. "You know what? I'm not even asking." She looked around the lobby and froze when she saw me staring. After a long moment, she cocked her head to the side and said, "Melody?"

Now, it was *my* turn to freeze. She knew me?

Was that Luna?

CHAPTER 15

Five minutes later, I was inside the elevator, riding up toward the top floor. As it turned out, she *was* Luna, and she'd recognized me from some photos she'd seen on the internet.

Imagine that. For once, all of that unwanted media attention was doing me some good.

Inside the elevator, it was just the two of us, and the upward momentum wasn't helping my stomach. Luna gave me a concerned look. "Hey, are you feeling alright?"

"Yeah." I swallowed. "Sure."

But from the look on her face, she wasn't buying it. "What, you don't like elevators?"

Elevators were fine. Gas station nachos, on the other hand, were something I'd be avoiding from now on. What on Earth had I been thinking? But I *hadn't* been thinking, and that was the real problem.

Unfortunately, it was one of those problems that *no one* would want to hear, especially someone I'd just met. I forced a smile. "Something like that."

Down in the lobby, I'd briefly explained that I was here because I was worried about Joel. That's all it took. Almost immediately, she was whisking me into the elevator and hitting the button for the penthouse.

Inside my pocket, my cell phone buzzed. Reluctantly, I pulled it out and took a look. *Damn it.* It was Derek of all people. Hadn't he bothered me enough for one day? With a sigh, I shoved the phone back into my pocket and let it to go to voicemail.

Luna said, "I know that look."

"What look is that?"

"It's the 'why-is-this-turd-calling-me' look." She glanced toward my phone, now tucked away in my pocket. "Ex-boyfriend?"

I shook my head. "More like an ex-friend." I considered everything that Derek had put me through. "But he's still a turd." It wasn't a word I'd normally use, but it definitely fit. "And actually," I added, "he's part of the reason I'm here."

"So he's a *jealous* turd?"

"Jealous? What do you mean?"

"Well, you already told me that you're worried about Joel. And *now,* you're telling me that the turd – who I *now* know is a guy – is one of the reasons you're here. So let me guess. The turd's trying to break you two up?"

"Me and Joel?" In my heart, I felt that all-too-familiar ache. "We *are* broken up."

"What?" She gave a little shake of her head. "You can't be."

"Why not?"

"Because he's so crazy about you. The last time I saw him, he was *so* happy." She paused. "Okay, he wasn't happy the whole time, because he was pretty mad at Jake. But he was definitely happy. I could tell." Her eyebrows furrowed. "You didn't dump him, did you?"

The elevator dinged, and the doors slid open to reveal a marble entryway that led to a single set of double doors. But Luna wasn't moving. "So, did you?"

"No. Not really. In a way, he dumped *me.* Sort of." I pushed a hand through my hair. "Actually, it's all really complicated."

She nodded. "I can relate to *that.*"

Finally, she turned and led us out of the elevator, heading toward the double doors. When she reached them, she pulled out a key card and swiped it across a nearby security panel, saying, "Jake's a real stickler about security."

Once we entered the penthouse, it was easy to see why.

I took a good look around, taking in the expensive furniture, the stylish décor, and the stunning riverfront view, visible through massive floor-to-ceiling windows.

I turned to Luna and said, "You have a beautiful place."

"Thanks," she said, motioning me toward a stylish sitting area. "But it's not mine. It's Jake's."

As we sat down, I said, "But you're engaged, right?" Even if I hadn't already known, the giant rock on her ring finger would've been a dead giveaway.

She gave me a sunny smile. "Yup."

"So why'd you call it *his* place?" Normally, I wouldn't be so nosy, but given the fact I was about to spill my guts – hopefully, not literally – I figured I might as well settle in for some serious sharing.

Luna gave it some thought. "I don't know." She looked around, as if seeing the place for the first time. "It's just that he had it before me, you know?" She gave a rueful laugh. "On my own, I could never afford something like *this*." She paused. "Or a place like yours for that matter."

At my confused look, she added, "I saw it on the internet."

"Really? *Where* on the internet?"

"You know. That feature on..." She paused as if thinking. "What was the show? Fanciful Living?"

"Oh. That." Around fifteen years earlier, my parents had given a televised tour for some charity thing. Little did they know that the footage would stick around forever, and now, thanks to the internet, offer virtual tours with just a few clicks.

"So," Luna said, "your house was built by some mobster, huh?"

"More like a bootlegger," I said. "You know, during prohibition and all that."

"Yeah, I saw." She leaned forward. "Any dead bodies in the basement?"

I tried to smile. "Not that I know of." Of course, I couldn't be certain, since I didn't have access to the basement. In truth, I hadn't been down there in years. And technically, it wasn't so much a basement as a wine cellar.

For all I knew, there could be a pile of corpses ten feet tall, stacked among the wine racks. Somehow, the thought didn't help my stomach.

Across from me, Luna lowered her voice. "You're not gonna be sick, are you?"

"Excuse me?"

"You were looking kind of green there for a minute." She studied my face. "Are you sure you're okay?"

I nodded. "I was just thinking, that's all."

"About Joel?"

"Something like that."

"So tell me," she said, "What's going on?"

"Well, like I said, it's really complicated." I bit my lip. There was no way I could explain the situation with Joel without also explaining what was going on with the estate. But the story was so long and convoluted that it would take at least an hour to tell.

Plus, as much as I appreciated her interest, she wasn't the person I'd come to see. Trying to be tactful about it, I said, "I don't suppose Jake's around?"

"Sorry, not for another hour. Why?"

"Because, well, I was hoping to get his help."

"Yeah. I know," she said. "That's why you're here, right?"

Of course. I'd pretty much said so downstairs. Still, I tried to explain. "So, I'd hate for you to have to hear it twice."

"Are you kidding?" she said. "I'd listen a dozen times if it helped. Do you know, I've known Joel for like ten years?"

"Really?"

"Sure. We grew up in the same hometown."

And just like that, everything made a lot more sense. I recalled Joel's animosity toward his brothers, which somehow didn't extend to their fiancées. I also recalled that Luna's sister was engaged to a different brother.

In a way, the whole thing made me feel just a little bit lonely. Here, they all had siblings and people on their side. But who did I have? It was a question I didn't want to consider.

Damn it. I didn't have time for a pity-party, especially now, when *I* wasn't the one in danger.

But Joel was. And across from me was someone who cared.

Soon, I was telling her everything.

CHAPTER 16

When I finished, she said, "Those cock-suckers!"

Startled, I drew back. Obviously, she was referring to Derek and his dad. "Uh yeah," I said. "Totally."

She gave an embarrassed laugh. "Sorry. I've had house-guests for like two whole weeks, and now I'm talking like them." She rolled her eyes. "Before you know it, I'll be watching Kung fu and tossing water balloons off the balcony."

My gaze shifted to the balcony. We were like twenty floors up. Wasn't that dangerous?

Across from me, Luna sighed. "Don't ask." She took a quick look around. "Do you know, the cleaning service just left?"

I looked around. The place was absolutely gleaming. I said, "Well, it looks really nice."

"Oh sure, but it didn't this morning. My guests? Total slobs, by the way." She bit her lip. "I think Jake's ready to toss them out."

"Why? Because he's a neat-freak or something?"

"No. Because they keep wearing his clothes and drinking his beer." She glanced toward the open kitchen. "Don't get me wrong. He's a great sport, but with the beer, it's like, no matter how much we buy, when Jake goes to grab one, it's all gone." Under her breath, she added, "And I just pray they're not wearing his underwear."

I froze. "Why would they?"

"I dunno. Because they hate doing laundry?"

I hated doing laundry, too, but that didn't mean I'd jump into another girl's panties. "Uh, yeah," I stammered. "I guess that makes sense."

Sounding more distracted than ever, Luna said, "But they wouldn't *really* do that. I mean, sure, they might have boundary issues, but they wouldn't go *that* far." She gave me a hopeful look. "Would they?"

I had no idea. I didn't even know who she was talking about. The two guys from the lobby? That would've been my guess, but I didn't have the chance to confirm it, because just then, I caught movement from the corner of my eye. I turned to see the penthouse doors swing open, followed by the sight of Joel's brother, Jake, striding in through the now-open doorway.

Until now, I'd seen him only on my computer screen, thanks to his insanely popular video channel. From what I'd learned, the channel had millions of rabid subscribers ranging from frat boys to slobbering groupies who loved to watch him brawl with celebrities, particularly high-dollar sports stars.

Like Joel, Jake had dark hair, dark eyes, and a lean, muscular build that made it easy to see why all those groupies went so wild over him. But unlike Joel, Jake had cryptic tattoos, snaking up and down his well-defined forearms.

At the sight of me sitting across from Luna, he stopped and gave her a questioning look.

She said, "You remember Melody, right? You know? Joel's girlfriend?"

Hearing this, the sick feeling grew in my stomach. I wasn't his girlfriend. I wasn't anything except worried.

Jake gave me a quick glance. Sounding less than enthused, he said, "I remember."

Luna frowned. "What's wrong?"

I answered for both of us. "We talked a few weeks ago. It didn't go so great."

Turning to Jake, Luna said, "You weren't mean to her, were you?"

"Hell no." He flashed her a grin. "If anything, she was mean to *me*."

Luna eyed him with obvious suspicion. "You're joking, right?"

I spoke up. "Actually, he's not." I winced. "I *was* kind of mean." I turned to Jake. "Sorry." Looking back to Luna, I explained, "I was

SOMETHING TRUE   77

searching for Joel, and I guess I went a little crazy."

Under his breath, Jake muttered, "Got that right."

I cleared my throat. "But in my defense, I thought I heard Joel in the background."

Jake looked to Luna. "But what she *really* heard was Steve and Anthony fighting over the last donut."

I sank lower on the sofa. "Yeah. Um, sorry about that." I tried to explain. "But I had the worst connection. I could hardly hear." Glancing away, I murmured, "And Joel *does* like donuts, so you know..." I let my words trail off and didn't bother finishing. At the time, I'd been so frantic to find him that I hadn't been thinking straight.

In hindsight, I'd been a total idiot. It was becoming a common problem.

Across from me, Luna gave Jake a perplexed look. "Why didn't you tell me?"

"About the phone call?" he said. "I *did* tell you." He moved toward the open kitchen, heading for the refrigerator. "But you were distracted by the thing with the boxes."

She frowned. "Was I? Sorry." She turned to me and said, "Pizza boxes. Don't ask."

Jake opened the refrigerator and paused for a long moment before turning to ask, "Where's all the beer?"

Luna groaned. "It's gone? Again?"

"I don't know." Jake's mouth twitched at the corners. "Is it?"

"No." She gave him a shaky smile. "Not *all* of it."

His eyebrows lifted. "You sure about that?"

"Definitely." She pointed down the hall. "I, uh, hid some in the linen closet."

He gave her a look. "Cold?"

"Not really." She perked up. "But we've got ice, right?"

Jake gave a slow shake of his head before closing the fridge and walking over to join us. He sat down next to Luna and wrapped an arm over her shoulder. Looking half-amused and half-irritated, he told her, "You're lucky I love you."

She gave him a sunny smile. "I know. And so are you."

He grinned. "Don't I know it."

Luna turned back to me and said, "About the thing with Joel, do *you* want to tell it? Or do you want me to?"

I still wasn't feeling so great. At something in my expression, she said, "Never mind. I'll do it."

Relieved, I listened as Luna gave Jake the rundown on why I was here.

I had to give her credit. The story had taken me nearly an hour to tell, and yet, she managed to summarize it in under ten minutes. She finished by saying, "And the scary thing is, he's fighting tomorrow night." She gave Jake a pleading look. "So you've got to stop him."

Jake looked oddly unconcerned. "Why?"

"Weren't you listening?" Luna said. "Because of the suspended sentence. If he gets caught, they'll be dragging him off to prison." Her voice held a twinge of panic. "No trial, no nothing."

Jake shook his head. In an overly reasonable tone, he said, "Baby, that's not the way it works."

I spoke up. "Actually, in this case, it is. I heard it from a lawyer-friend."

Jake turned to me and said, "Then your friend's exaggerating. I mean, yeah, it *could* happen that way. But in a case like this? Nah, I'm not seeing it."

His calm demeanor grated on me, and besides, Derek had promised to *make* it happen. I gave Jake an irritated look. "Are you willing to take that chance?"

"No."

"So?" I prompted. "What are you gonna do?"

"Nothing."

Damn it. "Why not?"

"Because I already did." □

CHAPTER 17

I gave Jake a perplexed look. What was he saying? That he'd *already* solved Joel's legal problems? "How?" I asked. "And when?"

"A few months ago."

I shook my head. "Did you say *months*? Seriously? Does Joel know?"

Jake made a scoffing sound. "Hell no."

"But why not?"

Before he could answer, Luna turned to ask, "And why didn't you tell *me*?"

"I did," he said. "It was part of the Vince thing."

Vince. I recognized that name from something Joel had told me, back when we'd been together. I said, "You mean that sports agent?"

Jake nodded. "That's the one."

I recalled what I'd heard from Joel. Vince was a hotshot agent who'd been planning to sign Joel as a client, right up until Jake stepped in and ruined everything. I recalled the exact terms of the deal. Jake had agreed to stop messing with Vince's clients, and in return, Vince had agreed to drop Joel like a hot brick.

Probably, it had cost Joel a fortune.

But I still didn't get the connection. I asked, "But what would a sports agent have to do with a court case?"

"Lemme put it this way," Jake said. "The guy's crooked as hell. The thing with Joel? That was nothing compared to some other stuff the guy's fixed."

"When you say fixed," I said, "what do you mean?"

"I mean it's gone," Jake said, "like it never happened."

"But how?" I asked. "I mean, how could Vince do it?"

"Trust me. The guy's willing to be creative – bribes, threats, blackmail – you name it, he'd do it."

Next to Jake, Luna chimed in, "Yeah, he's a total snake."

"But if he's such a snake," I said, "can you really trust him?"

"Vince?" Jake said. "Hell no."

I frowned. "But—"

"But I checked," Jake said. "And triple-checked. It's all legit."

I was still trying to process everything I'd just learned. "So what are you saying? That Joel *won't* be arrested?"

Jake gave a humorless laugh. "He might get arrested, but it won't be for that."

That was far from comforting. "What do you mean?"

"I mean, it's no get-out-of-jail-free-card." Jake gave me a penetrating look. "Let's say he does something stupid, like steals a car, he'd still find himself in trouble."

When I first met Joel, he'd been driving a priceless movie prop that he'd borrowed – without any sort of permission – from Jake.

I said, "Do you mean the Camaro?"

Jake shook his head. "I'm not talking about *my* car. I'm talking about *your* car."

Instantly, I felt color rise to my cheeks. "Oh. That." A few weeks earlier, my car had been towed away to some unknown garage. From what I learned afterward, Joel had been planning to steal it back, until Jake beat him to the punch.

I asked, "Is that why you stole it back, to keep Joel out of trouble?"

"Me?" Jake said. "Nah. I did it for kicks."

I studied his face. I couldn't tell if he was joking or being sarcastic. I looked to Luna for clarification.

She said, "Don't let him fool you. He'd do anything for his brothers."

Next to her, Jake muttered, "Yeah, right."

Ignoring this, Luna gave me a solemn nod. "He would." She smiled. "Just like I'd do anything for mine." Her smile faded. "When I don't want to strangle them, that is."

My mind was racing. Recalling the original reason for my visit, I looked back to Jake and said, "So, let's say someone *wanted* to cause trouble for Joel, could they resurrect that court case? Like if they knew the prosecutor or something?"

Jake didn't hesitate. "No. When I say it's gone, I mean it's gone for good."

I stared at him. "So why didn't you say something?"

"To Joel?" Jake gave a humorless laugh. "Lemme ask you something. You know him, right?"

At the moment, I wasn't so sure. But I nodded anyway.

"So *you* know what *I* know." Jake leaned back on the sofa. "If he knew I was behind it, he'd probably get himself arrested just to piss me off."

I started to object, but then thought better of it. I couldn't honestly deny what Jake was saying. For whatever reason, Joel seemed to truly despise him.

After meeting Jake in person, I couldn't really see why. The jerk he played for the camera seemed nothing like the guy sitting across from me.

But that was something to think about later. Now, all I could think about was Joel and the original reason for our breakup. It was all because of that stupid suspended sentence – which meant it was all for nothing.

The sentence wasn't just gone. It had been gone for months, long before Derek's threat, long before I'd given Joel up, long before everything went so terribly wrong between us.

Stunned by everything I'd just learned, I sank back on the sofa and let a horrible realization sink in.

I'd given Joel up for nothing.

I felt like throwing up. True, I'd been feeling that way for a while, but now, the vague queasy feeling had morphed into something worse, something that made me stand up and blurt out, "Can I use your bathroom?"

CHAPTER 18

As it turned out, I didn't throw up. But a half-hour later, as I rode the elevator back down, I was almost wishing I had. If nothing else, I might've felt better – in body, if not in spirit.

Over my objections, Luna had insisted on escorting me back to the lobby. It was so thoughtful, and yet, so terribly misguided. Just because I hadn't thrown up in the penthouse was no guarantee that I wouldn't lose it somewhere on the way down. And the motion of the elevator wasn't helping.

Luna gave me a concerned look. "Are you sure you're feeling okay?"

Already, she'd asked me this at least ten times. I forced yet another smile. "I'm fine, really."

Her brow wrinkled. "No, I don't think so."

Hoping to ease her concerns, I said, "I'm just worried. That's all."

"About Joel?"

I nodded. It wasn't even a lie. "If he keeps on fighting, he could still get in trouble."

"I guess so. But trust me, I've seen them do a lot scarier things than *that* and get away with it."

In spite of my queasiness, I was intrigued. "Like what?"

She rolled her eyes. "Don't ask." With a sudden smile, she added, "But I swear, they have the luck of the devil. It must run in the family or something."

I wasn't so sure. From the little Joel had told me about his childhood, I wouldn't have called any of them lucky. Still, I said, "Let's hope so."

"So what are you gonna do?" she asked.

It was a good question, and one I'd been asking myself non-stop for the past thirty minutes. My first instinct was to drive down to where Joel was fighting tomorrow – someplace in Cincinnati – and tell him everything that I'd just learned.

Maybe we could start over, and this time, Derek would have nothing to hold over our heads.

But even as I considered this, a little voice in my head reminded me that I'd tried such an approach not too long ago. True, I didn't have all the information *then* that I had now, but I'd practically begged Joel to come back with me.

And he hadn't.

At the memory, I blinked long and hard. Didn't he love *me* the way I loved *him?*

Across from me, Luna said, "Are you sure you don't need to lie down?"

I tried to laugh. "I don't look *that* bad, do I?"

She hesitated. "You don't look bad exactly, but you've been looking queasy ever since you showed up."

Heat flooded my face. "Oh. That? I'm just tired. That's all."

She looked far from convinced. "If you want, we could go back upstairs. You could take a nap or something."

I didn't need a nap. I needed a new life.

I needed Joel.

But did he need me?

And why wasn't I thrilled? The dark cloud that had been hovering over us had just vanished. *Poof. Gone.* And yet, I couldn't help but wonder if that truly changed anything between us. If I sought him out yet again, would it be a repeat of what had happened the last time?

And why was it, I wondered, that it was always *me* seeking *him* out, and not the other way around? Had I no dignity at all?

I looked to Luna and said, "Can I ask you something?"

"Sure, what?"

"If you were me, what would you do?"

She gave me a tentative smile. "I didn't want to be pushy, but since you asked…" She glanced down at my stomach. "I'd just tell him."

Something about her look made me pause. In a carefully neutral voice, I said, "Tell him what?"

"Nothing." And then, she made a point to look at everything *except* my stomach.

Oh, crap. Talk about embarrassing. My face was burning now. I said, "There's nothing to tell. I mean, not like that, anyway."

"Oh. Of course." She cleared her throat. "Sorry. My mistake."

I studied her face. She *did* believe me, right? I sure hoped so, because I definitely wasn't pregnant. And yet, a small part of me almost wished that I was. I wanted a whole bunch of kids, and I could think of nothing better than to have them with a guy I loved.

And only one guy fell into *that* category – Joel.

Of course, in my fantasy world, Joel felt the same way, and would move heaven and earth for us to be together. But it wasn't really like that, was it?

Besides, I hadn't seen Joel in weeks, and my cycle had been obnoxiously normal. In spite of my daydreams, this was definitely a good thing. I was alone, babies were expensive, and I couldn't even pay to get my sewer fixed.

It was almost enough to make me cry. But now wasn't the time or the place. So I summoned up a shaky smile and tried not to throw up.

Luna eyed me with continued concern. "Is there anything I can do to help?"

From the look in her eyes, I didn't want to speculate on what kind of help she was offering. But if it involved knitting baby booties, I wouldn't have been surprised.

It was so thoughtful and so awkward all at the same time. Suddenly desperate to change the subject, I forced a laugh. "Sure, you know a good sewer contractor?"

"Why? Do you need one?"

I looked heavenward. "You have no idea." My stomach twisted at the mere thought. Where on Earth was I going to get the money? Trying not to sound as worried as I felt, I forced another laugh. "So if you know anyone with a backhoe, you know where to send them."

With a ding, the elevator stopped, making my stomach lurch with the change in momentum. When the doors slid open, I thanked Luna for all of her help and rushed into the lobby, leaving Luna to ride back up alone.

The doorman was still there, but this time, he was obnoxiously polite. It shouldn't have mattered, but I couldn't help but feel the tiniest bit of satisfaction by his change in demeanor.

See, I'm not a groupie. So there.

Of course, I might've felt *more* satisfaction if I didn't end up sprinting for the lobby bathroom, where I said goodbye to my nachos, along with any hope of leaving with my dignity intact.

Five hours later, I arrived home, exhausted from everything – my stupid food choices, the long hours on the road, and too much thinking along the way. Long-term, I still didn't know what to do, but short-term, there was something that simply couldn't wait.

I *had* to call Joel.

CHAPTER 19

I didn't call him from the road. Instead, I waited until I arrived home, where I took a quick shower, brushed my teeth, and threw on some fresh clothes. And then, feeling almost human again, I pulled out my cell phone, only to pause at what I saw on the screen – a voicemail from Derek.

Reluctantly, I hit the play button and listened as Derek's voice said, "Alright, fine. You win, alright? I talked to my dad, and he's agreed to drop the thing with Joel. And just so you know, I had to really sell it. So you owe me. Remember that."

Listening to this, my jaw dropped. I owed him? For what? Living up to what he originally promised?

Talk about nerve.

And besides, it didn't even matter, not anymore. Thanks to what I'd learned from Jake and Luna, the suspended sentence was no longer an issue, which meant that Derek and his dad could take a flying leap for all I cared.

Even a day ago, Derek's message would've gone a long way in easing my concerns. Now, it was just plain annoying. As the voicemail droned on, mostly with reminders that I should be grateful, I muttered, "Thanks for nothing."

The message ended with Derek's promise to stop by early the next day to discuss something else. I sighed. *Just great.* On top of all my other troubles, I'd be getting nice dose of Derek first thing in the morning.

I checked the time. Already, it was past midnight. And late or not, I still wanted to call Joel.

The odds of him answering were almost zero, but I was reasonably certain that, at the very least, he'd listen to whatever message I left. As expected, my call went straight to his voicemail. At the prompt, I took a deep breath and tried to pack as much as possible into a brief message. "Listen, it's me." I hesitated. "Uh, Melody…."

I winced. That didn't *really* need to be spelled out, did I? I sure hoped not.

Pushing aside the distraction, I went on. "Anyway, I just wanted to let you know that your suspended sentence, well, it's gone. I mean, pretty much like it never happened."

Again, I hesitated. There were so many things I was longing to say, starting with "come back" and ending with, "don't ever leave."

But the words died on my lips. It felt too much like begging, and I'd done plenty of that already. So instead, I briefly outlined what I'd learned from Jake and Luna, and summarized by saying, "So the thing with Derek, meaning all of his threats, well, they're pretty pointless now."

I forced an awkward laugh. "I mean, it's not like he can have you dragged off to jail or anything." In a quieter voice, I said, "I hope you're okay, and um, if you want to talk, let me know."

With that, I ended the call and stared down at my phone. Maybe Joel was listening to my message right now. And maybe, he'd call me right back and tell me all of those sappy things that I'd been reluctant to tell *him.*

But none of that happened, at least not right away. So against all hope, I sat there, clutching my phone, for at least an hour, praying that he'd call.

In the end, it was a total waste of time. I received no call, no text, and no sign whatsoever that he'd even gotten my message. I shouldn't have been disappointed or even surprised. After all, he'd made it pretty plain that a happy reconciliation wasn't in our future.

And yet, I kept telling myself that there was always tomorrow. Maybe he hadn't gotten my message. Or maybe he *had* gotten it, and was still deciding what to do. Or maybe – and this was the best one yet

– he wasn't going to call at all, but rather, was going to show up here and surprise me like I surprised him outside that warehouse.

Sure, it was a long shot, but anything could happen, right?

Finally, exhaustion caught up with me. Still clutching the phone, I curled up on the sofa and drifted off, only to be startled awake by the doorbell.

I bolted upright and looked around. I'd fallen asleep with the lights on, but now they were drowned out by the sun's rays filtering in through the front window. From what I could tell, it was just past sunrise – a fact that was confirmed with a quick glance at the clock.

Recalling Derek's promise to stop by, I stood on shaky legs and peered out the front window, only to freeze in mid-motion. It wasn't Derek's car in the driveway.

It was Joel's.

CHAPTER 20

Unable to stop myself, I practically ran to the door and yanked it open. Sure enough, there he was, looking as good as I remembered. As if in a dream, he moved forward and pulled me into his arms, saying, "I got your message."

I was so overwhelmed by the feel of him, I could hardly think. Somehow, I managed to ask, "So why didn't you call?"

"Screw calling," he said. "I didn't wanna wait."

I wasn't quite sure I followed, but I really liked the sounds of what he was saying. I swallowed. "Really?"

He nodded against me. "It was almost three in the morning when I got the message." He ran a soothing hand along my back. "And I didn't wanna wake you. So I said, 'Screw it.' I got in my car and hit the gas."

I gave a small laugh. I could totally see it.

Maybe this *was* a dream. But if it was, I was determined to enjoy it while it lasted. Wordlessly, I soaked up the feel of him as he cradled me close, just like he used to, back before everything fell apart.

Into my hair, he said, "Would you believe I've been driving all night?"

"Really?" Against his chest, I asked, "Where were you?"

"Cincinatti. But forget that." He pulled slightly away and said, "I've got a question."

"What?"

"Wait, I wanna do this right." And then, right there in the doorway, he sank slowly to his knees. "Melody—"

My breath caught. "What are you doing?"

His gaze met mine in a look so intense, the force of it almost sent me reeling. "You *know* what I'm doing."

My heart was hammering, and my knees felt weak. Suddenly, I was afraid. It was official. This *had* to be a dream.

Damn it. Probably, any second, I'd wake up, only to find myself alone in my bed, longing for him like I always did.

In front of me, he reached out, taking both of my hands in his. And then, in a voice that sounded surprisingly real, he said, "Will you marry me?"

And just like that, the world stopped spinning. I wanted to pinch myself, but I didn't dare. Again, I swallowed. "What?"

"I don't have a ring," he said. "But we'll get one this week, I swear." He gave me a crooked smile that melted my heart. "Not much open at seven in the morning."

I almost didn't know what to say. Even in my wildest dreams, this wasn't anything like what I'd been expecting.

I'd been missing him for weeks. I'd been thinking of him every day. I'd been longing for him every night. And yet, all this time, I'd received no sign whatsoever that he'd been thinking of me at all – no calls, no texts, no nothing.

And now, he was proposing? Against all logic, I wanted to say yes. I loved him. I loved him so much, it hurt. But the mental whiplash was making it hard to think. I gave a confused shake of my head. "You can't mean that."

"Why not?"

"Well, because, you've been gone, and –"

"And miserable."

I stared down at him. "What?"

"Without you?" He gave a slow shake of his head. "I've been a miserable bastard. You don't believe me? Ask Cal. He'll tell you."

I recalled Cal, his friend from the parking lot. At the moment, I couldn't even remember what he looked like. Cripes, I could hardly remember what *I* looked like. My head was too filled with images of Joel. The images spanned our entire acquaintance, from the day I'd first met him, to the night he'd broken my heart.

And here he was, kneeling in my open doorway, offering me the promise of forever.

In front of me, the cold air was rushing in. Behind me, the heat was rushing out. Between us, the air crackled with that huge question – *his* question – which I still hadn't answered.

I'd dreamed of this. I'd wanted this. I'd even fantasized about this, just last night, in fact.

Deep in my heart, I knew with absolute certainty that Joel was the guy I wanted to spend the rest of my life with. And yet, I couldn't help but recall that he'd left me – not just once, but twice, without giving us the chance we deserved.

I still didn't know what to say. But I *did* know that we couldn't stay out here forever – so with a light tug, I tried to pull him to his feet, saying, "We should go inside."

He didn't budge. "No."

I was almost too breathless to speak. "No?"

"No," he repeated. "Not 'til you say yes." He gave my hands a tender squeeze. "I *know* you want to."

"How?"

He gave me the promise of a smile. "I can see it in your eyes."

He was right. I *did* want to. I let out a ragged breath. "You're right. But…" I paused. How could I explain?

His gaze probed mine. "But what?"

"But when I saw you last, you said—"

"What *needed* to be said."

"What?"

With no trace of a smile, he added, "It was the hardest fucking thing I ever did."

"It was?"

"Baby, you've gotta ask?" His voice softened. "That was for you. Not for me."

I recalled some of the things he'd said – in particular, something about not wanting to drag me down into the mud. In my mind, I could still see the look in his eyes as he'd pushed me further and further away. They'd been anguished beyond description.

And now he was here, looking at me with eyes filled with so much love, it almost made me want to cry. I bit my lip and tried to think. What if this *was* a dream? If I said yes, would I wake up?

Joel gave my hands another squeeze. "Baby, just listen. Everything's different now. You *know* it is."

It was then that I realized something. He was right. Everything *was* different now. Back in that deserted parking lot, the suspended sentence had been hanging over both of our heads, like a dark, dangerous cloud.

For him, it had meant the very real possibility of prison, surrounded by strangers who wanted him dead. For me, it had meant a long public spectacle regardless of which way it went. Even if Joel had beaten the charges, it would've been a train wreck of epic proportions.

Suddenly, my heart felt lighter than it had in forever. The way it looked, Joel had wanted to spare *me* in the same crazy way that I had wanted to spare *him*.

If that wasn't true love, what was?

Joel's voice, more urgent now, broke into my thoughts. "No one – and I mean *no one* – could ever love you like I do. You're everything to me. Just give me the chance. I'll prove it. You won't regret it. I promise."

His words drifted over me like a warm, wonderful dream.

But it wasn't just his words that made it impossible to say no. It was the deep realization that, before Derek's awful threats, I knew exactly how I would've answered this life-changing question.

I would've said yes without a moment's hesitation, and I would've counted myself the luckiest girl on Earth.

I felt my shoulders relax. I could *still* be that girl.

As time stood still, I gazed deep into Joel's eyes and saw, once again, a truth I couldn't deny. His love for me, like mine for him, had been there the whole time.

Suddenly, I wanted to cry, but this time, it wasn't with sadness. I opened my mouth, but was too choked up to speak.

Into my silence, he said it again, "Marry me." He gave my hands another squeeze. "Say yes."

Finally, I felt myself nod. And then, I couldn't help but smile. My voice, when I found it, was just above a whisper. "Yes."

The word had barely left my lips when Joel practically jumped to his feet and pulled me into his arms. A choked sound escaped my lips. But I wasn't crying. I was laughing – with relief, with surprise, and with so much happiness that I could hardly think.

This was real. *And* it was a dream. How incredible was that?

Together, we stood in the open doorway, letting the heat out, and the cold in. But I didn't care. I couldn't help but tease, "If this is a dream, I'm going to be so mad."

"*You're* the dream." His voice grew quiet, and he pulled back, gazing deep into my eyes. "I don't deserve you, but I'm gonna spend the rest of my life trying." With that, he lowered his head and pressed his lips to mine, tenderly at first, and then with an intensity that left me trembling with a newfound need.

This was better than a reunion. It was like he'd never left, like nothing bad had ever happened, and like nothing or no one could ever tear us apart. Pulling back, he picked me up, kicked the door shut behind us, and carried me up the stairs, just like he'd done on our very first time.

As we celebrated in the most intimate way, he told me loved me at least a hundred times, and I said the same thing right back, over and over, until I was too lost to say much of anything.

Later that morning, as we lay together in a naked, happy embrace, I couldn't help but compare this time to the last time, in the darkened parking lot outside that nondescript warehouse.

In its own way, that time had been amazing too. And probably, if it hadn't ended in such heartbreak, I would've spent an embarrassing amount of time reliving it in my fantasies, if not in real life.

Still smiling, I drifted off with my head on his chest and his arm wrapped protectively around my naked back, only to wake up who-knows-how-long later in an empty bed, listening to the sounds of angry male voices somewhere in the house below.

I sat up and threw aside the covers. One of the voices was definitely Joel's. I listened more carefully. *Damn it.* The other one was

Derek's.

And the way it sounded, they were ready to kill each other.

CHAPTER 21

I jumped out of bed and struggled into the first clothes I could find. Breathlessly, I scrambled into the hall, only to stop in mid-stride when I heard a door slam, followed by the sounds of tires squealing in the driveway.

By the time I reached the front door, the only person standing there was Joel, looking surprisingly unruffled in jeans and a T-shirt.

I glanced toward the door. "Was that Derek?"

"Yup."

"What happened?" I asked.

"Nothing. I told him to fuck off."

I stifled a giggle. It shouldn't have been funny, but for some reason, I wanted to laugh like a crazy person. "You didn't."

"I did."

"But why?"

Joel flashed me a grin. "Do I need a reason?"

In truth, I wasn't sure. I still wanted to laugh. "Uh, yes?"

He reached out and pulled me tight against him. "Alright, here's a reason. I don't want him bothering you. You're done with that."

Maybe I should've objected, but I'd been thinking pretty much the same thing. Somehow, I was going to get control of the estate and stop Derek *and* his dad from having any say at all.

Leaning into Joel I said, "Do you wanna hear something funny?"

"What?"

I pulled back to meet his gaze. "The last time I saw him, I told him the exact same thing."

He stared at me for a long moment. "You?"

I nodded.

The corners of his mouth twitched. "No way."

I couldn't decide if I was proud or embarrassed. "It's true," I confessed.

"Well, aren't *you* full of surprises?" He glanced down. "By the way, your shorts are on backwards."

I looked down to check. He was right. They were. I gave another giggle. Summer was long-gone. Probably, I shouldn't have been wearing shorts at all. But they'd been the first thing I could find in my top drawer.

I had to tease him. "It's *your* fault, you know."

His eyebrows lifted. "*My* fault?"

I nodded. "You took my clothes."

"I didn't take them. I threw them in the laundry."

"Why?"

His gaze warmed. "Maybe I wanna see you naked."

I felt a slow smile spread across my face. "Again?"

Now, he was smiling, too. "Always."

We spent the rest of the day in and out of bed, making up for lost time. Maybe we were crazy, but I couldn't bring myself to care. Without him, I'd been lost, and here he was, almost like he'd never left.

In spite of the frigid weather, everything around me felt warm and wonderful. When darkness fell, I grabbed my favorite quilt out of the closet and carried it out to the lower balcony. Together, Joel and I sank onto an oversized lounge chair and lay there, snuggled under the quilt, gazing up at the stars and listening to the waves crashing below the bluff.

In all the fun of getting reacquainted, we hadn't done a lot of talking, at least not about anything serious. But now, the questions were piling up, and I almost didn't know where to begin.

"I'm curious," I said. "What have you been doing over the past two weeks?"

His arms closed tighter around me. "Other than missing you?"

"Yes." I smiled in the darkness. "Other than that."

"The truth?" he said. "I've been racking up some favors."

"What kind of favors?"

"The legal kind."

I wasn't following. "You mean related to your suspended sentence?"

"No. Something else."

"Really?" I said. "What?"

In what felt like a change of topic, he said, "I know this guy in Troy. Utterly ruthless."

"Oh. What does he do?"

"He's a lawyer."

Of course. *The legal kind.* I should've guessed that. "You mean like a criminal lawyer?"

"No." Joel gave a low laugh. "And yes."

"Okay, now I'm really confused."

"He's an estate lawyer." Joel paused. "And let's just say some of his clients are on the shady side."

"How shady?" I asked.

"As shady as they get, which means that sometimes, this guy's gotta get creative."

"But you said he's an *estate* lawyer?" I paused. "Wait a minute. Are you thinking of *my* estate?"

In a tone filled with humor, Joel said, "Well, *I* sure as hell don't have one."

"So what are you saying? You talked to him about my situation?"

"You might say that."

"And?"

"Like I said, the guy owes me."

"For what?" I asked.

"Trust me. You don't wanna know."

I tensed. The last thing I wanted was to see him in trouble again. "But it wasn't anything illegal, was it?"

Joel paused as if thinking. "Illegal? Couldn't tell ya. Unethical? No. Not in my book."

The distinction wasn't exactly comforting. I was almost afraid to ask, "So, what did you do?"

"Nothing that didn't need doing. But forget that. This guy's gonna look at your stuff. That was the deal."

Now, I was more confused than ever. "But wait a minute," I said. "You said this happened during the last two weeks? We weren't even together."

"So?"

"So why would you bother? I mean, you had your own legal troubles, right?"

"Me?" He gave a humorless laugh. "I'm a lost cause. But you? Shit, I had to do *something*. The way they were treating you…" Joel's voice hardened. "And what the hell were they gonna do next?"

I didn't even want to speculate. And the way it sounded, neither did Joel.

To my utter astonishment, he went on to tell me that the lawyer had already done some preliminary research and was confident that he could help me regain control of the estate.

I could hardly imagine.

When Joel finished, I said, "And you said he's really good?"

"The best," Joel said, "especially if you're willing to fight dirty."

I bit my lip. "How dirty?"

"Lemme rephrase that," Joel said. "If you're willing to let *him* fight dirty." He paused. "With some help."

"From who?"

"Me."

"But what would *you* do."

"Whatever it takes."

On the nearby side table, something vibrated. It was my phone again. I was almost afraid to look. Already, Derek had called me a dozen times, not that I'd answered.

If I weren't expecting a call from Cassie, I would've turned off my phone hours ago. Unfortunately, that wasn't an option, because she might need me to work tomorrow, and with no other job-prospects, I couldn't risk missing the opportunity.

I snagged my phone and checked the display. It wasn't Cassie *or* Derek. It was Mike of all people.

I gave Joel a nervous glance and let the phone go to voicemail.

Joel said, "Lemme guess. Derek?"

"Uh, no. Actually, it's someone else." I was still holding the phone. A moment later, a short vibration announced a new message.

Joel asked, "What's wrong?"

"Nothing. Not really." I gave the phone another glance. "It's just that I know what that was about." I sighed. "And you're not gonna like it."

At Joel's insistence, I gave him a quick rundown of the Mike situation. When I finished, Joel said, "That's it?"

"Well, yeah," I said. "And now I don't know what to tell him."

Even now, after relaying the story, I was embarrassed for a whole host of reasons. Not only had I promised Mike an autograph, I'd also supposedly promised some sort of meet-and-greet, involving burgers, beer, and who-knows-what.

Next to me, Joel said, "If you want, tell him yes. Not a big deal."

I blinked. "You don't mind?"

"What I mind," he said, "is seeing you worry about it."

At this, I had to laugh. "Of course I'm worried. The last time I asked, you practically flipped out."

"Yeah. And you wanna know something?"

"What?"

"If he sends you anywhere dangerous again, I'll do *more* than flip out again. The guy's an idiot."

"He is not," I said. "He graduated with honors."

"I don't care if he's a brain surgeon," Joel said. "Sending you to that fight alone? Makes him dumber than a box of rocks."

I bit my lip. "So you're still mad about that?"

"Hell yeah."

"But you'd *still* be willing to give him an autograph?"

He reached out and ran a finger along the side of my cheek. "I would if it made you happy."

Even as I leaned into his touch, I couldn't resist pushing my luck.

"And what about the cheeseburger thing?"

He grinned. "Now, you're pushing it."

"Is that a yes?"

He gave something like a laugh. "You're lucky I love you."

It made me think of Jake and Luna, and I couldn't help but smile. "Yeah," I said, "I am *lucky*."

"You know who else is lucky?"

I was still smiling. "Who?"

"Him."

My smile faded. "You mean Mike?"

"Hell yeah."

"You mean to get your autograph?"

"Nah. That's nothing. What I mean is, he's lucky that nothing happened to you that night." His voice softened. "And he's not the only one."

Smiling again, I pulled up my voicemail and listened to Mike's message. Sure enough, it was exactly what I expected. Eager to seal the deal, I called him back and gave him the good news. The next time he was in town, he could swing by, and I'd make good on all of my promises.

Maybe it was a little thing, but it was a big deal to Mike, and an even bigger deal to me, because it was just one more sign that Joel and I had finally put all that confusion behind us.

And soon, we'd be married. Throughout the day, we'd been discussing lots of possibilities – ranging from a big formal affair to a quick getaway in Vegas. Either way, neither one of us wanted to wait.

Joel was especially eager, which made everything that much more wonderful as we began planning for our happily-ever-after.

I was so happy, I felt like telling the whole world. And first, I was dying to tell Cassie. But when I did, her reaction was nothing like what I'd been expecting.

CHAPTER 22

Cassie wasn't smiling. "Are you sure he means it?"

It was early in the morning, and we were assembling trays of cookies in the back room of her shop. I stopped and stared at her across the prep table. "Of course he means it. What are you getting at?"

"It just seems kind of sudden, that's all. I mean, he's gone forever–"

"It wasn't forever," I said. "It was just a couple of weeks."

"I know." She glanced at my empty ring finger. "But – I hate to say this – but it didn't seem like he really planned it, you know?"

I almost didn't know what to say.

So what?

It had been spontaneous and wonderful. Even if I could, I wouldn't have changed a thing. Why couldn't Cassie, of all people, see that?

I tried to smile. "You *know*, he wanted to shop for rings today, but…" Recalling where I was, I let the sentence trail off, unfinished.

Across from me, Cassie spoke the words I'd been too polite to say. "But you had to work?" She looked toward the front of the shop. "If you wanna go, just go. I totally understand."

I studied her face. She didn't mean it. And besides, I didn't want to go. Sure, I'd love to be out with Joel, regardless of what we were doing, but Cassie needed nearly a thousand cookies for some bridal show in a neighboring city.

With tourist season long-gone, this was a big deal for her. In fact, it was probably the only reason she could justify having me work today at all. Technically, my seasonal job had ended weeks ago.

But all of this was beside the point. Her reaction to my engagement stung. Oh, sure, she'd given me the perfunctory congratulations, but I could tell that her heart wasn't in it. And now, she was questioning Joel's sincerity?

I didn't like it.

She was my employer, but she was also my friend. Probably, she was my best friend, especially now, with everyone else gone away to college. And yet, she wasn't acting anything like the friend I thought I knew.

If you wanna go, just go?

As her words hung in the air, I recalled everything that she'd done for me over the past few weeks. She'd listened to me cry. She'd dragged me out for coffee, whether I wanted it or not. She'd cajoled me into smiling and handed me tissues when I couldn't.

Through everything, she'd been the one person who seemed to truly get it. And now, she didn't.

Trying not to sound as hurt as I felt, I said, "I don't want to go."

She gave me a dubious look. "Are you sure?"

"Of course I'm sure. You *do* need the help, right?"

With a shrug, she turned away, heading toward the storage area. When she disappeared behind a row of packed shelves, I returned my attention to the cookies. They were shortbread cookies, decorated to look like flowers – wedding flowers, obviously.

I wanted to smile, but my heart wasn't in it. So far, Cassie had been the only person I'd told. Aunt Gina was still in France, and we'd been playing telephone tag over the last day or so. I was beyond eager to tell her, but not by email or text.

My aunt was a walking bundle of energy. I wanted to hear her excitement and listen to her squeal in surprise, like she always did when she received happy news. And this *was* happy news, wasn't it?

I felt my jaw clench. Yes. It was, regardless of Cassie's reaction. When she returned a few minutes later, I asked, "Is something wrong?"

She gave an irritated sigh. "There is *now*."

Bracing myself, I asked, "What?"

Frowning, she pointed toward the front of the shop. "You've got company."

CHAPTER 23

I turned and peered around the corner. And sure enough, there he was, Derek, standing just outside the front entrance. He was peering in through the glass door, as if searching for activity inside.

It was early. We were still closed. But of course, that never stopped *him*, did it?

I glanced at the clock on the far wall. It was only nine-thirty. Even if I *did* want to talk to him, which I didn't, I couldn't justify taking a break just yet. I said, "Maybe if we ignore him, he'll go away."

"Or maybe," Cassie said, "he'll pound on the glass 'til it breaks."

Was that a joke? Just in case, I tried to laugh, but it didn't come out quite right – not that it mattered, because soon, just like Cassie had predicted, Derek was banging ferociously on the glass.

I bit my lip. Cripes, maybe it *would* shatter.

Looking more irritated than ever, Cassie said, "Just so you know, if he breaks the door, I won't be the one paying for it."

Color rushed to my face. "Of course."

At something in my expression, she sighed. "I wasn't talking about you. I was talking about him." Under her breath, she added, "Ass-hat."

Choosing to believe she was referring to Derek, I said, "Do you want me to get rid of him?"

"From the looks of it, you'd better." Her mouth tightened. "And if you need to, grab the bat."

We kept a baseball bat behind the front counter. Although the thought of clubbing Derek was oddly satisfying, I skipped the bat and marched straight to the door.

When I pulled it open, he barged in and said, "What the hell is going on?"

From the back room, Cassie called out, "We're making cookies, dipshit!"

Derek stopped and looked around. From where he was standing, he couldn't see Cassie, but he'd obviously heard her just fine. He lowered his voice. "Was she talking to me?"

Cassie called out again. "You see any *other* dipshits in the store?" Her head poked out from around the corner of the back room. "And just so you know, that door you were banging on? It was four-hundred bucks."

Derek frowned. "So?"

"So, you break it, you buy it." Without waiting for a response, she pulled back, disappearing, once again, into the prep area.

Derek turned and gave me a questioning look.

Was he expecting sympathy? If so, he was looking at the wrong person. "Listen," I said, "we've got a lot of work to do, so whatever you're gonna say, just say it and get it over with."

"Or what?" he said. "You'll tell me to fuck off again?"

From the back room, Cassie called out, "If *she* doesn't, *I* will."

Derek turned and glowered in her general direction. "What's *her* problem?"

I didn't answer. Obviously, there *was* a problem. Maybe the problem was me. But that was none of Derek's business.

I asked, "Why are you here?"

Now, he was glowering at *me*. "Well, I can't exactly go to your house, can I?"

Obviously, he meant because of Joel, who'd made it perfectly clear that *he'd* be the one dealing with Derek from now on, because he didn't want me stressing about it.

It was sweet, even if it *was* a little overprotective.

"Well?" Derek demanded. "Don't you want to say something?"

"Like what?"

"Like you're sorry, for starters."

Now, it was my turn to scoff. "Why would *I* be sorry?"

"For what you said."

"You mean cursing you out?" I wasn't sorry, and I saw no reason to pretend. "You totally had it coming."

"I did not," Derek said. "And while we're talking, a thank you would be nice."

My jaw almost hit the floor. Over the past few weeks – no, *months* – he'd caused me nothing but misery. If I weren't so irritated, I might've laughed in his face. "You can't be serious."

"Sure, I am. You owe me."

"For what?"

He gave me a what-the-hell look. "You *did* get my message, right?"

I tried to think. And then it hit me. On my way back from seeing Jake and Luna in Detroit, Derek had called to tell me that he and his dad wouldn't be trying to get Joel arrested for violating the terms of that suspended sentence.

But of course, by the time I'd received that message, I'd discovered something that had changed everything. The suspended sentence was toast.

I had to wonder, did Derek know? And if he *didn't* know, should I tell him?

No, I decided. Definitely not.

The less Derek knew, the better. I gave him a thin smile. "I shouldn't *have* to thank you for living up to your promise."

"Oh, that's funny," Derek said. "What about *your* promise?"

"To give up Joel?" Now, I smiled for real. I didn't *have* to give him up, and I wasn't planning to, ever. Feeling suddenly cheerful, I said, "That's none of your business."

"Are you forgetting, we had a deal?"

What a joke. "You mean the deal you tried to break?"

Derek stiffened. "Well, I'm not breaking it now. So you're gonna get rid of him, right?"

I smiled. "Nope."

Derek stared at me. When I said nothing else, he said, "Nope?"

"That's right," I said. "And I might as well tell you, this interference, or whatever it is, I'm not having it, not anymore. Joel's staying." I lifted my chin. "And there's nothing you can do about it."

Derek gave me a nasty smile. "Wanna bet?"

I smiled right back. "Sure."

Derek blinked. "What?"

I made a breezy motion with my hands. "Bet away. Knock yourself out."

His eyebrows furrowed. "Knock myself out?"

From the back room, Cassie called, "If it helps, we've got a bat!"

Derek glanced in her general direction. "What does *that* mean?"

I looked toward the door. "It means I've gotta get back to work." When he didn't move, I added, "That's a hint, by the way."

He still didn't move. "But we're not done talking."

"Oh, we're done," I said. "And that goes double for your dad."

"What do you mean?"

"I mean, go ahead. Sue me, kick me out of my house, whatever. I'll work it out." As I listened to my own words, spoken out loud for the first time, it suddenly struck me that I meant everything I was saying.

What was the worst thing that Derek or his dad could do? Have me physically evicted? Drag me to court and make a giant spectacle of this whole sorry situation?

Well, my life was already a spectacle. And if he booted me from the house? Well, I'd find a way to get it back. I wasn't alone anymore, and I was tired of being bullied.

Derek's gaze narrowed. "It's because *he's* back, isn't it?"

Maybe. But it wasn't the only thing.

I'd been only sixteen when my parents had died. I'd been a scared teenager, looking for guidance from the people I knew. But I wasn't a kid anymore, and it was long past time for me to seize some control.

Feeling suddenly inspired, I said, "And by the way, that endowment? I'm making sure that Joel gets it."

Derek's mouth fell open. "The art endowment?"

As if he didn't know. I smiled. "That's the one."

"But you can't."

"Sure, I can," I chirped. "Remember? I refused to give his slot to anyone else."

It was true. And it wasn't only due to sentimental reasons. Joel was by far, the most talented painter I'd ever seen, with the possible exception of my dad. None of the other candidates had a prayer of filling Joel's shoes, and I saw no reason to pretend otherwise.

I thought of my dad and all that he'd been able to accomplish in the fifty-plus years he'd been on this Earth. He'd been amazing – as a dad *and* as a painter.

But Joel was just starting out. What could he accomplish if he focused on it full-time? Suddenly, my heart felt lighter than it had in forever. Thanks to the endowment, Joel would finally have that chance.

Feeling embarrassingly smug, I said, "Oh well. The cookies are waiting." I made a little shooing motion with my hands. "Off you go."

Derek was staring again. "What's gotten into you?" He leaned closer to study my face. "Are you on something?"

Yes, I was. And his name was Joel.

By the end of my shift, I was practically squirming with excitement. I'd spent my lunch hour conferring with Claude, the art critique who oversaw most of the endowment activities. He was thrilled, to say the least, to hear that Joel was back in the picture.

But when I bounded in through my front door to give Joel the happy news, something in his expression told me that he had news too. But unlike mine, it wasn't going to be good.

☐

CHAPTER 24

Obviously, Joel had been waiting for me. Either that, or he'd heard my car and decided to greet me at the front door. Either way, the look on his face was making me just a little bit nervous.

At something in my expression, he paused. "Baby, what's wrong?"

It was a funny question, but I didn't feel like laughing. I should be asking *him* the same thing, because it was pretty obvious that something wasn't quite right.

Stalling, I turned and pulled the door shut behind me. Night had already fallen, and I should've been home hours ago. But between Derek's interruption and a long, tense conversation with Cassie, followed by an impromptu trip to the grocery store, I'd been delayed well past my expectations.

I still had my purse dangling from one hand and a couple of plastic grocery bags dangling from the other. Joel looked to the bags and said, "Here, lemme get those."

When he moved forward, I silently handed over the bags and watched as he set them – not in the kitchen as I might've expected – but on the floor beside us.

I gave the bags a perplexed look. In them were all of the ingredients for homemade pizza, along with a bottle of the best champagne I could afford, meaning, of course, that it was the cheap stuff.

But it was the thought that counted, right? Between our engagement and my news about the endowment, I'd been in the mood for a celebration.

Now, I wasn't so sure.

I was still looking at the bags when Joel took me into his arms. He felt warm and wonderful, and I couldn't stop myself from leaning into him.

Into my hair, he said, "Bad day?"

"No. Not really." *Not yet, anyway.*

"So, what is it?" he asked.

I pulled back to say, "When I walked in, you looked like you had bad news."

He gave me a smile filled with regret. "Sorry, but I do." He glanced toward the front door. "I've gotta go."

Something like panic seized at my heart. "You mean *now?*"

He hesitated. "No. But soon."

"Why?" I asked.

Briefly, Joel explained that Cal had just called him, asking for help. Apparently, he'd broken his leg trying to move a dresser down a stairway alone, and now, he was in a bind, because he'd made some commitments that he couldn't break.

When Joel finished, I realized I was smiling – *oh, crap* – because nothing says smile like a nice, broken leg. I wiped the smile from my face and said, "Poor Cal."

Joel gave me a perplexed look. "What'd you think I was gonna say?"

"I don't know," I admitted. "It's just the way you were looking, I thought it might be something worse." I smiled up at him. "So you offered to help?"

"I wouldn't go *that* far," Joel said. "But he needs a favor, and I sure as hell can't say no."

"Because you feel sorry for him?"

"No," Joel said. "Because I owe him."

"For what? Letting you stay at his place?"

"Not just that." Joel pulled me closer. "For keeping you safe when I was too pissed off to think."

I smiled against him. "You mean in the parking lot?"

Joel's voice held no hint of humor. "Don't remind me."

Feeling suddenly flirtatious, I couldn't help but tease, "The night wasn't *all* bad."

Joel refused to be teased out of it. "I was so damn stupid."

Again, I pulled back. "Forget that. We've got a new beginning, right?" With total sincerity, I said, "And just so you know, with Cal, I think you're doing the right thing."

"Hell, I'm doing the *only* thing, because if something had happened to you…"

"But it didn't."

"I know. And it's not gonna." Finally, he smiled. "Because I won't let it."

As we made our way into the kitchen, Joel gave me some good news, followed by the opposite kind. The good news was that he could delay his departure until early the next morning. The bad news was, he'd be gone for at least a week, maybe even two.

My footsteps faltered. "Why so long?" I asked. "You're just helping him move, right?"

"Cal? Nah. He's not moving."

"Really? So why was he moving the dresser?"

"I dunno. I didn't ask."

Huh. That was weird. "So what *are* you helping him with?"

"Just some stuff out of town."

It felt like a non-answer, and in spite of my earlier relief, I had a terrible feeling about where this was going. Cal was a fighter. He had a broken leg. And now Joel was keeping some out-of-town commitment.

Standing at the kitchen counter, I began unpacking the bags, even as the questions piled up. *Which town? And what kind of favor?*

Finally, I just asked, "What aren't you telling me?"

Joel frowned. "What do you mean?"

I recalled the look on his face when I first walked in. I said, "Something's wrong, isn't it?"

"Yeah," Joel said. "The thought of leaving you…" He shook his head. "It made me wanna break his other leg."

Sweet or not, this felt like another non-answer. "Oh come on. You don't mean that."

"Wanna bet?" His gaze shifted to my hand, and he smiled. "I was gonna take you shopping tomorrow."

At this, I couldn't help but smile back. "Oh really? For what?"

"You *know* what." His gaze met mine. "If you want, I'll ask you all over again – this time, *with* the ring."

I recalled my conversation with Cassie. It was her final comment that really hurt. *"You might be smiling now, but if you're not careful, you'll be crying before you know it."*

It had been an awful thing to say, especially coming from Cassie, who'd always been so supportive. I didn't get it. She really liked Joel. I *knew* she did.

Would it make her feel better if Joel proposed all over again in a more traditional way? Maybe. But this wasn't about Cassie. This was about me and the guy I loved.

So I pushed all those doubts aside and told Joel with utter sincerity. "It was perfect the way it was, and I wouldn't change a thing."

He smiled. "Yeah?"

I nodded. "Definitely." I considered the situation with Cal. I still had those questions. Before the night ended, I was determined to get those answers. But first, I was dying to tell Joel about the endowment.

So, standing right there in the kitchen, I did – only to be further confused by his odd reaction.

CHAPTER 25

When I finished talking, Joel paused for a long moment before saying, "Alright."

We were still standing at the kitchen counter. Beyond eager to tell him, I'd explained everything in a rush – how I'd refused to give up his endowment slot, how Claude was thrilled to hear that Joel had returned, and how we were just a few signatures away from making everything official.

It was exciting news. And yet, Joel didn't look excited.

Wondering what I was missing, I said, "So, that's good news, right?"

He glanced away. "Yeah."

I recalled his obvious happiness the last time around. I saw none of that now. But of course, I was being unreasonable, wasn't I? After all, the last time hadn't ended so great. Shortly after that initial burst of happiness, he'd lost the endowment *and* me, all in the same day.

But that wasn't going to happen, not this time. Looking to drive the point home, I said, "And just so you know, it's a total done-deal. We just need to sign the paperwork, that's all."

He reached up to rub the back of his neck. "Alright."

Alright?

Again?

I bit my lip. "I'm sorry, but I've gotta ask something."

"Yeah? What?"

"Are you honestly excited? Or are you just saying that?" I gave a nervous laugh. "I mean, after the last time, I was kind of worried you'd give up painting for good."

He looked away, as if seeing something on the distant horizon. But there was no horizon. There was just the two of us, standing here in my oversized kitchen. As the silence stretched out, it became increasingly obvious that I'd been right. He wasn't thrilled with the prospect of painting again.

Finally, he returned his gaze to mine. "Alright, you want the truth?"

I nodded. After all, I *had* asked for it.

He shrugged. "I don't care either way."

"What do you mean?"

"You need the money, right?"

"The endowment money? But that's for you, remember?" I smiled. "Since you're the actual artist and all."

"It's not for me," he said. "It's for *us*."

In a way, I saw what he meant. Soon, we were going to be married, which meant that we'd sink or swim together.

The endowment was a generous one. If we weren't too extravagant, it could pay for months of living expenses, maybe even *more* than months if we were really careful.

But more than that, it would give Joel the chance to do something he loved. I gave him a nervous glance. He *did* still love it, right?

I had to ask, "But you're not doing it *only* for the money, are you?"

He gave a tight shrug. "Better than fighting."

I couldn't argue with that, but it wasn't exactly a glowing endorsement. "True," I said. "But there must be more to it than that."

"There is." His gaze met mine. "I wanna be here for you." He gave me the ghost of a smile. "Hard to do that if I'm off, beating the hell out of people."

It was a nice sentiment, but vaguely unsatisfying. I was so happy, and I wanted him to be happy, too.

Hoping to get the ball rolling, I forced a smile. "We should celebrate." I reached into the nearest grocery bag and pulled out the bottle of champagne. I lifted it in Joel's direction and said, "You know what I think? We should drink the whole bottle."

He eyed the bottle. After a long pause, he said, "What's that?"

Wasn't it obvious? I looked to the label. The handwriting was ultra-fancy, even if the champagne itself wasn't. "Well, it's not the good stuff, if that's what you're asking." I forced a laugh. "But who cares, right? By the third glass, we won't even notice."

I wasn't a huge drinker, but tonight, I was determined to make an exception.

I was still holding the bottle. I'd expected Joel to take it, but he hadn't. I cleared my throat. "So, do you want to open it or do you want me to give it a try?"

Silently, Joel took the bottle from my outstretched hand. He lifted it higher to study the label.

And then, he frowned.

I felt my face grow warm. Okay, so I'd bought the cheapest bottle I could find. But it's not like I was asking him to drink motor oil. I asked, "What's wrong?"

He was still looking at the label. "There's alcohol in here."

"Well, yeah," I said. "It *is* champagne, even if it isn't the best stuff."

He gave me an odd look. "You're not having any, are you?"

"Sure." I hesitated. "Why wouldn't I?"

His gaze drifted to my stomach. "You know why."

It took me a moment to realize the significance of that look. But when I did, I almost felt like throwing up – but not for the reason that Joel obviously thought.

CHAPTER 26

Standing in the kitchen, the silence stretched out between us. He lifted his gaze to mine and gave me a look that I couldn't quite decipher.

Around us, the house felt eerily big and unnaturally quiet. Under the weight of his stare, I had no idea what to say.

Well, at least, he wasn't looking at my stomach anymore.

As we stood there, watching each other with wary eyes, scenes from the last few days raced through my mind. I recalled that final elevator ride with Luna. For a minute there, she'd obviously assumed that I was pregnant. But I'd set her straight on that. Hadn't I?

Suddenly, the kitchen felt way too hot. I recalled Joel showing up out of the blue and proposing right there in my open doorway, like he'd been far too eager to wait. At the time, I'd chalked it up to unbridled love.

Obviously, I'd been wrong.

He was still holding that stupid bottle of champagne. I had a sudden urge to rip it out of his hands and fling it against the far wall. But I didn't. Instead, I reached out and gripped the bottom of the bottle. I gave it a tug until he finally let go.

I set the bottle on the counter and let out a long, shaky breath. We wouldn't be needing *that* anymore. Obviously, neither one of us felt like celebrating.

Maybe Cassie was right. Maybe I *would* be crying before it was all over. But I wasn't going to cry now, not if I could help it.

I took a deep, steadying breath and said, "I'm not pregnant, if that's what you're thinking."

Again, his gaze drifted to my stomach.

I felt my jaw clench. "Just stop it, okay?" My voice sounded sharp, even to my own ears. "There's nothing to see." With a muttered curse, I turned away. I felt like such a fool. I should've realized this. Or, at the very least, I should've known that my fairy tale ending was just a sham, based on a lie, whether intentional or not.

Looking to do something, *anything*, to keep myself from crying, I yanked the remaining groceries from the plastic bags and started putting the items away. As I moved, I felt Joel's gaze following me around the kitchen, haunting my steps like a dark apparition.

He still hadn't said anything, and maybe that was for the best. After all, what could he say?

Of course, I could think a few things that might've helped – starting with "That wasn't the reason I proposed" and ending with, "It doesn't change a single thing."

But he didn't say either of those things, and I guess I couldn't blame him. But I *could* blame Luna. What on Earth had she been thinking? Even if I *were* pregnant, didn't *I* deserve the chance to tell him?

Putting away the final item, a lone can of pizza sauce, I found myself deep inside the pantry, staring at the barren shelves. Before my parents had died, the shelves had been nearly overflowing with all kinds of things that I'd taken utterly for granted.

Now, I had a few cans of soup, two boxes of pasta, and the lone can of pizza sauce. I'd been planning to use it tonight. But now, I wasn't remotely hungry, and from what I suspected, neither was Joel.

Out of groceries to put away, I just stood there, staring at the barren shelves. I don't know how long I was standing there before I heard movement behind me. I didn't even turn to look.

Still facing the back wall, I said, "If you want to leave tonight, I totally understand."

His voice was quiet. "Is that what you want?"

"Honestly? I don't know what I want." Finally, I turned to face him. His face was pale, and his eyes were dark. I sucked in a ragged breath. "And I guess I don't know what you want either."

This was his cue to say that he still wanted me, that nothing had changed, and that he proposed not because he felt he *had* to, but because he *wanted* to.

He said nothing.

I clamped my lips shut and waited for some sort of response. None came, and as the silence stretched on, I felt my frustration grow. Finally, I blurted out, "If that's what you thought, why didn't you say something?"

Again, his gaze drifted to my stomach.

Oh, for God's sake.

I made a sound of annoyance. "Seriously, you've been here for what? Two days? And you never thought to ask?"

His gaze returned to mine. "I was waiting for you to tell me."

"For how long?"

"What?"

Through gritted teeth, I said, "How *long* would've you waited?" I gave a bark of laughter. "Lemme guess. Nine months?"

His jaw tightened. "You think I didn't *want* to ask?"

"I don't know. Did you?"

"Hell yeah, I wanted to ask."

"So?" I said. "Why didn't you?"

He glanced away. "I didn't want you to think it was the only reason."

But obviously, it *was* the only reason, because he wasn't saying otherwise. I was mortified at the thought of asking him, and yet, I *had* to know.

I asked, "Was it?"

He shoved a hand through his hair. "Fuck."

"You know what? Forget I asked."

I lunged forward, intending to move past him. But as I did, he reached out and practically yanked me into his arms. "Don't."

"Don't what?"

"Don't leave." His grip tightened. "Not like that."

As a profession of love and devotion, it was utterly lacking. He was still holding me, but the embrace felt wrong. His arms were stiff, and his stance was rigid.

Feeling suddenly claustrophobic, I yanked myself out of his grip and stared at up at him. The pantry felt way too small, and I was having a hard time breathing.

We were standing so close, I had to crane my neck to stare up at him. "Just tell me," I said. "What do you want? Are you sorry you proposed? Do you want to take it back? Is that it?"

He gazed at me with anguished eyes. "I never said that."

I waited for him to say more.

He didn't.

I made a scoffing sound. "Well, that was informative."

Again, Cassie's words rang in my memories. *You'll be crying before you know it.*

I had to wonder, was Cassie the type to say those four awful words. *I told you so.* I'd never heard her say it before, but soon, she'd have the perfect opportunity.

If it weren't so pathetic, I might have laughed. I recalled all of the other points she'd made – that until Joel's surprise proposal, he'd been gone for weeks with zero contact; that he'd walked away once, which meant he was capable of doing it again; that I had no idea where he'd been or what he'd been doing.

But that last part wasn't true. He'd been with Cal, a guy I'd actually met.

So Cassie wasn't right about everything.

Was I grasping at straws? Probably.

In front of me, Joel reached for my hand. "I'm not gonna back out, if that's what you think."

I stared up at him. "Back out?"

He gave a tight nod.

"Like what?" I said. "Like out of some real estate deal that's gone south?" I blinked long and hard. This wasn't the way I wanted it. Probably, I should be giving him some credit. He was, after all, offering to live up to his end of the bargain.

Talk about humiliating.

I pulled my hand from his. "Forget it." I took a deep breath and said, "We can pretend it never happened." I forced a stiff smile. "See? All better."

It was a lie, and he'd be a fool to believe it. But now, all I wanted was to slink away and forget the last two days had ever happened. So I didn't wait for his reaction. Instead, summoning up whatever dignity I could muster, I lifted my chin and calmly walked past him.

This time, he let me go. Unsure what else to do, I walked through the kitchen and made a beeline for the main stairway. I had to give myself credit. I didn't start crying until I reached my bedroom. And then, I did it quietly, with the music on, behind my locked bedroom door.

Whether he heard me or not, I had no idea.

When I woke, he was gone.

CHAPTER 27

Surprised that I'd slept at all, I stood on the front porch, staring out over my long, mostly empty driveway. It was just past sunrise, and the only car in sight was my own.

There was no sign of Joel *or* his vehicle. This was the second time I'd checked. The first time had been around three in the morning. He'd been gone then, too.

I wasn't sure when he left or if he planned on returning. But I *did* know that I was done chasing after him. I was done pretending that he wanted me as much as I wanted him. I was just done, period.

When it came to Joel, I'd been a slow learner, but everyone wised up eventually, right?

Regardless, there was something that I wasn't going to let go. I pulled out my cell phone, turned away, and marched back into the house, slamming the door behind me.

As I walked toward the kitchen, I pulled up Luna's number and hit the call button. It went straight to voicemail – no surprise there. It was, after all, ungodly early.

That was fine by me. I wasn't looking for a conversation. I was looking to send a message.

At the sound of the beep, I took a deep breath and said, "Hey, remember me? The girl who almost barfed in your bathroom? Well, just so you know, it was just a stomach thing…" My tone grew sarcastic. "…and *not* a bouncing, bundle of joy. I *did* tell you that, didn't I? Wait, don't bother answering. I did. I *know* I did. And just so you know, I *wasn't* lying."

Feeling nearly unhinged, I forced a laugh. "So, anyway, if Joel shows up there – Hey, crazier things have happened, right? – you can all have a good, long laugh about it."

On some level, I seriously doubted that anyone would be laughing, especially Luna, who'd been surprisingly nice. But I was too far gone to care. I wanted to finish with a bang, but I had no idea what to say. In a fit of desperation, I blurted out, "So thanks a lot!"

I froze. *Thanks a lot.* God, I totally sucked at this. But so what? I'd made my point. With a sigh, I disconnected the call and tossed my phone onto the kitchen counter.

In the back of my mind, I realized that Luna probably meant well. But the emotional roller coaster ride had taken its toll. After too many ups and downs, I'd reached the point where all I wanted now was to get off this crazy ride and forget every single one of them – Luna, Jake, and especially Joel.

When the phone rang an hour later, I picked it up and studied the display, only to feel myself frown.

It was Jake.

Just great. I could only imagine why he was calling. I felt my jaw clench. *Fine.* If he wanted to chew me out, he could do it in a voicemail, just like I had.

I shoved a nervous hand through my hair. Who knows? Maybe when I cooled down, I'd be apologizing to Luna for leaving such a rude message. But for now, I was too angry, too tired, and too sick of all of them. When a beep announced a new voicemail, I eyed my phone with renewed dread.

If his message was anything like mine, I didn't want to hear it – not now, anyway. So instead, I marched upstairs to freshen up, only to pause when I caught sight of my shower drain.

There it was again – standing water, probably from my ill-advised 3 a.m. shower. I gave a long, weary sigh. In all the drama, I'd completely forgotten about my sewer problems.

Here, I had a whole bunch of bathrooms, and now, none of them were draining – or at least, not fast enough to matter.

I was still looking at the drain when the doorbell rang.

I froze.

Joel?

Doubtful.

And besides, what did it matter? I didn't want to see him, anyway.

Really, I didn't.

Probably, this was a good thing, because it *wasn't* Joel at the door. Instead, it was two strangers, a couple of guys in their early twenties, who looked vaguely familiar.

I was almost certain that I'd seen them somewhere before.

But where?

CHAPTER 28

From the open doorway, I looked from one guy to the other. They were both tall and lean, and wore grubby jeans and long-sleeved shirts. One was blond, and the other had hair so dark, it might as well have been black.

I gave them a perplexed look. I'd already said hello, which was *their* cue to tell me what they were doing on my doorstep at nine in the morning. When they didn't, I said, "Can I help you?"

"Sure," the blond said, "You got any beer?"

I blinked. "Excuse me?"

"Beer," he repeated. "You got any?"

"Uh, no."

"Shit." He looked to the dark-haired guy and said, "Told ya we should've stopped."

Again, I looked from one guy to the other. "And you are…?"

"Thirsty," the blond said, shouldering his way past me, into the house.

Startled, I whirled around to call after him. "Wait! You can't just barge in here."

He stopped and turned back to face me. "Why not?"

Did I really need to explain? "Because I don't even know who you are."

"Sure you do. You got the message, right?"

"What message?" I said. "From who?"

"From Luna. Maybe an hour ago?"

My phone was tucked into the pocket of my jeans. So far today, I'd received exactly one message – the one from Jake. I still hadn't listened. More confused than ever, I pulled out my phone and took a look.

I saw no call from Luna, which was probably a good thing. I could only imagine what kind of message she'd be leaving for me *now*.

I told the guy, "Sorry, but you're wrong." I held up my phone, screen out. "See? No message from Luna here."

Thank God.

Behind me, the other guy laughed.

I whirled to face him. "What's so funny?"

He was still laughing. "Not from *her* phone."

I didn't get it. "What do you mean?"

Now, the blond – who was still inside the house – was laughing, too. Feeling like a spectator at a cartoon tennis match, I kept looking from one guy to the other. Whatever the joke was, I sure as heck didn't get it.

On a more positive note, I finally realized where I'd seen these two guys before. They'd been with Luna, coming out of that elevator in Detroit. I vaguely recalled her threatening to turn the hose on them.

I bit my lip. I had a hose somewhere. Was it time to pull it out?

From inside the house, the blond said, "So, you got a bathroom in this place?"

From the porch, the dark-haired guy said, "Dude, she's probably got twenty. Pick one, and get it over with."

When I turned to look, the dark-haired guy explained, "We've been on the road since five." In a louder voice, obviously intended for the blond, he added, "And he's been griping since Kalamazoo."

Kalamazoo was an hour away, but that didn't mean I was any less clueless. I gave the dark-haired guy a perplexed look. "This message from Luna, what did it say?"

He held out his hand. "Here, lemme see your phone."

Instinctively, I drew back. "No."

"Why not?"

"Because I don't know you."

He gave me a look. "Well, you *would* if you listened to the message."

But there *was* no message. I hesitated. Unless, he meant the one from Jake?

From somewhere deeper within the house, the blond called out, "Found one!"

I didn't even turn to look. I was still clutching my phone. I looked down and eyed it with renewed dread. "You don't think she would've called me from Jake's phone, do you?"

The guy chuckled. "Well, she sure as hell wouldn't have called from hers."

I looked up. "Why not?"

He shrugged. "Eh, there was an incident."

My gaze narrowed. "What kind of incident?"

"Well, she's got that balcony, right?"

I recalled the balcony in Jake's penthouse. It was at least twenty floors up. "Uh, yeah?"

"So last night, me and Steve are out there, having some fun, you know?"

"Steve? Is that the guy in the bathroom?"

"Yeah. My brother." The guy went on to tell me that his own name was Anthony, and that Luna was their sister.

Feeling more awkward than ever, I now felt obligated to invite him inside. After all, his brother was already in there. What was one more invader in the big scheme of things?

After I shut the door behind us, I briefly introduced myself and once again, asked why they were here.

He held out his hand, palm-up. "Gimme your phone."

It was the second time he'd asked, and I wasn't any more eager than I'd been the last time. "Why?"

"Because I wanna hear the message, see what she told you."

I bit my lip. *He* might want to hear. But *I* sure didn't, especially in front of an audience.

I glanced down at his empty palm. "My phone?" I tried to make a joke of it. "I'm not sure I should. I mean, you still haven't told me what happened to Luna's."

To my surprise, the guy nodded like this actually made sense. He pulled back his hand and shoved it into the front pocket of his jeans. "Good thinking." He gave my phone a quick glance. "But if there's a message from Jake's phone, you should pull it up. I'm guessing it was from Luna."

Slowly, something was dawning on me. "Wait a minute. So Luna's phone isn't working at all?"

"Lemme put it this way," Anthony said. "Twenty floors, a bucket of water, and one pissed off sister. What do *you* think?"

I wasn't sure what the water had to do with it. But I *did* think I should hang onto my phone. I asked, "And when did this happen?"

Anthony gave it some thought. "I dunno…a couple hours past midnight?"

I considered the timetable. I'd left that enraged message shortly after sunrise. Based on what I'd just learned, odds were pretty good that Luna hadn't even heard it.

I wasn't sure how that made me feel. Relieved? Or frustrated?

I looked down at my phone. Either way, it meant that whatever message she'd left for *me* was probably ten times nicer than the one I'd left for her. Feeling a different kind of dread, I pulled up the voicemail.

I hit the play button and lifted the phone to my ear. Luna's voice, sounding remarkably friendly, informed me that she was sending over a terrific sewer contractor, just like I'd asked.

I felt my eyebrows furrow. I *hadn't* asked. Had I? Oh wait. I'd made some throwaway comment in the elevator, but I hadn't thought she'd take me seriously.

She went on to say, "Oh, and by the way, they're my brothers, so you can totally trust them." She paused. "Except with your phone. Oh, and your beer. And, um, come to think of it, you'll probably want to hide your good towels – don't ask."

Her voice picked up steam. "Anyway, they might not look it, but they're super good at what they do. They're licensed and everything, so whatever the problem is, I'm sure they can fix it."

She ended the call with a cheery suggestion that we all get together soon.

Well, that answered *one* question. She definitely hadn't gotten my voicemail.

I gave Anthony a worried look. Whether he and his brother were legit or not, it didn't matter. I couldn't afford to pay them.

Talk about awkward.

Before I could even think of how to explain, I heard movement behind me and turned to look. It was the blond, Steve, who said, "You're out of toilet paper."

"What?"

"Yeah," he said, moving to stand beside his brother in the entryway. "I had to wipe with the towel."

I stared at him. "You're kidding, right?"

He burst out laughing. "Of course I'm kidding. Shit, what kind of animals do you think we are?"

"Uh…"

"Eh, forget I asked." He shrugged. "Wasn't kidding about the toilet paper though. I *did* use the last of it." He looked to Anthony. "And we know how pissed-off girls get when you use it all."

I felt my gaze narrow. "Of course we get 'pissed off'. We need to use it every time."

Steve rolled his eyes. "So we hear." He looked to his brother and said, "So, did you plug it in?"

"Not yet," Anthony said.

Steve frowned. "Why not?"

Anthony glanced in my direction. "Because we were talking."

I spoke up. "Wait. Plug what in?"

Anthony glanced in the general direction of the driveway. "The job trailer."

I didn't know what a job trailer was, but I did know that I couldn't afford any of this. "Actually, that won't be necessary."

"Why not?" Anthony asked.

I didn't want to hurt their feelings – or confess how broke I was. I tried to smile. "Because my sewer's fine."

"The hell it is," Steve said. He looked to Anthony and added, "I had to flush like five times."

He had to be exaggerating. For one thing, he wasn't gone long enough for five flushes. Three maybe, but five was a bit much. Still, that was hardly the point. I tried again. "Yeah, well, I'm still getting estimates. And I think I'm gonna have to wait 'til spring." I gave them an apologetic smile. "So I'm really sorry you made a special trip."

Steve was frowning again. "Forget the estimates. You got us."

Already, my face was in flames. Reluctantly, I said, "So do *you* want to give me an estimate?"

He looked at me like I'd just said something incredibly stupid. "You don't need an estimate."

"Why not?"

"Because we were already paid."

I did a double-take. "What? By who?"

Steve grinned. "Jake."

CHAPTER 29

I looked from brother to brother. This wasn't making any sense. "Why would *Jake* pay you?"

Steve made a scoffing sound. "Because we don't do nothin' for free."

"Yeah," I said. "But, I mean—"

Anthony spoke up. "I got a theory."

"What?" I asked.

"It was the beer thing."

I gave a confused shake of my head. "What beer thing?"

Anthony grinned. "Me and Steve had this bet."

"What kind of bet?" I asked.

Anthony snickered. "How long before he'd pop."

"Who?" I said. "Jake?"

"Yeah," Anthony said. "We've been staying with them, you know?"

When I'd seen Luna, she'd complained of messy house guests who drank all the beer and tossed water balloons off the balcony. Apparently, I was looking at those guests now. I nodded. "And?"

"And," Anthony continued, "we kept hiding the beer." He shrugged. "Well, the stuff we didn't drink, anyway."

I felt my brow wrinkle. "Why would you hide it?"

"Because of the bet," Anthony said. "Steve said he'd pop in three weeks. Me? I gave it two."

I stared at them. I wasn't sure what to say. Finally, I had to ask, "So did he? Pop, I mean?"

Steve lifted his hand and made a waffling gesture.

I looked to Anthony who said, "Eh, I wouldn't say he popped. But he *did* give us a big-ass bonus to leave in a hurry." He looked to Steve and said, "So, you owe me."

Steve snorted. "Your ass. He didn't pop. He hired us for a job. That don't count."

Anthony gave it some thought. "I dunno. He looked like he was *gonna* pop."

"Sorry," Steve told him. "'Gonna' don't count."

I broke in, "That job? You mean here?"

Steve said. "Yeah. That's where we are, right?"

And here we were, back to square one. I had to be honest. "I can't accept this."

"Why not?" Steve asked.

I bit my lip. "Because it sounds expensive."

Steve nodded. "Got that right."

"And," I continued, "I don't even know Jake, not really. I can't let him pay for my sewer work."

"Too late for that," Steve said.

"What do you mean?"

"He already paid us." Steve frowned. "And there's no way we're giving the money back."

I looked to Anthony, who gave a solemn nod. "We've got a strict no-refund policy."

I asked, "Not even for family?"

Steve gave me a perplexed look. "You mean you? We're not related."

"I wasn't talking about *me*," I said. "I was talking about Jake."

Steve shrugged. "Sorry. Not related to him either."

I made a sound of frustration. "But you're related to Luna."

"Trust me," Steve said. "She was all *for* this."

Next to him, Anthony added, "Especially after the phone thing."

Listening to this, I had to wonder if Jake's real motivation for paying them was to get them out of his hair – and his penthouse. But that still didn't mean I could take his money. Plus, what kind of contractors were these guys, anyway?

Going for a change in tactics, I said, "Well, I hate to tell you something, but the plumber told me the job would need a backhoe."

Both guys burst out laughing.

I asked, "What's so funny?"

"You," Steve said. "What? You think we're gonna dig by hand?"

"So you *do* have a backhoe?" I glanced in the general direction of the driveway. By now, I was dying to see one. "Is it here now?"

"Hell no," Anthony said. "We don't bring it 'til we need it."

"Yeah," Steve added. "That thing's a bitch to haul."

Anthony nodded in agreement. "Right now, we're in the assessment stage."

Inside my pocket, my cell phone rang. I pulled it out and looked at the display. My breath caught.

It was Joel.

Indecision made me pause. On one hand, I was desperate to talk to him. On the other hand, hadn't I just vowed not to jump every time he called?

My fingers itched to answer. My heart begged to know what he wanted. My head reminded me that it was exactly this sort of eagerness that had caused me so much heartbreak in the first place.

I was still waffling when the call went to voicemail.

Probably, this was a good thing. Aside from any issues of self-respect, I couldn't exactly talk to him in front of two strangers.

Still, I was dying of curiosity. When the beep announced a new message, it took all my willpower to not bolt upstairs to listen in private.

In front of me, Anthony said, "Man, that's cold."

I gave a distracted shake of my head. "What?"

"Just ignoring the call like that. What if he's worried about you?"

"Who?" I asked.

"Joel. That was who called, right?"

"Yeah. How'd you know?"

"I looked. I can read upside-down, you know."

I *so* didn't need this. "Has it ever occurred to you that some things are private?"

At this, both guys burst out laughing.

"What's so funny now?" I demanded.

Steve said, "You sounded just like Luna."

I rubbed at my forehead. The mention of their sister reminded me of something. Whether Luna had good intentions or not, it wasn't that long ago that I'd left her a scathing voicemail. Maybe she hadn't gotten it yet, but odds were pretty good that she would eventually.

And then, what would happen?

I looked from one brother to the other and said the thing that needed saying. "It's not that I'm not appreciative, but honestly, I can't accept this."

"Why not?" Steve asked.

Deciding I might as well be honest, I confessed, "Well, for one thing, because your sister and I aren't exactly getting along." I bit my lip. "In fact, she's probably pretty mad at me. Or, if she isn't yet, she *will* be."

The two guys exchanged a look. Anthony asked, "Why?"

I didn't want to get into it. But, given the fact they drove all this way, I felt like I owed them at least *some* sort of explanation. "Well, you see, I, um, left a mean voicemail, actually."

Steve frowned. "Oh yeah? *How* mean?"

Inside my pocket, my cell phone rang again. I pulled it out and looked at the display, only to cringe. The caller was Jake – or more likely, Luna.

Well, this was awkward. Having no idea what to expect, I answered with a tentative, "Hello?"

But this time, it wasn't Luna. It was Jake.

CHAPTER 30

With barely a hello, Jake said, "Are they there?"

It was pretty obvious who he meant. I eyed Luna's brothers, standing just a few feet away. "Uh, yeah."

"Good," he said. "Keep it that way."

I spoke up. "But they won't be for long."

"Yeah? That's what *you* think."

Well, that wasn't bossy or anything. I felt my eyebrows furrow. "What are you saying?"

"I'm *saying* if you send them back, you're gonna regret it."

I stiffened. Okay, as much as I appreciated what he was trying to do, this was a bit much. "You're not seriously threatening me, are you?"

"No," he said. "I'm threatening *them.* And you seem like the type who'd care."

"About what?"

"I dunno." Jake paused, as if thinking. "Like if I launched them off the balcony."

"What?"

"Yeah," he said. "I'm betting you'd feel bad."

I was still looking at Luna's brothers. Actually, I would feel kind of bad. As weird as it sounded, they were kind of growing on me. Somewhere in the background, I heard Luna say, "Here, lemme talk to her."

My stomach sank. I didn't want to talk to Luna, and not only because I was still angry about the whole pregnancy thing. Sooner or later, she'd hear my message, which would put a distinct damper on our friendship.

And yet, a moment later, I heard her voice, coming through the phone. "You got my message, right?"

"Yeah." I sighed. "And I'm betting you *didn't* get mine."

"You left me a message? When?"

"A couple of hours ago."

"Oh. Sorry, my phone's like in a million pieces." She perked up. "So what'd you call me about?"

I bit my lip. I *so* didn't want to do this now. But I saw no way to avoid it. With another sigh, I turned away from her brothers and said in a low whisper, "Why'd you tell Joel I was pregnant?"

Behind me, one of her brothers murmured, "Holy shit."

The other one said, "Did you know?"

"Hell no. Did you?"

I whirled to face them. Through gritted teeth, I said, "I'm *not* pregnant."

They were both staring at my stomach. Without looking up, Steve said, "Are you sure?"

I glared at him, not that he appeared to notice. "What's that supposed to mean?" My voice rose. "Are you implying something?"

"Yeah," he said, still looking down. "You seem kind of moody." Finally, he looked up and asked Anthony, "Isn't that a sign or something?"

Anthony gave a slow nod. "Oh yeah. For sure."

Oh, for God's sake. Maybe they *weren't* growing on me. Giving up all pretense of politeness, I turned and stomped into the nearby den, slamming the door behind me.

Through the closed door, I heard one of the brothers say, "See? Moody."

I looked to the door and hollered out, "I'm not moody! I just want some privacy, that's all."

Sounding even closer now, one of them said, "Sounds moody to me."

"Yeah, totally."

With a sound of frustration, I stomped deeper into the room and said into the phone, "Well? You did, didn't you?"

Her response was a long time in coming. "Not exactly." She hesitated. "I might've given a little hint, but I didn't outright tell him or anything."

It sounded like a copout to me. "Well, it must've been a pretty big hint, because he showed up and proposed."

Luna gave a happy squeal. "Really? Congratulations! Oh, my God, that's so wonderful!"

Talk about ironic. Her response was everything that I hadn't gotten from Cassie, which only made it more irritating.

"No," I said. "It isn't."

"Sure, it is," she said. "You guys make a great couple. You're gonna be so happy together."

No. We weren't. I blinked long and hard. "How would *you* know? You haven't even seen us together."

"Well, yeah," she said. "But he's a great guy, and you seem pretty nice—"

"Yeah? Well, you won't think so when you get my message."

"Oh." She hesitated. "So you were pretty mad, huh?"

"Of course I was mad."

"But why?"

"Well for one thing, because I'm *not* pregnant."

"Are you sure?"

Oh, for crying out loud. "Yes. I'm sure. A hundred percent."

"Oh." Funny, she actually sounded disappointed.

Did I need to point out the obvious? "That's good news, by the way."

"Are you sure?" she said. "Because Joel would make a great dad. He was really super excited."

Now, that made me pause. "What?"

"Yeah," she said. "After I gave him that little hint, you should've heard him. He was really happy." She hesitated. "Well, he didn't come out and say it or anything, but he was. I'm sure of it."

Maybe *she* was sure. But I wasn't. "Well, he wasn't happy last night," I said. "And just so you know, we're not getting married."

"But why not? You said he proposed…"

"Yeah, but he pretty much took it back when he found out I wasn't expecting." At the memory, I wanted to cry. "He was only doing it, because he felt he had to."

"No. I don't think so."

I wanted to scream in frustration. "You weren't here. *I* was."

"So, tell me. What'd he say?"

For the life of me, I couldn't even remember. But I *did* know that he wasn't overflowing with plans for the future. Mostly, it was what he *didn't* say that counted.

Into my silence, Luna said, "Is he there? Can I talk to him?"

I gave a bark of laughter. "No. He's gone."

"Oh. When will he be back?"

My heart gave that familiar ache. "For all I know, never."

Again, she said, "No. I don't think so."

I shoved a hand through my hair. This conversation was feeling less satisfying with every passing second. Obviously, she didn't get it. Probably, she never would. After all, she and Jake seemed perfect together. For all I knew, they never even argued.

Switching gears, I said, "And just for the record, I wasn't serious about the sewer contractor."

"You're kidding. You don't need the work done?"

"No, that's not it. It's just that—"

"What? You're worried they won't do a good job?"

"No. That's not it either. But—"

"Because like I said, they're *really* good at what they do. They're licensed and everything."

"I know," I said. "You told me in the message, but—"

"But what?" She hesitated. "Oh no. Was it the towel thing?"

"No."

"The beer thing?"

"No." I was so tired of dancing around the issue. In a fit of frustration, I finally just told her the truth. "I can't afford to pay them."

"So?" she said. "They're already paid."

"But I can't accept that."

"Why not?" she asked.

"Because it's too much."

"Then consider it a wedding gift."

I felt my jaw clench. "But I'm not getting married."

She made a scoffing sound. "Not for *you*. For me."

I gave a confused shake of my head. "What?"

She lowered her voice. "Yeah. I mean, they're my brothers, and I love them and all. But they've got like another week until their next big job starts. They can either spend that week with *you*, working. Or with *me*, making Jake crazy. And besides, they've already been paid. If you don't accept, you'll hurt their feelings. And they're um, *really* sensitive."

Sure they were.

Somewhere in the background, I heard Jake say, "And don't forget the balcony thing."

"Oh, stop it," she told him. "You wouldn't really."

"You wanna bet?"

She returned to the phone and chirped, "Alright, it's settled. Talk to you later. Bye."

And then, with a click, she was gone.

I felt my gaze narrow. I had the distinct impression that I'd just been massively manipulated. But for whose benefit? Mine? Or hers?

I decided to think about *that* later.

For now, while I had some semblance of privacy, I was dying to hear Joel's message.

CHAPTER 31

Standing in the den, I pulled up Joel's message and braced myself for whatever he was going to say.

But it wasn't quite what I expected.

His voice, quiet but intense, made my heart ache. "Listen, Melody. About last night, it wasn't what you think." He paused. "Fuck. I hate that I'm not there. Sorry. Anyway, just call me back, okay?"

And that was it.

I wasn't quite sure what any of it meant, but it sent an irritating surge of hope flooding through me.

And I hated myself for it.

In my mind, I could practically see myself on a roller coaster, heading slowly up the hill, accompanied by that annoying clickity sound. I knew exactly what that sound meant. It meant that eventually, I'd be heading for a steep fall.

I rubbed at my sore eyes and tried to think. If I were smart, I wouldn't even call him back.

But who was I kidding? I knew I would. It was just a matter of when.

With my phone in-hand, I sank into a nearby armchair and closed my eyes, hoping to clear my head. It was no use. My head was too filled with images of Joel.

I sighed. What else was new?

I was still sitting there, clutching my cell phone, when a different phone rang. It was the landline, which I almost never used. A moment later, the ringing stopped, and I heard one of the brothers call out,

"Hey, Melody!"

Damn it. I'd been so focused on Joel, I'd almost forgotten that anyone was here. I hollered back, "What?"

"It's for you!"

What the hell? They weren't seriously answering my phone?

A few seconds later, I heard pounding on the door, followed by one of the brothers calling through it. "It's some guy, won't give his name!"

I pushed myself up and marched to the door. When I yanked it open, there they were, both of them, standing within arm's reach.

Steve held out my cordless telephone. "Whoever the guy is, he sounds pissed off." With a sudden snicker, he turned to Anthony and said, "Maybe *he's* pregnant, too."

Oh, for God's sake. I yanked the phone out of Steve's hand and told him, "For the last time, I'm *not* pregnant."

"If you say so." He flicked his head in the general direction of the driveway and said, "So, you want us to get plugged in or what?"

I still had no idea what that meant. But if it got them out of the house, then yes, that's exactly what I wanted. "Fine," I said. "Go. Do whatever." Without waiting for their response, I ducked back into the den and shut the door firmly behind me. Into the phone, I said, "Hello?"

It was Joel, who wasted no time in demanding, "Who the hell was that?"

Well, this was just great. He sounded nothing like the guy who'd left that earlier message. But I couldn't tell if he was angry in general, or just unhappy that another guy had answered my phone.

Looking to move past this, I said, "That was Steve."

"Steve who?"

Funny, I had no idea. "You know. Luna's brother?"

"What the hell is *he* doing there?"

"It's not just him," I said. "There's two of them."

"Anthony too?"

"So, you've met them?" Even though I was pretty sure that the brothers were outside, I lowered my voice, just in case. "Are they okay?

Like, should I trust them?"

"With what?"

"I just mean, if I leave, are they gonna rob the place or anything?"

"No," he said, "but I'd keep an eye on your beer."

I hesitated. Was that a joke? I couldn't be sure either way, especially because Joel definitely hadn't been smiling.

Already, this whole conversation was incredibly frustrating. I still didn't know why Joel had called. I wanted to ask, but with the way he was acting, I felt compelled to first explain how Luna had sent her brothers to help with my sewer situation.

When I finished, Joel said, "And how about Jake?"

"What about him?"

"Is *he* there?"

"No."

"Good. Do me a favor, alright?"

"What?"

"If he stops by, don't let him in."

"Why not?"

"Because I don't trust him."

"So you trust *Luna's* brothers, but not your own?"

"Steve and Anthony? They're harmless. But Jake? Different story."

"Oh come on," I said. "I talked to Jake. He's not *that* bad."

"I mean it. You steer clear of him." And then, in a quieter tone, he added, "Alright?"

"But I don't get it," I said. "What do you think he's gonna do?"

"I don't know. And I don't wanna find out."

"Joel, seriously. You *do* realize how paranoid that sounds?"

"Yeah? Well, lemme ask you something."

"What?"

"If he screwed his dad's girlfriend, what's to stop him from putting the moves on *you*?" His voice hardened. "Especially with me out of town."

My breath caught. *Out of town?* Did that mean he was planning to come back? *Damn it.* There it was again, that annoying flicker of hope.

I was still trying to squash it down when Joel abruptly said,

"Lemme talk to them."

Startled, I asked, "Who?"

"Steve and Anthony."

"Why?"

"Because I wanna warn them."

"About what?"

"Are you gonna put them on the phone or not?"

I really didn't like his attitude. "No."

"Alright," he said. "Then, I'll call you back in five minutes."

"What? Why five minutes?"

"When I call, are you gonna answer?"

"Not if you're asking like *that*."

"Should I call your cell or the land line?"

"Did you even hear what I just said?"

"Your cell," he said. "You got it on you?"

"Maybe."

"Five minutes," he repeated. "And if you don't answer? I'll keep calling 'til you do." And with that, he hung up.

I pulled the phone away from my ear and stared down at the thing, wondering why Joel had bothered to call at all. As far as warm and fuzzy, the conversation had been seriously lacking.

On top of that, I had a pretty good guess on what he planned to do during the next five minutes. Looking to confirm my theory, I hustled out of the den and made my way to the front room, where I parted the front curtains and peered outside.

In my driveway, I saw a big, mud-splattered pickup, emblazoned with the words Moon Construction along the side. Behind the truck was a small bubble-shaped camper.

From the camper's far side, a long extension cord snaked its way over my front lawn and ended somewhere on the side of my house.

As far as the brothers themselves, I didn't see either one of them until Anthony emerged from the other side of the camper, holding a cell phone to his ear.

I pressed my face closer to the glass and studied his face in profile. Was he talking to Joel? I couldn't be sure. He wasn't smiling, but he wasn't cringing in terror either. I was still looking when Anthony turned abruptly in my direction and caught me with my face smashed up against the glass.

On instinct, I drew back and yanked the curtains shut again.

And then, realizing how unhinged I probably looked, I reopened the curtains and gave Anthony a little wave.

Yeah, that's me. Just adjusting the curtains.

When he waved back, I breathed a sigh of relief.

Maybe I wasn't acting nearly as crazy as I felt. I paused. Or more likely, he was chalking it up to my so-called pregnancy. On that disturbing note, I left the window and returned to the den to wait for Joel's call.

Regardless of whatever else was going on, he and I were due for a serious discussion, and I didn't want to do it in front of an audience. But to my infinite frustration, five minutes went by, and then ten more – all without a phone call.

After thirty full minutes, I was seriously miffed. Determined to get some answers, I left the house in search of the brothers. But now, neither one of them was in sight.

I looked around. From what I could tell, they weren't in their truck *or* in the yard. I eyed the camper. They wouldn't be in there, would they?

But sure enough, that's exactly where they were.

Unfortunately, what they told me after I knocked on the door didn't make me feel any less crazy.

CHAPTER 32

Standing inside the camper, I looked from brother to brother. "He said *what?*"

They were sitting on opposite sides of a narrow booth that *might* seat four, if the four people didn't mind squashing in next to each other.

Considering that I hardly knew these guys, I'd already declined their offer to sit. Instead, I was standing at the end of the booth, trying to make sense of everything they'd just told me.

At my request, Anthony repeated his last sentence. "He said that if anything happens, he's gonna kick our asses."

I gave Anthony a perplexed look. "If anything happens? Like what?"

Anthony shrugged. "He didn't say."

I wasn't buying it. For some reason, I just couldn't see Joel threatening these guys, unless – maybe it was some sort of inside joke? I asked, "Was he serious?"

Anthony gave it some thought. "Maybe. Hard to say."

I studied his face. "You don't look too concerned."

"Eh, we're used to it."

"Used to what?" I asked. "Being threatened?"

"Or whatever." Suddenly, he reached out and slapped the tabletop. "Wait a minute. That wasn't it."

Startled, I gave a little jump. "What?"

"What Joel *said* was that if some lawyer showed up, we should kick *his* ass." He paused, as if thinking. "Some guy named Dirk?"

I wanted to groan out loud. The last thing I wanted was more drama. Reluctantly, I said, "I think he meant Derek."

"Yeah, that's it."

I gave the two brothers a good, long look. They didn't look like fighters, but they didn't look soft either. In truth, I wasn't sure that Derek could handle either one of them, much less both.

But that wasn't the point. The last thing I wanted was a fist-fight on the front lawn.

Hoping to head off trouble, I summoned up what I hoped was a smile. "I'm sure it was just a joke."

Anthony gave me a dubious look. "You think?"

I kept my smile plastered in place. "Definitely."

Across the table, the two brothers shared a look. It was Steve who said, "The aunt and uncle – was that a joke, too?"

Damn it. I knew exactly who he meant. My Uncle Ernie and Aunt Vivian, who had who had this annoying tendency to show up and swipe my stuff when I wasn't home. In a carefully neutral voice, I said, "What about my aunt and uncle?"

"Yeah," Steve said. "What about them?"

I felt my jaw clench. "That's what I'm *trying* to find out."

"Yeah," Steve said. "Me, too."

It was enough to give me a headache. "So Joel mentioned them, too?"

"Hell if I know," Steve said. "*I* didn't talk to him."

I turned and gave Anthony a questioning look.

He said, "Hey, that was like a half-hour ago."

"So?"

"So I didn't take notes or nothing."

I looked back to Steve and said, "But you were the one who mentioned it. So *you* remember, right?"

He gave me a look. "You *see* a pen and paper?"

I glanced around. Inside the trailer, I saw piles of dirty laundry, a few discarded pizza boxes, and some crushed beer cans in the far corner. Unless it was buried under the clutter, there was no pen and paper. Grudgingly, I said, "No."

Steve said, "Well, there you go."

Yes. There I went.

Across from him, Anthony said, "Oh, and there was something about Jake."

I tensed. "What about him?"

"If *he* shows up, we're supposed to call Joel and tell him."

"Why?" I asked.

Anthony stroked his chin as if thinking. "Maybe *that's* where the ass-kicking comes in."

I looked from brother to brother. I had the distinct impression that they were giving me the runaround. I felt my gaze narrow. "Did he say anything else?"

"Oh yeah," Anthony said. "I was supposed to tell you that something came up, and he'd call you later."

Oh, that was nice. So much for calling and calling until I answered. I asked, "Did he say when?"

"Yeah," Anthony said. "Later."

Well, that was informative.

Unsure what to do next, I glanced around the trailer, trying to see through the clutter. When I turned to look behind me, I saw a lower and upper bunk, covered with a mess of blankets and pillows, along with more dirty laundry.

Or who knows? Maybe the laundry was clean.

Think positive, right?

I asked, "Is this where you plan on staying?"

"Sure," Steve said, "unless you got someplace better."

My house was huge, and they *were* the brothers of someone I might call a friend, in a new-acquaintance sort of way. But inviting them to sleep in the house seemed a bit premature.

Thinking out loud, I murmured, "Well, there's always the guest house."

In some ways, it wasn't even mine to offer. After all, it was still filled with all of Joel's things. And yet, I was absolutely certain that, if given the choice, Joel would point them to the guest house long before he'd send them into *my* house for a sleepover.

Or who knows? Maybe he wouldn't care either way. For all I knew, he wasn't even coming back.

CHAPTER 33

I spent the next two days on pins and needles, waiting for a call that never came. And with every passing hour, the more I kept telling myself that I didn't want to hear from him anyway.

Seriously, who did he think he was?

The only upside was that the brothers were proving to be a good distraction, if only because they were making me crazy. They had serious boundary issues, and although they were staying in the guest house, they were constantly in and out of my kitchen, where they made themselves utterly at home.

Already, they'd gone to the other side of the state to retrieve their backhoe and were now tackling my sewer problem, just like they'd promised.

After watching them work, I had to give them credit. They actually seemed to know what they were doing. They'd found the problem, which, oddly enough, was Derek's fault in a roundabout way, and were now in the process of fixing it.

During the first couple of days after their arrival, I'd made it a point to stay close to the house. But today, I'd had a job interview in a neighboring city and had been tied up for nearly three hours.

Plus, I'd somehow managed to let the brothers talk me into stopping for beer and takeout pizza on the way back. Between that and a few other errands, it was already dark by the time I was finally heading home.

I was just a few miles from my house when my cell phone rang. I reached for it and gave the display a quick glance, only to feel that familiar – and yes, pathetic – disappointment. It wasn't a certain guy who I didn't want to talk to anyway. It was Aunt Vivian, my least-favorite relative.

She almost never called me, and on the rare occasions when she did, it was never for anything good. As it turned out, this time was no exception.

I'd barely said hello when the shrieking started. I couldn't understand a single word, but it was pretty obvious that something was terribly wrong. Desperate to make out what she was saying, I pulled my car off to the side of the road and cut the engine.

When she paused for air, I said, "Excuse me? What'd you say?"

This time, my aunt's voice came through loud and clear. "I *said*, they turned the hose on me!"

"What?" I gave a confused shake of my head. "Who?"

She sounded nearly unhinged. "*You* put them up to it, didn't you?"

My mind was going a million miles a minute. *They wouldn't. Would they?* I chewed on my lower lip. "Uh…"

"Aha!" she yelled. "I knew it!"

In the background, my uncle said, "Go on. Tell her about my hair."

My aunt replied, "For the last time, forget *your* hair! What about *my* hair!"

My uncle muttered, "Well, at least *yours* is still attached."

What on Earth did *that* mean? I was still trying to figure it out when my aunt returned to the phone and hollered, "So I hope you're satisfied!"

And with that, she hung up.

I sat there in my quiet car for a long moment, asking myself an odd question. *Was I satisfied?*

A sudden snicker escaped my lips, and I gave a little gasp. *Oh, my God.* I was, even if I wasn't quite sure what had happened.

Did that make me a horrible person?

I was still trying to decide when I pulled into my driveway a few minutes later. Outside the house, I saw no sign of the brothers, but I *did* see the garden hose rolled out to its full length. Slowly, I got out of the car and confirmed that yup, sure enough, the porch was dripping wet.

When I walked in through the front door a minute later, Steve and Anthony were waiting in the foyer.

Steve said, "Hey, you just missed your aunt."

Anthony snickered. "Yeah, but *we* didn't." He stopped and looked down at my empty hands. "Hey, where's the pizza?" He was frowning now. "You didn't eat it in the car, did you?"

Funny, in all the excitement, I'd neglected to bring it in. "Forget the pizza," I said. "You didn't *really* hose down my aunt and uncle, did you?"

The two brothers exchanged a look. It was Steve who said, "Let's say we did. Were we not supposed to? Because if that was some sort of rule, you should've told us."

"Yeah," Anthony said. "And besides, it's not like we didn't warn them."

They went on to tell me that my aunt and uncle had tried to barge into the house, in spite of being told it was off-limits. My aunt, with her usual charm, had claimed she wasn't about to be deterred by a couple of two-bit flunkies who weren't even related.

Continuing the story, Anthony said, "which made her look like a giant dumb-ass, because we're brothers, you know?"

I hesitated. "I think she meant related to me."

"Eh, whatever," Anthony said. "Anyway, we told 'em, you try it, and you'll get the hose."

I was almost afraid to ask. "So then what happened?"

He grinned. "Guess."

I cleared my throat. "They, uh, tried it?"

He was still grinning. "You got it."

By now, I almost didn't know what to say. We were still standing in the foyer. I looked from brother to brother. "So you turned the hose on them? Just like that?"

Steve gave me a look. "Well, yeah. Once you threaten it, you gotta do it, you know?"

Funny, I *didn't* know, at least not from experience, but it made a weird kind of sense.

"Yeah," Anthony agreed. "If you don't, they won't believe you the next time."

"By the way," Steve said, "someone dropped off a cake."

"Who?" I asked.

"Some chick. I didn't get her name."

I could think of only one person who might drop off a dessert. Cassie. I gave Steve a worried look. "You didn't turn the hose on *her*, did you?"

"Hell no," Steve said. "Jeez. What? You think we're stupid?"

I held up my hands. "Sorry."

"You should be." He made a scoffing sound. "No way we'd ruin a cake."

I stared at him. Was that a joke? From the look on his face, I couldn't be sure either way.

When I looked to Anthony, he said, "Yeah. You get it wet, you gotta eat it with a spoon. Totally sucks."

Steve said, "And if it gets *too* wet, you gotta pull out a straw."

I felt my gaze narrow. "Where's the cake now?"

Steve flicked his head toward the kitchen. "The counter near the fridge."

While I made my way toward the kitchen, the brothers headed outside to retrieve the pizza and groceries from my car.

When they returned five minutes later, I was still staring at the cake. I had to ask, "Where's the rest of it?"

"Where do you think?" Steve said. "We ate it."

The cake had definitely come from Cassie. Even if I hadn't guessed already, the box with her shop's logo would've been a dead giveaway. As far as the cake itself, it was chocolate with white frosting. It looked absolutely delicious – well, what was left of it, that is.

It was even decorated. Along the top was a message, written in fancy purple icing. But with half of the cake missing, I wasn't sure what it was supposed to say. I read the remaining part out loud. "I'm so...?"

"Hungry," Steve said, opening the nearest pizza box.

I turned to him and demanded, "How can you be hungry? You just ate half a cake."

"I did not," he said. "I ate a quarter of it. Big difference. Jeez."

When I looked to Anthony, he pointed to the cake and said, "I'm sorry."

I sighed. "That's alright. It's not like I would've eaten the whole thing anyway."

"No," Anthony said. "What I mean is, that's what the cake said. I'm sorry." He reached into his pocket and pulled out his cell phone. I took a picture, in case you wanted to see."

Well, that was thoughtful. I guess.

As I watched, he started scrolling through the images on his phone.

Watching, I said, "Wait! What's that?"

He looked down at his phone. "This? It's your aunt and uncle."

"Well, obviously," I said, staring down at the image. My uncle was stocky with thick red hair, while my aunt was thin and ferret-faced, with a look of perpetual annoyance.

In the photo, both of them were impeccably dressed as usual. He was wearing a suit and tie, while she was wearing a formal black dress with long, lacy sleeves and a big, poofy skirt. They were both standing on my porch, glaring at the camera. But at least, they were dry.

When I looked to Anthony, he grinned. "That's the before picture."

As I watched, he scrolled to the next image. In *this* one, my aunt and uncle were utterly drenched. My aunt's mouth was wide open, like the photo had caught her in mid-screech. As for my uncle, he looked mostly confused and – now *this* was weird – bald.

I felt my brow wrinkle in confusion. "He wears a toupee?"

Anthony snickered. "Not anymore."

With a mouthful of pizza, Steve added, "But I think he found it in the bushes."

I didn't know whether to yell at them or congratulate them on their aim. It was awful and oddly pleasing all at the same time. I decided to think about that later.

I asked, "But what about the cake photo? You said you had one?"

"Oh, yeah. Sorry, almost forgot." Anthony scrolled to the next image, and there it was – the cake in all its uneaten glory.

Not only did it say, "I'm sorry." It also had one painful word written in big, bold letters on the bottom with multiple exclamation points.

That word was, "Congrats."

I felt a sad smile tug at my lips. After all, it was the thought that counted, right?

CHAPTER 34

Cassie stared at me from across the small table. "So you're broken up?"

It was the morning after she'd dropped off the cake, and we were sitting in the front room of her cookie shop. On the way over here, I'd picked up two lattes, along with a couple of frosted cinnamon rolls, which neither one of us were eating – me, because I wasn't hungry and Cassie, because she'd been too engrossed in my latest tale of woe.

Last night, rather than telling Cassie the story over the phone, I'd suggested meeting for coffee before her shop opened.

As far as her question – whether Joel and I were broken up – I didn't even know how to answer. "Honestly, I'm not sure. I guess so. I mean, I don't think we're exactly together."

Probably, this was a massive understatement. It had been four whole days since that one short phone call, and he never did call me back. As far as me calling him, I'd resisted, in spite of some pretty strong urges otherwise.

As miserable as I was, I was actually pretty proud of myself.

Across from me, Cassie still looked stunned. "Seriously? So you're not engaged anymore?"

"Actually, I don't think we ever were." I sighed. "After all, it wasn't a real engagement. It was more of an obligation thing, on his part, I mean."

It hurt to say, but at some point, I had to accept reality and move on.

But Cassie was shaking her head. "You don't know that for sure."

It was a nice sentiment, and I tried to smile. "If you want to say it, I'll totally understand."

Her eyebrows furrowed. "Say what?"

"I told you so."

"Why would I say that?"

"Because you tried to warn me." At her blank look, I said, "You know. That I'd be crying before it was over?"

"Oh, that?" She winced. "Forget I said that, okay? I was totally wrong."

"You were not," I said. "You called it perfectly." In truth, I *had* been crying, more than I cared to admit. Happily, this was mostly at night, when I didn't have an audience.

Across from me, Cassie looked anything but smug. "Listen, there's something I've got to tell you."

"What?" I asked.

"There's a reason I was so crabby that day." She glanced away and let out a long, shaky breath. "It was Angelina the Skank. I ran into her just that morning, and she told me something that set me off."

"Really? What?"

Cassie hesitated. "Okay, before I tell you, I want you to know something. What she told me, it wasn't true. I'm absolutely sure of it."

Now, I was getting nervous. "What's not true?"

"Well, according to Angelina, she and Joel hooked up like five minutes after you two broke up."

True or not, my stomach clenched. "When?" I asked. "You mean like a few days ago?"

"No. A few *weeks* ago. After that whole moving-truck fiasco."

"Oh. Right." Based on the timing, I should've been able to figure that out for myself.

Cassie continued. "Anyway, the way Angelina tells it, Joel was on his way out of town and stopped at that gas station off the highway." Cassie paused, as if afraid to continue.

"And…?" I prompted.

"And Angelina happened to be there. And she, uh, hitched a ride to Detroit with him."

My gaze narrowed. "What kind of ride?"

"Well, it wasn't the kind that Angelina claimed."

"How do you know?"

"Because after you and I talked, I asked around."

"And...?"

"And I learned that he *did* give her a ride, I mean in his car, but it only lasted like two miles."

I felt my brow wrinkle. "What happened after two miles?"

Cassie leaned forward. "Get this. He kicks her skanky ass out and makes her walk."

"To where?"

"To the gas station. You know, where he picked her up."

I shook my head. "I don't believe it."

"Which part?" Cassie asked.

"I don't believe any of it," I said. "But especially about him making her walk."

"Why not?"

"Because he's a lot nicer than that."

Cassie laughed. "To you, maybe."

"What's that supposed to mean?"

"Look, I'm not saying he isn't a great guy. But how he treats you and how he treats Angelina are two different things." She gave me a wistful smile. "I've seen you two together, remember? He's crazy about you. Anyone can see that."

It was a nice thought, but I couldn't take much comfort in it. True, Joel hadn't ditched me on the roadside. But he *had* left my house in the middle of the night. In the big scheme of things, it wasn't a whole lot better.

Still, there was something that I didn't quite understand. "So let me get this straight," I said. "When I told you that Joel and I were engaged, you were under the impression that he hooked up with Angelina? Why didn't you tell me?"

"Because I wasn't sure it was true, and I didn't want to say anything until I knew for sure."

I tried to laugh. "Well, you did say *some* things."

She looked utterly mortified. "I know. And I'm really sorry."

I sighed. "That's alright. Besides, you were right. Probably, I should've listened."

But Cassie was shaking her head. "No. I *wasn't* right. Mostly, I was in a rotten mood and took it out on you."

I gave her a concerned look. "Is something wrong?"

She waved away the question. "Nah, everything's fine."

I studied her face. I wasn't so sure.

As if eager to change the subject, Cassie leaned forward again. "Hey, you wanna know how I'm sure that Joel kicked the skank out of his car?"

"Sure, how?"

Cassie laughed. "You know that chicken shack just outside town?"

"Yeah?"

"Well, *that's* where he dropped her off. She made a big stink about it too."

"How do you know?" I asked.

Cassie grinned. "Because I got it straight from Dorothy the Librarian, whose niece works at the chicken shack. Anyway, I'm really sorry about how I acted. I was awful, wasn't I?"

"Nah, you weren't that bad," I said.

She smiled. "Liar."

As I watched, her smile faded into a look of confusion.

"What's wrong?" I asked.

Cassie was facing the front window. I wasn't.

She said, "He's here."

"Who?"

"Joel."

CHAPTER 35

I turned to look, and there he was, gazing at me through the glass. He wasn't smiling, but then again, neither was I.

Still, my pulse jumped as I devoured the sight of him. His grey T-shirt clung to his pecs and fell loosely over his waist as he stood, still and silent, watching me watching him.

In the background, I heard Cassie say, "I'll just check on that thing in the kitchen." A moment later, I heard her footsteps receding toward the back room, where they ended with the sudden sound of the radio, cranked up to some oldies station.

Almost in a trance, I stood and walked slowly to the door. As I did, I reminded myself of every vow I'd made over the last few days.

I was done falling into his arms every time he showed up out of the blue. I was done acting like no matter what happened, I'd always be there, waiting like the sap I was. But was I done with him, period? As in forever? I honestly didn't know.

My brain said one thing, but my heart said something else entirely.

As I pulled open the door, I put my brain firmly in charge and waited for him to speak first.

He still wasn't smiling when he said, "You got a minute?"

Wow, a whole minute. Lucky me. I shrugged. "I guess."

He looked toward the shop's interior. "Want to talk in there? Or in my car?"

I spotted his car, parked at the curb across the street. A little privacy would've been nice, but why bother, given the time constraints? I gave him a thin smile. "How about right here?"

His voice was flat. "In the doorway."

"Sure," I said, "I mean, we've wasted thirty seconds already. The time's half gone, right?" I met his gaze head-on. "Or, does the timer start ticking *when* we reach your car?"

If he was amused, he didn't show it. "There's no timer."

Maybe not. But there *was* a calendar. And even though I didn't have a calendar *on* me, I did know that it had been several days since he'd promised to call me back. I wanted to bring it up, to demand to know why he hadn't called, and to throw his own words in his face. *"If you don't answer, I'll keep calling 'til you do."*

But that would just be more of the same – me, being pathetic.

So all I said was, "Alright. You pick – the car, here, whatever – it's all the same to me."

With a frown, he glanced down at his watch.

I felt my jaw clench. *No timer, huh?* I gave a bitter laugh. "In a hurry?"

He shoved a hand through his hair. "Alright, you want me to say it? Yes. I am." His gaze met mine, and I saw a flash of emotion – raw and fierce, burning across the short distance. "But I don't wanna be."

I made a sound of frustration. "Then why are you even here?"

"You can't guess?"

"I don't want to guess. I'm tired of guessing." My voice rose. "And why didn't you call?"

Damn it. So much for playing it cool.

"When?" he asked.

"Oh, come on," I said. "You know when. You said, 'I'll call you back in five minutes.' But you never did. That was what? Four days ago?"

He shook his head. "Didn't they tell you?"

It took me a few seconds to realize who he meant. "Who? Steve and Anthony?" Oh yeah. They said you'd call me later. But let me ask you something. What does 'later' mean to you?" I held up a hand. "You know what? Don't even answer. How about this? I'll tell you what it means to me *and* practically everyone else on the planet. 'Later' means, later on that night, or maybe the next day. It doesn't mean *never.*"

"You think I didn't *want* to call?"

He was still standing in the open doorway. Outside, the early December morning was cold and blustery – not quite freezing, but pretty darn close. Joel, like an idiot, wasn't wearing a jacket or even a shirt with long sleeves.

Behind me, I could feel the heat pouring out of Cassie's shop. I was wasting not only time, but money too – money that wasn't even my own, at least when it came to Cassie's heat bill.

Obviously, Joel and I couldn't argue in the doorway forever. Besides – I felt my mouth tighten – he was in a big, stupid hurry. And what was he doing with our limited time? He was waiting for the answer to his incredibly dumb question. Did I think he didn't want to call?

"Okay," I said. "You want an honest answer? Yes, that's exactly what I think, because if you *wanted* to call, you would've." Trying hard not to look pathetic, I took a deep breath and continued. "And look, it's not like I've been sitting around waiting or anything, but you were the one who told me that I *had* to answer the phone, so I'm just saying, it's pretty hard to answer a call that never comes."

When I finished, he looked at me for a long, silent moment. And then, he turned his head to look at his car.

I forced a laugh. "Oh. So my minute's up, huh?"

He looked back to me and said, "Alright, you want the truth?"

I gave another shrug. "I don't know. Do I?"

His voice was tight. "Probably not."

I stiffened. What did *that* mean? I didn't want to speculate, but I *did* want to know, so I said, "Look, whatever it is, just tell me." I lifted my chin. "Or don't. I guess it's up to you."

He was quiet for another long moment. His muscles were rigid, and his eyes were hard. And then, he said something I didn't expect. "I was in jail."

CHAPTER 36

The door handle slipped from my fingers and started to swing shut between us. I caught it just in time and said, "What?"

Joel let out a long breath. "And I just got out."

I had no idea what to say, other than to ask the obvious question. "For what?"

"What do you mean?"

"Why were you arrested?"

"For being in the wrong place at the wrong time."

My gaze narrowed. "And where was that, exactly?"

"A fight."

Damn it. I knew it. Still, hoping for the best, I said, "Were you watching a fight, or–?"

"No."

"So you were fighting?"

"Almost."

"What does *that* mean?"

"It means the fight was busted before I went on."

"But you were still arrested?"

He gave a tight shrug. "Like I said, wrong place, wrong time."

I sighed. "You were filling in for Cal, weren't you?"

His gaze grew intense. "I had to."

"Why?"

"Because I owed him."

I knew what he meant. He owed him because of me. And as a result, he'd ended up in jail.

I had no idea how I felt. Relieved that he had a decent reason for not calling? Horrified that he'd been in jail? Or scared to death that he was still in some sort of trouble?

My head was swimming. It was all of those things and more. I said, "So, what are you? Out on bail or something?"

Joel shook his head. "No. I'm out, period."

"How?"

"The charges were dropped."

"Against everyone?"

"No. Not everyone."

It suddenly struck me that we were still standing in the open doorway. I had a million questions, but the way it looked, no time to ask them. But why *was* that? I just had to know. "And why are you in such a rush?"

Right on cue, a flashy red sports car rounded the corner and squealed to a stop behind Joel's car. A moment later, the driver's side window rolled down, and his brother, Jake, leaned his head out to holler, "Nice try, dickweed!"

With a muttered curse, Joel gave Jake and his car a quick glance before turning back to me. A ghost of a smile crossed his features. "I tried to lose him."

"Why?" I asked.

"Because I *had* to see you."

And just like that, my heart turned to jelly. Did that make me pathetic? Probably. "So what are you? His prisoner now?"

"No. But they're helping me with something, and we're running late."

"So there's more than Jake?" The words had barely left my mouth when, across the street, Jake's passenger's side door opened, and his other brother, Bishop, stepped out of the car. He turned and gave us a long, cool look before shutting the car door behind him.

I muttered, "Never mind. I think I know." As I watched, Bishop sauntered over to Joel's car and leaned his hip against the passenger's side door. He watched us with a look that wasn't exactly hostile, but wasn't terribly friendly either.

I was still looking when I felt a hand close over mine. It was Joel's hand, and it felt like a warm balm to my wounded heart. I looked up to meet his gaze.

His voice was quiet. "Promise me something."

"What?"

"You'll wait."

"For what?"

"For me."

I had no idea what he meant. I tried to laugh. "You're not joining the foreign legion, are you?"

"No. But there's something I've gotta do. And I've gotta finish it now, because it's already started."

I felt my brow wrinkle. "That makes no sense."

"I know. But I'll explain it when I get back."

"When will that be?" I asked.

"A few days, maybe a week."

I breathed a sigh of relief. "And what do you mean by wait?"

"I just mean, don't give up on us. Everything's a cluster right now, but I'm working it out. Just trust me, okay?"

I wanted to trust him, but I wasn't sure where this led. I let out a long, frustrated breath and admitted a sad truth. "I'm not sure I should."

"Why not?"

Humiliating or not, I wanted to be honest. "Because it just seems like I'm always chasing after you, like I want you more than you want me."

He made a low scoffing sound. "You're kidding, right? You know what it took to get here?"

I didn't want to split hairs, but I had to say it. "But you didn't *have* to come here. You could've called." I tried to make a joke of it. "I mean, you get one phone call, right?"

His mouth tightened. "You think I'm gonna call you from jail?"

"Why wouldn't you?" I tried to smile. "I could've bailed you out."

"No fucking way."

"What?"

"You heard me. That kind of shit? It's not for you. And I'm not dragging you into it."

"Alright, fine," I said. "Even if you didn't want me involved, you still could've called."

"And say what?" he said. "Shit, I didn't even want you to know."

"So you weren't gonna tell me?"

"Not if I could help it."

That *wasn't* what I wanted to hear. "Why not?"

"Aside from it's fucking embarrassing?"

"Yes." I straightened. "Aside from that."

"Alright. How about this? I'm not getting you involved, because I'm done with that."

"You *can't* be done," I said, "not if you're still fighting."

"I'm *not* still fighting," he said. "It was a favor for Cal. A one-time deal."

A loud, honking sound made me jump practically out of my skin. I looked across the street and saw Jake, eyeing us with obvious impatience. As for Bishop, he was still leaning against the passenger's side door of Joel's car.

Annoyed with both of them, I hollered out, "He'll be there in a minute. Jeez!"

When I looked back to Joel, he was almost smiling. He said, "You forgot to call him an asshole."

"Oh, please. I would never say that."

At least not out loud.

Joel gave me a look filled with regret. "The truth is, he's not completely wrong. There *is* someplace we've got to be."

"Where?"

"The airport."

"Why? Where are you going?"

Joel smiled. "If you wanna know, you'll have to see me again."

My gaze narrowed. "Are you bribing me?"

"You know it." With a low curse, he added, "And sorry, but I've really gotta go."

"Wait," I said. "I have a question."

"What?"

"Will you call me before then?"

Joel shook his head. "I can't."

"Why not?"

"No phone."

"No phone coverage, you mean?"

"No. I mean my phone's gone."

"Like lost?"

"No. Like destroyed."

"Really? From what?"

"From me."

"Sorry, but I'm not following."

"When things started going south, I didn't know what was gonna happen. But I *did* know that I didn't want anyone getting ahold of your stuff."

"What stuff?"

"Numbers, messages." He paused. "Pictures."

I saw what he meant. It's not like Joel had any nude pictures of me, but he *had* used his phone to take quite a few pictures that I wouldn't want to see splashed across some internet gossip site. Still, it struck me as overcautious. I said, "You think someone would've busted into your phone?"

"No. But I *did* think I'd rather smash it myself than take that chance."

I had to smile. It was vintage Joel, and I loved him all the more for it, even if I couldn't quite agree. I asked, "Are you going to get a new one?"

"Yeah. As soon as I get time."

Oh yeah. Time. It was something we were sadly lacking. Still, I said, "Sorry, but I've got another question."

"Yeah? What?"

"Why'd you leave?"

"When?" he asked.

"The other night."

He gave me a look. "Is that a serious question?"

"Of course."

"I left because you locked me out."

In spite of the cold air rushing across my face, I felt a slow warmth creep across my cheeks. "You mean the *bedroom* door?" I paused. "Wait a minute. How'd you know?"

"I tried the doorknob."

I didn't *hear* him try the doorknob. I glanced away. "Well, maybe I wanted some time to think."

"Yeah? You wanna know what I wanted?"

"What?"

"To kick in that door and make you talk to me whether you wanted to or not."

"You wouldn't have."

"Wanna bet? Five more minutes, and that's *exactly* what I would've done." His voice grew quiet. "I knew I messed up. And I sure as hell didn't wanna make it worse."

"So you just left?"

"Better than scaring the shit out of you."

I wasn't so sure. But for some reason, I *did* feel better. Sort of.

When I said nothing, Joel added, "When I'm done, you gonna be there?"

"Where?" I said. "At my house? Sure. I mean, where else would I be?"

His voice was almost a caress. "And when I show up, are you gonna let me in?"

I recalled all those promises I'd made to myself – that I was done waiting. And yet, I couldn't tell him no. And even if I did, I knew it would be a lie, so instead, I murmured, "Probably."

"Good," he said. And he turned away without even a kiss goodbye. Silently, I stared after him, wondering if I was making a huge mistake. Maybe. Maybe not.

But I did know one thing. Stupid or not, I'd be waiting.

CHAPTER 37

"What you should do," Steve said, "is shit in a fancy vase."

I stared at him from the other side of the kitchen counter. We'd been talking about my aunt and uncle, and their annoying tendency to show up and swipe my stuff.

But what this had to do with using a vase as a toilet, I had no idea. I was still staring. "What?"

He looked utterly sincere. "Yeah, and like, when they come in to steal it, splat, they get shit all over them."

Next to him, Anthony was shaking his head. "Dude. No."

I breathed a sigh of relief. Thank God *one* of them wasn't completely insane – or so I thought until Anthony added, "If you're going for the splat thing, you don't shit in a vase. You shit in a water balloon."

Steve made a sound of derision. "Get real. You can't shit in a balloon."

"Well, yeah," Anthony said. "Not directly. But you could shit in a bucket and fill the balloon using a pump or something. I mean sure, you'd have to add water–"

I threw up my hands. "You know what? Forget I said anything."

They both turned to look. Steve said, "You sure you're not pregnant?"

It was only the hundredth time he'd asked. After days of this, I was reasonably certain that he was only doing it to get a rise out of me, which of course, it did, every single time.

"For the millionth time," I told him, "I'm *not* pregnant. And stop asking, okay?"

He gave me a look that was all wide-eyed innocence. "Why?"

"Because it's irritating."

He grinned. "I know."

I was heading out for groceries. As I dug through my purse in search of my car keys, I said, "Gee thanks."

They'd been working on my sewer for days now – although the amount of hours they spent actually working wasn't terribly impressive. In truth, they seemed to spend most of their time eating pizza, drinking beer, and giving me a hard time.

By now, it was pretty obvious that they weren't fixing things as fast as they could, which for some weird reason, I didn't mind. As strange as it was, I liked having them around, temporarily, anyway – even if they were making me a little crazy.

Across from me, Steve said, "If you don't want to *personally* shit in a vase, you could pay a hobo to do it."

I rolled my eyes. "I'll think about it."

Steve leaned forward. "Seriously?"

"No." I pulled my keys out of my purse. "While I'm out, do you guys need anything?"

"Yeah," Steve said. "Beer."

Oddly enough, I *was* planning to get beer – only because they seemed to like it so much. "Anything else?" I asked.

Anthony said, "Pizza. Get a couple, alright?"

"Again?" If we ate pizza tonight, it would be the third night in a row. "Don't you guys ever get tired of it?"

"Not if you're buying," Steve said.

I had to laugh. In truth, they'd been treating me to pizza for the last few days. Already, I felt incredibly guilty and was trying to keep track of everything they were spending. Someday, I vowed, I'd pay all of them back with interest.

True to form, Anthony reached into his wallet and pulled out a fifty. "While you're out, get some donuts or something, will ya?" He made a face. "If I eat one more bran muffin, *I'm* gonna be shitting in a vase."

Well, that was an image I didn't need.

I waved away the money. "That's alright. It's my turn to treat." True, I was seriously short on funds, but I couldn't let them pay for *everything.*

But Anthony was insistent. He thrust the money closer. "Take it, or I'll hear about it later."

"From who?" I asked.

"Luna. Who else? You wouldn't believe it to look at her, but she can be pretty scary sometimes."

Somehow, I just couldn't see it.

But Steve was saying, "Yeah, especially after the phone thing." He looked to me and said, "You wanna know what I think?"

"What?" I asked.

"I think they wanted to get rid of us."

I recalled something that the brothers had told me when they first showed up. "Well, you *were* trying to make Jake…" I paused. "…how'd you put it?"

Steve was grinning again. "Pop." He looked to Anthony and said, "Funny to think Luna popped first."

I had to ask, "But why would you even do that? Don't you like him?"

"Jake?" Steve said. "Sure. But that don't mean we're not gonna give him shit once in a while."

I felt my gaze narrow. "Are you doing that to me?"

"What do you mean?" Steve asked.

"Well, you keep asking me if I'm pregnant."

"So?"

"So, are you waiting for *me* to pop?'

The two brothers exchanged a look, but neither one replied.

I looked from one to the other. "Oh, my God. You are. Aren't you?"

Steve looked to Anthony and said, "If she pops *now*, does it count?"

Anthony shook his head. "Hell no. She's gotta pop right when you're asking her."

Steve said, "Hey Melody."

"Don't even—"

"Are you pregnant?"

"Oh, for God's sake," I muttered, turning to head for the door. By the time I reached it, he'd asked me that same question three more times.

I didn't know whether to laugh or to kill him.

But on the upside, all the teasing made the house feel a little less empty while I waited for Joel to return.

In spite of all our troubles, I was dying to see him, or heck, even a phone call would've been nice.

So far, I hadn't heard from him, not that I'd expected to. But then, as if by magic, just as I was pulling into a grocery store parking spot, I got my wish.

CHAPTER 38

Just the sound of Joel's voice was enough to send my heart fluttering. And yet, I had to confess, "I almost didn't answer."

"Yeah? Why?"

"Because I didn't recognize the number." In truth, there *was* no number. The call had come through as "unknown."

"Sorry," he said. "Burner phone."

"Oh," I said. "You mean like a temporary one to tide you over?"

"Something like that." He paused. "Listen, I don't have much time, but I wanted to let you know that we'll be back on Saturday."

I felt myself smile. "Really?"

"Yeah, but do me a favor. If Jake gets there first, don't let him in, okay?"

And just like that, my smile was gone. "Wait. Jake's coming over, too?"

"He's not gonna stay, if that's what you're asking."

I wasn't sure what I was asking. It's not that I objected to Jake or any of Joel's brothers stopping by. But Joel's attitude was more than a little confusing.

I was still pondering that when Joel said, "So promise me, alright?"

"But why?" I asked.

"Because I don't want him alone with you."

Now, I was frowning. "You don't trust me?"

"I trust *you*. It's *him* I don't trust."

I wasn't quite sure I believed him. "Is this because of that thing with Jake and your dad's girlfriend?"

"That's part of it."

"What's the other part?"

"He's a dick."

"Oh come on," I said. "He's your brother."

"Yeah. Which means that I know him. You don't."

This whole conversation was incredibly frustrating. Of all the things we could be talking about, why this? I tried to laugh. "It's pretty hard to get to know him when you guys are always fighting."

"We're not fighting," Joel said. "He's here with me now."

So Jake was hearing this? I just couldn't see it. "You mean in the same room?"

"No. In the same country."

"Wait. You're in a different country?"

"Long story," Joel said. "But you promise, right?"

It was only like the tenth time he'd asked. Maybe I should've said yes and been done with it. But after everything Jake had done for me, I just couldn't see myself refusing to let him in.

Looking to sidestep the issue I said, "The thing with your dad's girlfriend, that was what? Ten years ago."

"Yeah. So?"

"So people change."

"No. They don't. Especially Jake."

"But honestly," I persisted, "he seems really happy with Luna. And let's say he *was* like that as a teenager, I don't think he's like that now."

"Maybe not, but he's still a dick. I don't want him bothering you."

I *so* didn't want to get in the middle of this. I sighed. "If that's the case, why don't *you* tell him?"

"I did."

"And…?"

"And he was a dick, like always."

I thought of Steve and Anthony. They were brothers, and they gave each other grief all the time. Heck, they'd given *me* tons of grief, too. But there wasn't any real malice there.

I said, "Maybe he was just teasing you."

His voice was flat. "Teasing me."

"Yeah. Like to make you pop. You know. Lose your temper." I tried to smile. "Come on. Admit it. He was probably just goading you."

"You think that makes a difference?"

"Doesn't it?"

"Listen. My dad's girlfriend? She was a skank twice his age. And you wanna know what else? He *loved* pissing my dad off."

I wasn't following. "So?"

"So Jake screws her right there in my dad's house, *with* my dad in the other room."

My jaw dropped. "You're kidding."

"No. I'm not. And when my dad catches them—"

"Oh, my God," I said. "In the act?"

"No. But close enough. Anyway, when my dad walks in, Jake looks to my dad and says, 'What's the big deal? It was like screwing sandpaper.'"

I sucked in a breath. "He didn't."

"He did," Joel said. "Starts calling her Sandpaper Sally, right to my dad's face."

I shuddered at the implication. "So what'd your dad do?"

"What do *you* think? He takes a flying leap, looking to beat Jake's ass. This is in Jake's bedroom, by the way. But before you know it, the whole thing spreads to the kitchen."

"Why the kitchen?"

"Who knows. But give it five *more* minutes, and it's not just Jake and my dad fighting. It's *all* of us."

"You too?" I did the math. "So you were what, twelve years old?"

"Give or take."

At the image, my heart went out to him. "But why were you involved at all?"

Joel gave a humorless laugh. "Why were any of us involved?"

"I don't know," I said. "Why?"

"At first, it's because we're trying to separate my dad and Jake, but then, someone throws a bad punch, and before you know it, it's hard to say who's fighting who. And right there in the mix, there's

Sandpaper Sally, naked except for this ratty-ass blanket, and all this time, she's still screaming that nothing happened."

"Did your dad believe her?"

"What do *you* think?" Joel said. "Forget she's got no clothes on. Jake's bragging about it."

I gave another shudder. I wasn't quite sure it could be counted as bragging, considering the whole sandpaper aspect. But that was probably beside the point. Bracing myself, I asked, "So how'd it all end?"

"For me," Joel said, "it ended with a broken arm and a whole lot of stitches."

I winced. "Really? How?"

"Long story," he said. "But there was this glass table—"

"In the kitchen?"

"Hell no. We're long past the kitchen. By now, we're in the living room, heading out the front door…" His words trailed off. "Anyway, you get the picture. I'm just saying, Jake? The guy's a dick. And if you let him in, he'll get under your skin – or worse."

"Worse?" I said. "Like what?"

"I don't know." His voice hardened. "And I don't wanna find out. So just promise me, alright?"

Desperately, I wanted to promise. But I knew it would be a lie. I heard myself sigh. "I can't."

Sounding less than thrilled, Joel said, "Why not?"

It should've been obvious. "Because if he stops by with Luna or something, I can't just be rude about it. I mean, they just did me this huge favor."

"So?"

"So I owe them. And besides, you guys should patch things up."

"There's nothing to patch up," Joel said. "It's just the way it is."

"But it doesn't have to be."

Sounding more unhappy than ever, Joel gave a low curse.

At first, I thought he was cursing at me, but then said, "Sorry, but I've gotta go."

Now, *I* felt like cursing. We'd talked for what? Five whole minutes?

And we'd spent most of those minutes arguing.

Joel's voice, softer now, carried across the distance. "Listen, I want you to know something."

"What?"

"I love you, and we're gonna work this out."

In spite of everything, I smiled into the phone. I couldn't help but say it back. "I love you, too."

And then, he was gone.

I sat in the parking lot for a long moment, wondering where all of this would lead. I only prayed that Jake *didn't* stop by – not because I was truly concerned, but because there was no way on Earth that I could refuse to let him in.

But with Derek, it was another matter entirely, as he soon found out.

CHAPTER 39

From my open doorway, I gave Derek an annoyed look. "For the tenth time, no."

"Oh, come on," he said, "I'm trying to make it up to you."

Ten minutes earlier, he'd shown up in a suit and tie, uninvited, to ask me out to dinner.

I gave him an annoyed look. Dinner with Derek was the last thing I wanted. Cripes, I didn't even want to be talking to him.

I *had* told him that. Hadn't I?

Apparently, it was time to tell him again. "Seriously, just get in your car and leave, okay?"

He turned and looked out toward the driveway. Near the road, the brothers were laying a huge pipe in the massive trench they'd dug with the backhoe.

Derek said, "So you're having some work done, huh?"

I recognized this for what it was – a stalling tactic. Probably, under that cool façade of his, he was planning his next attack. Sadly for him, he'd chosen the worst possible topic.

I said, "Funny you should mention that."

He turned again to face me. "Oh yeah? Why?"

"Because it's *your* fault."

"Why mine?"

"Remember that giant moving truck? The one *you* sent?"

"Yeah. What about it?"

"It missed the driveway and crushed the main sewer line."

His eyebrows furrowed. "Like what? You saw it happen?"

I recalled what the brothers had showed me a few days earlier – a crushed pipe directly below deep ruts left in my lawn, courtesy of the wayward moving truck. "I didn't *have* to see. I've got the evidence, right there in my front yard."

"Sorry," Derek said, "but even if the truck *did* crush it, *they'd* be liable, not me."

"I don't care who's officially liable," I said. "It's your fault."

"What are you saying? You want *me* to pay for it?"

I knew the odds of that – just about zero. Still, it was worth a shot. "Well, the truck wouldn't have been here if it weren't for you."

"Alright," he said. "How about this? I'll file suit, see if they pay up. Then we'll split the proceeds, okay?"

Well, that was attractive. "I don't want you to *sue* them," I said. "I want you to stop interfering with my life."

His jaw clenched. "In case you haven't noticed, we've backed off considerably."

I rolled my eyes. "You backed off for like five days. What do you want? A medal?"

"No," he said. "I want to take you to dinner. Is that too much to ask?"

"Yes. It is."

"Why?"

"Because there's nothing we need to talk about."

"Sorry, but you're wrong." He glanced around before lowering his voice to say, "I've got something you'll want to hear. Just trust me on this, okay?"

"Trust you? You've got to be joking."

"I'm not joking," he insisted. "You'll want to hear this."

I crossed my arms. "Fine. Tell me now."

"I can't."

"Why?"

"Because there's a process."

"Then forget it."

Now, *he* was crossing *his* arms. "I'm not leaving 'til you say yes."

I wanted to scream. The way it looked, he actually meant it. *What now?* My gaze strayed to the nearby garden hose, and I felt myself smile.

I looked back to Derek. "Are you sure about that?"

Derek glanced around. "Why are you smiling?"

"You'll see." I stepped forward and shut the front door behind me. I elbowed my way past Derek and made my way down the front steps.

He said, "You're not leaving, are you?"

I called out over my shoulder. "Nope."

"Then where are you going?"

But I was already there. The faucet for the hose was just a few paces away from my porch. I leaned down and gave the handle a twist. I glanced toward the far end of the hose. I saw no water coming out, but that didn't mean anything.

The hose had a complicated nozzle with ten settings. It wouldn't do anything until I gave the handle a squeeze. I began striding toward the nozzle.

Derek said, "You're watering the flowers *now?*"

It was an incredibly stupid thing to say. For one thing, the flowers were long dead. For another, *they* weren't standing on my porch refusing to leave. I gave Derek a cheery smile. "Nope."

"Then what are you watering?"

"You."

His mouth fell open. "What?"

I reached down to swoop up the nozzle. I looked to Derek and asked, "Should I go for a fine mist or master-blaster?"

"Master-blaster?" Derek took a small step backward. "That's not a real setting."

He was right. It wasn't. But I really liked the sound of it. I gave the nozzle a quick glance. "Jet spray." I shrugged. "I guess that'll have to do."

I squeezed the handle and sent a stream of water splashing low in his direction, just enough to dampen his shoes.

He stepped back like he'd been scalded. "What the hell?"

I lifted the nozzle higher and squeezed again. This time, it hit the bottom of his pant legs.

He yelled, "Watch the suit!"

"What suit?" I asked, aiming the water just a bit higher. "*That* suit?"

He scrambled backward until his backside hit the porch railing. "You're nuts! You know that?"

"Totally," I said, flicking the hose nearly to waist level.

"Son of a bitch!" he yelled, looking down to his newly dampened groin. "That's freezing!"

When I squeezed the nozzle again, he dove sideways, vaulted over the porch railing, and hit the ground running, sprinting toward his car.

By the time he peeled out of the driveway a moment later, the faucet was off, and I was already coiling up the hose. But I didn't put it away, not completely, because if he came back, I'd definitely be using it again.

CHAPTER 40

Two days later, my sewer was finally fixed, and everything was working just like new. As far as the yard, yeah, it was pretty torn up. But that, I decided, was something to worry about later.

Like spring.

Spring would be good.

At noon, I left the house for yet another job interview and returned later that afternoon to a surprisingly quiet house. The brothers were nowhere in sight, but on the kitchen counter was something I hadn't seen before – a sturdy-looking portable safe, not much bigger than a small microwave.

I gave the safe a closer look. It was dark gray with a classic combination lock. I couldn't be sure, but the safe looked brand new. What it contained, I had no idea.

Obviously, it belonged to the brothers, but for the life of me, I couldn't figure out what valuables they'd want to secure, or why they'd leave the safe just sitting there, out in the open.

When they showed up a couple of hours later with yet more pizza, I pointed to the safe and asked, "Is that yours?"

Steve set the pizza boxes on the nearby counter and said, "Yeah. For now."

I gave him a perplexed look. "What does that mean?"

"Eh, nothing," he said. "But leave it there, will ya?"

I looked to Anthony for a better explanation, but all he said was, "And when he says don't move it, he means don't move it. Like not at all."

I wasn't exactly thrilled with the idea. "For how long?"

"As long as it takes," Anthony said.

"But you're leaving in just a couple of hours."

"I know," Anthony said. "That's why we're leaving it."

The more they talked, the less I understood. By now, I should be used to this sort of thing, but I couldn't stop myself from saying, "So you're not taking it with you?"

Steve gave me a look. "Why would *we* want it?"

"Well, it *is* yours, isn't it?"

Steve said, "For now."

And there we were – full circle. Again, I looked to Anthony. "Why shouldn't I move it?"

He said, "It's sort of fragile."

"It doesn't *look* fragile."

"Well yeah," Anthony said, "I'm not talking about the safe. I'm talking about what's *inside* the safe."

I made a forwarding motion with my hand. "Which is…?"

He grinned. "Fragile."

Well, I should've seen that coming.

After several more attempts, I finally gave up. But *they* didn't. Somehow, they managed to wheedle a promise out of me that I wouldn't touch the safe until they came back for it.

The promise had barely left my mouth when I thought better of it. "Wait a minute," I said. "When you say you'll come back for it, you *do* mean in a couple of days when you stop by to pick up backhoe." I gave the safe another glance. "Right?"

Anthony said, "I don't think it'll be that quick."

"So you're not picking up the backhoe on Friday?"

"Oh, we're picking up the backhoe," Anthony said. "But the safe? Eh, it's hard to say."

I wasn't liking the sound of this. "But you're not going to just leave it on the counter, are you?"

"Sure we are," Steve said, "where else would we put it?"

"I don't know," I said. "Maybe in a closet or something?"

"Nah," Steve said. "A closet's no good."

I felt my gaze narrow. "It's nothing illegal, is it?"

"Hell no," Steve said, looking almost insulted. "How dumb do you think we are?"

"Sorry," I stammered, "it's just that—"

"If it were illegal," Steve said, "we'd put it in the basement, maybe dig a hole down there or something."

"Yeah," Anthony agreed, "I mean, we wouldn't just leave it out *here*, for anyone to see. You think we're nuts?"

Choosing to believe this was a rhetorical question, I opened the nearest pizza box and took a slice. Before biting into it, I said, "I don't even have a basement."

"Sure you do," Steve said. "I can tell by the structure."

"Well, yeah," I said. "Technically, I guess I do. But it's not like a basement-basement."

"No kidding?" Anthony said. "What is it?"

"Well, actually, it's a wine cellar."

Steve grinned. "No way. You got a wine cellar?" He leaned forward. "Is it just wine? Or beer, too?"

I gave it some thought. "As far as *I* know? Just wine."

Steve was no longer smiling. "Well, that sucks."

Anthony said, "As far as you know? What does that mean?"

Briefly, I relayed the story of my wine cellar. Shortly after the death of my parents, Derek's dad had hired a locksmith to secure the door that led to the wine cellar steps. At the time, he'd claimed it was a liability issue, because I'd been under the legal drinking age.

But looking back, I wasn't sure this was the real reason. After all, Aunt Gina, who'd been my guardian at the time, had been in her thirties. And she *did* love her wine.

Then again, maybe that was the problem.

Before I knew it, we were all standing around the wine cellar door. It was located off a small hallway near my kitchen. The door was made of thick, ancient oak and secured with a much newer lock, which had been drilled a couple of inches above the doorknob.

Even though I was now weeks past my twenty-first birthday, I still didn't have a key. And given my newly hostile relationship with Derek,

I knew the odds of getting one.

They weren't good.

Thinking out loud, I said, "Maybe I should call a locksmith."

"Screw a locksmith," Steve said. "We can get this."

"You can?" I said. "How?"

"Like with an ax." He shrugged. "Or maybe a crowbar."

I was absolutely horrified. "What?"

"Or," Anthony added, "there's always a chainsaw. You got one?"

"No," I said. "And even if I did, I wouldn't let you use it."

"Why not?" Anthony asked.

"Because I don't want the door destroyed. I just want it opened."

Steve gave me an annoyed look. "*Now*, you tell us?"

"I shouldn't *have* to tell you."

"That's what *you* think," Steve said, looking distinctly disgruntled. "If you change your mind, let us know."

I wasn't going to change my mind, and I told them so in no uncertain terms. But I did make a mental note to ask Derek about it, assuming I was unlucky enough to see him in the near future.

As it turned out, I *did* see him, early the next morning after being summoned to his family's law firm for an emergency meeting. But what happened there was so shocking that I completely forgot to ask about the wine cellar – or anything else for that matter.

CHAPTER 41

It was seven in the morning, and I'd just walked into the law firm. I'd slept terribly the night before, and was barely awake, much less ready to take on Derek and his dad.

I was greeted at the front desk by a receptionist who I'd never seen before and then ushered into their nicest conference room. She said, "Mister Mitchell will be with you in a few moments."

"Wait," I said, "*Which* Mister Mitchell? The father or the son?"

She looked surprised by the question. "The son, of course."

I wasn't sure why she'd be surprised. But then again, I still had no idea why we were meeting at all. I only knew that it was supposedly urgent.

I said, "Did he say what the meeting was about?"

"I'm sorry. I'm just the receptionist." She gave me a smile that looked a little tense. "I'll let him know you're here."

The whole situation was unnerving to say the least. I'd been summoned to this meeting not by Derek, but by his dad, who had called last night and insisted that it was important.

And yet, the guy wasn't even going to be here?

Even as the thought hit me, I reminded myself that probably, this was a good thing. Dealing with the son was bad enough.

I'd been sitting there alone for almost fifteen minutes when my cell phone rang. I pulled it out and took a look.

It was my aunt Vivian – the one I loathed. I had no idea why she'd be calling me so early, but I did know that I'd rather deal with her now than later. Besides, what else was I going to do while waiting for

Derek?

When I answered the call, she said in a tightly controlled voice, "I suppose you think you're funny."

I frowned. "What do you mean?"

"Don't play dumb with me," she snapped. "I know exactly what you want."

"Well, that makes one of us."

"Oh, so you *want* me to lose my temper? Is that it? You want a nice big laugh at my expense? Well let me tell you something, missy. I'm *not* going to give you the satisfaction. But I *will* say this. I was wearing my favorite dress, and now it's ruined. So, go ahead. Laugh it up. It won't be so funny when you get the bill."

I sighed. *Not this again.*

I heard my uncle say, "And don't forget my suit."

My aunt hissed back, "Like she'd care about your suit. The little snot doesn't care about anything."

Well, that was nice. Apparently, the little snot was me. To think, all along, I'd been a lot nicer to Aunt Vivian than she ever deserved. I said, "Oh, I care, alright."

My aunt paused. "Pardon?"

"Yeah." My voice rose. "I care about you staying out of my house. So you got a little wet. Big deal. It happens to all of us, right?"

She gave a little gasp. "Wet? It was more than wet! It was disgusting!"

So much for not losing her temper. "Oh come on," I said. "You're blowing this way out of proportion."

"You think so, huh? Well, let me tell you something, you little snot. You might think you're clever now, but *you're* paying for it. And I don't mean for the dry-cleaning."

I almost laughed. "I'm not paying for anything."

"Oh, yes you are. And you know what? I want new shoes, too."

In the background, my uncle said, "Don't forget *my* shoes."

My aunt yelled back, "Forget *your* shoes! *Mine* were Jimmy Choos!"

My uncle said, "You mean the guy in our bridge club?"

"Oh, for God's sake," my aunt hissed. "That's Jimmy *Woo.* The banker." Under her breath, she muttered, "Oh, forget it." Returning to the phone, she said, "So when you get the bill, I suggest you pay it, pronto."

And with that, she hung up.

That was fine by me. She could rant all she wanted. I couldn't – and wouldn't – be paying for her shoes.

Cripes, I could barely afford cheap shoes for myself, much less shoes for someone else, especially the kind that would set me back a small fortune. I was just tucking my phone back into my purse when something made me pause.

It was the sound of music – violins maybe? – coming from somewhere down the hall. As I listened, it became louder, until a moment later, the conference door swung open, and a trio of musicians playing – yup, violins – sauntered into the room, followed by Derek, holding a bouquet of red roses.

As they all approached, I eyed them with growing trepidation. I didn't know what exactly was going on, but I did know that I wanted no part of it.

CHAPTER 42

Already, I was on my feet. Ignoring the musicians, I looked to Derek and said, "What's going on?"

His face was pale, and his eyes were red-rimmed around the edges, like he'd just gotten off a two-day bender. He took a deep breath and said, "I'm proposing."

My mouth fell open. "What?"

He looked to the musicians, who were still playing. I didn't recognize the tune, but it was slow and obviously intended to be romantic.

It didn't sound romantic to me, not under the current circumstances. It sounded more like the soundtrack to a horror movie, starring myself – because I *was* horrified.

I eyed the door to the conference room. If I bolted now, would they all chase after me? Cripes, if they kept on playing, we could form our own little parade.

But before I could make any such move, Derek dropped to one knee, pulled out a small black box, and opened it up to reveal a massive diamond engagement ring. He visibly swallowed before saying, "So, will you marry me?"

I stared down at him. "No."

Instantly, the music stopped, ending on a jumble of notes that didn't quite mesh.

Into the silence, Derek said, "Are you sure?"

"Of course, I'm sure." I made a sound of frustration. "Now, will you *please* stand up?" I looked to the musicians, who were now making a point to look at anything but us. I cleared my throat. "That was really nice, but, um, would you mind giving us some privacy?"

I didn't have to ask twice. They practically bolted for the door, carrying their now-silent instruments with them, I looked back to Derek. He was *still* on one knee, and he was still holding the ring box. In his other hand were the roses, gripped loosely, as if he'd forgotten they were there.

He wasn't getting up. Instead, he took another deep breath and said, "Just listen. We've always been good friends, right?"

"Not lately," I muttered.

"And if we get married," he continued, "we'll be even better friends. And just think, your money problems, they'd be gone. We could fix up your house, and do whatever you wanted." He gave me a smile that looked half-crazed. "Wouldn't that be nice?"

If I'd been hoping for words of love – which happily, I wasn't – I would've been sadly disappointed.

Nowhere in my wildest dreams, did I ever envision getting a marriage proposal that centered around finances and home-improvement projects.

I couldn't help but compare all of this to Joel's proposal – so raw and wonderful, right there in the open doorway to my house. There'd been no violins or flowers, or even a ring. But it was a million times better than this.

Joel's proposal had touched my heart. Even at the time, with everything else going on, I could clearly see the love in Joel's eyes – a love he must've seen mirrored in my own.

But with Derek, I had no idea what I was seeing. I didn't even know why he was doing this. No matter how I sliced it, it was pretty obvious that something was terribly off.

I squinted at his face. "Have you been drinking?"

"No."

I leaned a little closer. "You are such a liar."

"Alright, fine," he said. "So I've been drinking. Big deal. A guy has to get up a certain amount of nerve to propose, you know."

Well, that was sexy.

"Yeah," I said, "especially when he doesn't want to."

"What's that supposed to mean?"

I had a theory. And the more I thought about it, the more it made sense. I said, "Your dad made you do this, didn't he?"

"What?" Derek gave an awkward laugh. "No."

Sure, he didn't. I gave Derek a pleading look. "Will you *please* stand up?"

"Not 'til you say yes."

"Well then you'll be kneeling there forever," I said, "because the answer isn't just a no. It's a hell no. And you know what?"

"What?"

"Somewhere, in that thick skull of yours, you're doing a little happy dance, because you don't want to marry *me* any more than I want to marry *you.* Just admit it."

But he *didn't* admit it. Instead, he launched into another marriage sales pitch. This one centered on uniting our two families like our parents had always wanted.

What a crock. My parents had mentioned no such thing, at least not to me. And even if they *had* wanted this, so what? I knew for a fact that they'd want me to be happy. And there was no way on Earth I'd be happy with Derek.

Besides, he wouldn't be happy with me either.

If this were a genuine proposal from someone who truly loved me, I'd feel terrible saying no. But all I felt now was pure annoyance.

I said, "Get up."

"No."

I looked at him for a long moment. Part of me – an evil, twisted part of me – wanted to kick him in the face. But instead, I stepped around him, grabbed my purse off the table, and stalked toward the conference room door.

When I passed through it and turned toward the reception area, I spotted a silver-haired man – Derek's dad – poking his head out of a nearby office. At the sight me, he flashed a hearty smile and said, "So, are congratulations in order?"

What an asshole.

"No," I said, and kept on walking, passing him without another word. Stalking past the reception desk, I saw the musicians milling around, as if waiting to be called in for an encore. Or who knows, maybe they were just waiting for their check.

Either way, I was done with the whole scene. As I drove back to my house, I considered my theory – that Derek's dad had been behind the whole thing.

The more I thought about it, the more I decided I'd been right. In that case, Derek owed me a huge favor.

Someday, maybe I'd collect. But for now, all I wanted was strong black coffee and a dozen chocolate donuts. But in my kitchen, I found no donuts – even though I'd picked up a couple dozen yesterday – and the only coffee I had was decaf.

Deciding it was better than nothing, I made a pot anyway and stood in the kitchen waiting for it to finish brewing. While waiting, I happened to glance around and noticed something that made me curse for a whole new reason.

The safe – the one the brothers had left – it was missing.

Holding my empty coffee cup, I stared down at the bare countertop, where the safe should've been. I tried to think. When was the last time I'd seen it? Last night? Or was it yesterday morning?

I couldn't be sure either way. But it was definitely gone.

I squeezed my eyes shut and tried to think. The timing was awful. As luck would have it – meaning *bad* luck – the brothers were planning to swing by later this afternoon to pick up the backhoe and take it to the other side of the state.

I still had no idea what the safe contained, but I *did* know that the brothers had been adamant about it not being moved. Now, it wasn't just moved. It was gone entirely.

I wasn't looking forward to telling them. Deciding I'd rather tell them in person than on the phone, I waited nervously for them to show up. I wasn't sure when they were coming, but I prayed it would be soon, only to get this over with.

It was nearly four o'clock when my doorbell finally rang.

But when I went to answer it, it wasn't the brothers at all. It was their sister, Luna.

CHAPTER 43

Standing in the open doorway, I glanced around. I saw no sign of her brothers, just her. I said, "Uh, hi."

She gave me a sunny smile. "Hi."

For some reason, I felt almost awkward. It's not that I was unhappy to see her. In fact, I owed her, bigtime, for the help with the sewer. And yet, I wasn't blind to the fact that she lived on the other side of the state, so there had to be a particular reason for this visit.

Given my luck lately, I didn't want to speculate. With more than a little trepidation, I stepped aside and said, "Would you like to come in?"

"Sure, if you don't mind." And then, as if sensing my nervousness, she added, "I'm meeting my brothers here. They *did* tell you that? Right?"

Well, that was a relief.

Trying to be diplomatic, I said, "They might've, but there's been a lot going on, so I probably lost track."

"With them around? I can imagine." She gave me a tentative smile. "Speaking of which, you weren't *too* mad, were you?"

"For the pregnancy thing? Oh, I was definitely mad." I smiled. "But I'm pretty much over it now."

She cleared her throat. "Thanks. But, um, actually, I meant the other thing."

"Oh." I was almost afraid to ask. "What other thing?"

"My brothers. I sort of pawned them off on you."

My shoulders relaxed. Maybe that was true, but she'd also done me a huge favor, and not only with the sewer. In truth, the brothers had been the perfect distraction during what would've otherwise been a pretty lonely time.

As we made our way into the kitchen for coffee, I explained this to her as best as I could. "So, actually," I concluded, "they were kind of nice to have around."

"Don't tell *them* that," she said, "or they'll never leave." She rolled her eyes. "Don't ask me how I know. Oh, and get this. You know all that beer they were drinking?"

"You mean at your place?"

"Right. Jake's beer. Well, after they left, I found a whole bunch of it in the guest room, under the bed, no less. You know what I think?"

"What?"

"I think they were just doing it to get a rise out of Jake." She sighed. "Knowing them, they probably had some stupid bet on when he'd finally pop."

I didn't know what to say. Would it be snitching if I confirmed her theory? I was still debating that when she spared me the decision by changing the subject.

As I listened, she went on to explain that she was on her way back from Chicago, and that my house was practically on the way. Aside from seeing her brothers, she was here to pick up a family heirloom that they'd retrieved from their grandparents' house.

She finished by saying, "And it's kind of fragile, so I figured I should get it before it ends up in the back of their truck or something."

Something fragile? My stomach sank. She *had* to mean whatever had been inside the safe. I glanced at the nearby countertop, where the safe had been sitting until just last night.

Talk about bad timing.

If only she'd stopped by yesterday, she'd be getting the heirloom – whatever it was – instead of bad news.

How on Earth was I supposed to tell her?

As if reading something in my expression, she asked, "What's wrong?"

I winced. "If you're talking about what they were storing in that safe, it went missing. And just so you know, I mean the whole safe, not just what was inside it. I'm *really* sorry."

She frowned. "So they put it in a safe?"

"I think so. I mean, I didn't see what was in there, but they warned me that it was fragile and made me swear not to move it."

The more I explained, the more confused Luna looked. "What do you mean it went missing?"

"It was stolen, just last night, in fact."

"By who?"

"Probably my aunt and uncle." I gave her a brief overview of the situation with my relatives, including the fact that I had an alarm system and everything, but nothing seemed to stop them.

Again, I glanced at the empty countertop. "I should've insisted on hiding it or something."

Now Luna was looking at the countertop, too. She asked, "How big *was* this safe?"

I gave it some thought. "About the size of a microwave, or maybe a little smaller."

She shook her head. "I don't think that's big enough." She gave a shaky laugh. "Of course, knowing my brothers, they might've crammed it in there." She hesitated. "Or chopped it into a million pieces."

I couldn't tell if she was joking, but it was pretty obvious that she was disappointed, and rightfully so. I felt compelled to say it again. "I'm really sorry."

She tried to smile. "Don't be. It's not *your* fault. If anything, it's mine."

"Yours?" I said. "How?"

"Because I should've picked it up myself."

I still didn't what the heirloom was, and it seemed beyond rude to ask, especially since it was partly my fault that it was gone.

I tried to think. "Maybe if I call my aunt and uncle and explain that it wasn't mine…" I bit my lip and let the words trail off. "Of course, I doubt they'll admit they took it. They never do."

As if shaking off the gloom, Luna said, "Well, for all we know, it wasn't even in there."

I gave her a hopeful look. "You think so?"

"Well, we *are* talking about my brothers," she said. "For all we know, the safe contained old beer cans or something."

It was a cheery thought, but it was pretty obvious that she didn't believe it any more than I did.

Still, in the interest of not adding to her disappointment, I offered her a tour of the house while we waited. When I'd seen her in Detroit, I'd promised her one if she was ever in the neighborhood.

I could see why she was interested. The place had a history, even before my parents had bought it. Nearly a century ago, a Chicago bootlegger had built the house to serve as his summer residence during the height of prohibition.

As I led Luna from room to room, I tried to envision the house through the eyes of a stranger. It really *was* amazing, with its high ceilings and classic woodwork. But the size – not to mention the maintenance – was a huge problem, especially for me, an unemployed college dropout.

Probably, I'd have to sell the house eventually, but for now, I was determined to enjoy it. It was, after all, my childhood home.

When the tour was over, we returned to the kitchen, where Luna surprised me by saying, "I have a confession."

"You do?"

She nodded. "I had another reason for stopping by."

"Really? What?"

She leaned forward. "I have a secret, and I want you to blab it."

CHAPTER 44

By the time Luna finished talking, I realized that she was right. Normally, I was a stickler for keeping secrets, but not in a case like this.

The secret involved Jake and his dad's girlfriend. From what Luna had just told me, I couldn't help but agree with her that everyone – Joel and Jake, in particular – would be better off once the truth came out.

Still, I had to ask, "If you feel so strongly about it, why haven't *you* told him?"

"Joel?" she said. "I would. But I can't seem to find the chance. And besides, it's not something you just blurt out. You've got to ease into it, you know?"

I saw what she meant. The whole thing sounded like a total train-wreck. And to think, the train had jumped the track over a decade ago, and no one had ever bothered to set it straight.

"Plus," Luna added, "I don't see Joel that much, and with him and Jake getting along so terribly all the time, it's like I'm walking on eggshells." She gave me a shaky smile. "But the wedding's coming up, and it would be really nice if they weren't fighting anymore."

Obviously, she meant her wedding to Jake. And yet, I couldn't help but feel that familiar pang in my heart. Not too long ago, I'd been thinking of my own wedding. And it wasn't even the wedding itself that I was looking forward to. It was the prospect of having Joel forever.

Now, I had no idea where we stood. Still, I promised Luna that if I had the chance, I'd try to set things straight. After all, it was the least I could do after everything she'd done for me.

As we returned to the kitchen, I said, "So, do you know where they were going?"

"Who?" she asked.

"Jake and Bishop. They practically dragged Joel away. They had to catch a flight or something?"

"Oh. That." She gave me an apologetic smile. "Sorry, but it's a secret."

I had to laugh. "Wait a minute. That's not fair."

"What do you mean?"

"You just asked *me* to 'blab' a secret. And now, you have *another* that you won't tell me?"

She smiled. "Yup."

"But you *do* know where they went?"

She nodded.

I made a sound of frustration. "And you're not gonna say?"

"I would," she said, "but it's better if you hear it from Joel."

"But Joel hasn't told me either."

She gave a breezy wave of her hands. "Oh, but he will."

"When?"

"Probably when he gets back."

"Can you at least give me a hint?"

"No way," she said. "The last 'hint' I gave? Got me in a world of trouble."

Well, there was that.

As it turned out, we were out of time, anyway. Outside, I heard a vehicle pulling up to the house. A moment later, I opened the front door to see Luna's brothers getting out of their truck.

Already, I was dreading giving them the bad news – that their safe had been stolen right off my countertop. But when I led them to the scene of the crime and explained what happened, they did something that caught me totally off-guard.

They laughed.

I looked from brother to brother. "What's so funny?"

They were still laughing. Steve turned to Anthony and said, "Oh man, I wish I could've been there."

I asked, "Where? Here?"

They didn't answer. They were too busy doing some complicated high-five, low-five hand thing with each other.

I looked to Luna. "Do *you* know?"

She shook her head, and turned to her brothers. "Hey! Butt-munches!"

They turned to look. Anthony said, "What?"

She said, "Where's the veil?"

Anthony asked, "What veil?"

She gave them an exasperated look. "Grandma's veil? The one you promised to bring me?"

"Oh, that?" Anthony said. "It's in the back of the pickup."

Luna's gaze narrowed. "Please tell me you're joking."

I broke in, "Wait a minute. Was *that* the family heirloom?"

Steve made a scoffing sound. "I wouldn't call it an heirloom. It's just a bunch of lace and stuff."

"It is not!" Luna told him. "It's a piece of family history – *and* it's the 'something borrowed' for my wedding." She looked to Anthony. "It's not really rolling around in the truck bed, is it?"

Anthony rolled his eyes. "Did I *say* the truck bed?"

"Yes," Luna said. "You did, in fact."

"No," he said, in an overly calm voice. "I said the back of the truck, like behind the seat."

Luna frowned. "With the soda cans?" She threw up her hands. "You know what? Never mind. I'm gonna go get it myself." And with that, she turned and marched out of the kitchen. Over her shoulder, she called out, "If it's damaged, I'm making one of *you* wear it."

When we heard the front door slam, Steve turned to me and said, "I don't know what she's so cranked about. We put it in a box and everything." His gaze drifted to my stomach. "Oh hey, are you pregnant?"

For once, the comment bounced right off me. I looked at the spot where the safe had been. "So you're not mad about the safe?"

"Hell no," Steve said. "We wanted them to take it."

I felt my brow wrinkle. "You mean my aunt and uncle?"

He gave me a look. "What, you got someone else stealing your stuff?"

I waved away his question. "But why would you want them to steal it? What was in there, anyway?"

Steve and Anthony shared a look. And then, they started to snicker.

"Oh, my God," I said. "You didn't do that thing with a vase, did you?"

"You mean shit in a vase?" Steve said. "Hell no. What kind of animals do you think we are?"

This wasn't the first time he'd asked me such a question. And just like always, I wasn't quite sure how to answer.

When I looked to Anthony, he shrugged. "It wasn't a vase. It was a plastic bag." He grinned. "Except we didn't seal it so good."

Suddenly, I recalled my aunt's latest phone call. I didn't know whether to laugh or throw up. In spite of my best intentions, a snicker escaped my lips.

"See?" Anthony said. "Pretty cool, huh?"

I wiped the smile from my face. "So you seriously…?" I didn't want to say it.

Steve grinned. "Shit in a bag? Hell no."

For some reason, I just had to know. "So was it dog poop or something?"

"Nah," Anthony said, "it was, what we call in the trade, sewer sludge."

I made a face. "Sewer sludge?"

"Yeah," he said. "Like when you're digging up a broken sewer, and you've got all this crap that seeps up. You just scoop it up, and there you go. You don't even need to add water. Pretty cool, huh?"

Immature or not, I had to agree. It *was* pretty cool, in a totally disgusting sort of way.

When they all left a couple of hours later, I was still smiling, and not only with amusement. It was in anticipation. Tomorrow was Saturday – the day Joel promised to return.

I didn't know what would happen when I saw him next, but I did know that I was dying to see him. □

CHAPTER 45

It was long past dark, and there'd been no sign of Joel. For what felt like the millionth time, I wandered to the front window and pulled aside the nearest curtain. Outside, it was raining buckets. It had been raining like this for at least three hours now.

I saw the flash of lightning and heard the crack of thunder. Staring out the window, I stifled a shiver. It was the perfect kind of night to curl up in front of a warm fire with someone you loved.

But the person I loved wasn't here, even though today was Saturday, the day he was supposed to be back. Just like so many times before, I wasn't sure if I should be worried or angry.

I waited until midnight before giving up – at least until tomorrow. I trudged through the house and turned off all of the lights, leaving only the porch light on – not for Joel, I told myself, but because that's what I always did.

And then, I went up to my bedroom, took a shower, and threw on some sleeping shorts and a loose t-shirt over them. I crawled into bed and lay there, gazing up at the darkened ceiling. Around me, the house felt too big and too lonely.

I shut my eyes, trying to block out the time, along with everything else. It was then that I heard it – a loud metallic sound that made me bolt upright in the bed.

A moment later, I heard it again. My heart was racing now. The way it sounded, it was coming from *inside* the house, somewhere on the main floor.

Joel?

No. It couldn't be him. He wouldn't just barge in on his own and start clanging around downstairs. He'd ring the doorbell, or at least knock.

Wouldn't he?

Regardless, I couldn't just lie here like an idiot and hope for the best.

From under the covers, I reached for my nearby cell phone and called the police. In a hushed whisper, I explained what was happening, and they promised to send someone right away.

Still, I couldn't help but flinch when the same sound rang out again. Hoping for some clue of what was going on, I crept silently out of bed and tiptoed to my partially open bedroom door.

And then, I listened.

I heard nothing, except for the pounding of my own heart and the ragged sounds of my nervous breathing. Determined to get a grip, I took a deep, steadying breath and counted to ten.

Outside, the rain had stopped, leaving the house eerily quiet until I heard something that almost made me groan out loud. It was the sound of Uncle Ernie, calling out, "Hey Viv, was it the *silver* punch bowl? Or the crystal one?"

Oh, for God's sake.

I bolted out of my bedroom and practically flew down the stairs, flicking on the lights as I went. I found my uncle in the kitchen, crouched behind the center island. He had his whole head poked into the cupboard underneath it and was rummaging around inside.

Without looking, he said, "I know you like silver, but the crystal's probably worth more." He gave a low chuckle. "You know what? Heck with it. I'll just grab both."

I rolled my eyes. "Don't forget the ladles."

"Good thinking," he said, and then suddenly froze. Slowly, his head emerged from inside the cabinet. He twisted his neck to gaze up at me. His eyes were wide, and his hair – or should I say his toupee? – was slightly askew. He was wearing a green sports jacket with matching green pants.

He looked like a crazed leprechaun.

I crossed my arms. "Hi."

He gave me a shaky smile. "Oh hey, Melody. Funny seeing you here."

"Yeah," I said. "Funny."

From somewhere deep inside the house, I heard Aunt Vivian's voice echo off the walls. "Hey Ernie! Don't forget the little cups!"

Unable to stop myself, I called back, "Which ones? Silver? Or Crystal?"

The words had barely left my mouth when I heard the sounds of cars roaring into the driveway.

The police?

I sure hoped so.

A few feet away, my uncle was still crouched like a dog on all fours. I glared down at him. "Stay!" And then, I turned toward the front of the house.

Continuing to flick on lights as I went, I hurried from room to room, heading toward the front window. Once there, I pushed aside the heavy curtains to peer outside.

I squinted in confusion. In front of the house, I saw two pairs of headlights. But as far as I could tell, none belonged to the police.

I shielded my eyes from the glare and tried unsuccessfully to figure out who was here. There were no sirens, no flashing lights, no swat team, rushing for the front door.

Praying it was Joel, I moved away from the window and started heading toward the front door. I was halfway there when the doorbell rang several times in quick succession. And then, the pounding started.

Moving faster now, I rushed to the door and hit the intercom button. "Who is it?"

I heard Joel's voice. "It's me. You alright?"

My shoulders sagged in relief. *I was now.* After disengaging the alarm, I unlocked the door and flung it open.

And there he was, Joel, with Jake and Bishop standing just behind him.

Joel strode forward and pulled me into his arms. "Sorry I'm late. Are you okay?"

I couldn't help but lean into him as his arms closed tighter around me. In the back of my mind, I realized that nothing was truly settled between us, but for now, I couldn't bring myself to care.

He was here, and his body felt amazing, hard and tight against mine. "Yeah. I'm fine." I sighed. "But guess who showed up."

"I *know* who." He pulled back and asked, "Where are they?"

I blinked up at him. "Wait, how would you know?"

"I saw their car."

Before I could ask where, Aunt Vivian's voice drifted out from somewhere behind me. "Melody, darling, I'm *so* relieved to see you."

Startled, I whirled to face her. "Yeah, I bet."

She offered up a smile that looked more like a grimace. "And I see you have company." Her eyes narrowed to slits. "How nice."

I didn't bother smiling back. "What are you doing here?"

"Why, making sure you're okay, of course. That storm was awful, wasn't it?"

"Seriously?" I said. "That's the best you can do?"

She drew back. "Just what are you implying?"

"I'm not implying anything. I'm telling you flat-out that I know you're lying." My voice rose. "You're not here to check on me. You're here to check on…" I made a little fluttering motion with my hands…"the freaking punchbowls!"

Somewhere behind me, I heard Jake, ask, "What's a punch bowl?"

Bishop said, "It's a party thing. Don't ask."

Ignoring all of them, my aunt trotted out her overly patient voice and said, "No. Darling. We're here to check on *you.*"

I gave her a hard look. "Is that so? Then why, exactly, were you wanting the punch bowls?"

My uncle wandered up behind her and said, "To, uh, water your cat?"

I stared at him. Even from Uncle Ernie, that had to be the dumbest excuse I'd ever heard.

I didn't *have* a cat. And even if I did, I sure as heck wouldn't be 'watering' it with a bowl that could hold ten kittens and enough yarn to knit a sweater.

Again, Jake's voice carried across the short distance. "What's with the leprechaun?"

My uncle looked around. "What?" His eyes gleamed with interest. "Like a new statue or something?"

Slowly, my aunt turned to face him. Through clenched teeth, she said, "I *told* you that suit looked ridiculous."

He looked down to study his clothes. "What? This?" He looked up. "But it's my favorite."

Next to me, Joel asked, "Want me to toss 'em out?"

My aunt gave a little gasp. "Are you referring to us?" Her voice rose. "Unlike *you*, we're family!"

From somewhere behind us, Jake muttered, "And here, I thought ours sucked."

My aunt's gaze swiveled in Jake's direction. "And who, exactly, are you?"

"Me?" He grinned. "I'm the guy who's gonna toss ol' Lucky out on his ass."

Joel spoke up. "The hell you are."

My aunt gave Joel a grateful look. "Thank you."

But then, Joel said, "If anyone's tossing him, it's me."

CHAPTER 46

Together, Joel and Jake studied my uncle, who was slowly backing away, as if planning to bolt.

Jake turned to Joel and said, "We could toss him together. You grab his legs. I'll get his arms."

My aunt made a little huffing noise. "That's it! We're leaving!" She turned to my uncle and barked, "Get the car."

He frowned. "You want me to use the *front* door, or…?"

With a tight smile, she said, "Of course I want you to use the front door. What other door would you use?"

My uncle's mouth opened, but before any words came out, my aunt barked, "For Pete's sake, just go!"

My uncle gave a little jump, and then scurried toward the front door. But when he neared it, the guys made no move to get out of his way. My uncle practically skidded to a stop and stared up at them. "Would, uh, you mind moving?"

"That depends," Joel said. "You coming back?"

My uncle lifted his left wrist and pushed back the sleeve of his green sports jacket. He studied his watch. "It's pretty late, so, uh—"

"I don't mean *tonight*," Joel said.

My uncle turned to give my aunt a questioning look.

Joel's voice cut across the short distance. "Hey, Lucky! I was talking to *you*."

My aunt stepped forward. "Melody!" she snapped. "Are you going to just stand there and let these…" Her mouth tightened. "…*hooligans*, speak to your uncle like that?"

I turned and studied the hooligans in question. In spite of their clean-cut faces and normal clothes, they looked dark and dangerous as they eyed my uncle with open hostility.

My uncle took a couple of steps backward and glanced around as if seeking a quick escape.

My aunt looked to me and demanded, "Well?"

I gave her my brightest smile. "Yes."

"What?" she sputtered.

"Yes. I *am* going to let them." I stepped toward her. "No. Not just *let* them. *Encourage* them."

Her jaw dropped. "But I'm family!"

She was wrong. She wasn't family. Yes, technically, she'd married my dad's brother, so that made her family in the legal sense. But she'd never been family in any way that mattered.

"And while we're on the topic," I said, "how'd you get in?"

She looked toward the front door. "The door was open."

I knew otherwise. "It was not."

"Well, I don't mean open, open," she clarified. "But it *was* unlocked."

I gave a decisive shake of my head. "Nope. Not even close."

My aunt lifted her chin. "How would *you* know?"

"I know, because I locked it myself. *And*, I set the alarm."

My aunt's gaze darted from me to the guys and back again. She gave a little sniff. "What *is* this? An interrogation?" She threw back her shoulders. "Well, I don't like it."

Joel spoke up. "You'd like it less if *we* handle it."

My aunt drew back. "Are you threatening me?"

This time, it was Jake who answered. "Does a leprechaun shit in the woods?"

My aunt gave a dramatic gasp. "What are you saying? You'd mistreat me?" Her voice became shrill. "A woman? What kind of people are you?"

Joel looked unaffected by the theatrics. "Keep stalling, and you'll find out." His gaze shifted briefly to my uncle. "And we don't need to hurt *you*." He gave her a cold smile. "We can beat it out of Lucky."

My uncle croaked, "What?"

My aunt turned to give my uncle a long, speculative look. I could practically see the wheels turning in her head. *How bad would they hurt him, anyway?*

The way it looked, it was a risk she was willing to take.

In truth, I would never let it get that far. But a little fear would do both of them good.

I said, "Just tell us. I deserve to know."

My aunt snorted. "Deserve? What does *that* have to do with anything?" Her lips curled into a nasty sneer. "Haven't you gotten enough already?"

I knew exactly what she meant. In their will, my parents had left nearly nothing to my uncle. I recalled his face when the document was read. My uncle hadn't been happy. And as far as my aunt? Well, let's just say her reaction hadn't been pleasant.

That was years ago, and they'd been trying to even things up ever since.

If they only knew. Sure, I was the primary beneficiary of my parents' estate. But I had zero control and nearly no cash to speak of. As far as the property itself, it was so deep in debt that it hardly mattered.

In the end, *I'd* be lucky to get a punch bowl. Forget the little cups. *And* the ladle.

At the sound of sirens, my uncle perked up. He cupped his hands around his mouth and yelled out, "Help! Police! Over here!"

Joel gave a low laugh. "Hey Lucky, they can't hear you. Not over the sirens."

My uncle dropped his hands from his mouth and muttered, "How would *you* know?"

Joel gave a loose shrug. The way it looked, he knew plenty. But I'd known that already, hadn't I?

Pushing that distraction aside, I stared at my uncle. "And besides," I reminded him, "the police are here to *arrest* you, not *rescue* you."

My uncle's face froze. "Us? Why?"

Did I really need to explain this? I threw up my hands. "Because you broke into my house. That's why."

My aunt gave another gasp. "You wouldn't seriously prosecute us?"

Funny, she hadn't denied breaking in, not within the last two seconds anyway. Was that progress? I had no idea.

I looked to the guys standing in my doorway. And then, I turned to look at my aunt and uncle.

I tried to see things how the police would see them. The guys in my doorway looked dark and dangerous. My aunt and uncle looked like a pissed-off socialite and her lucky mascot.

I sidled closer to Joel and peered around him out the open doorway. If I wasn't careful, the police would be arresting the wrong people.

CHAPTER 47

Officer Nelson had barely made it through the front door when my aunt cried out, "Thank God you're here!" She pointed toward Joel and his brothers. "I want them arrested!"

I made a scoffing sound. "Oh, please. *You're* the ones who broke in."

My aunt gave a toss of her hair, making her earrings glitter in the foyer light. She hoisted her designer purse higher on her shoulder and asked Officer Nelson, "Do we *look* like thieves?"

The words had barely left her mouth when something slipped from the inside of my uncle's jacket. It clattered to the floor, and we all turned to look. It was a silver ladle with gold trim. My uncle looked down and said, "Huh. Where'd that come from?"

Aunt Vivian was glaring at him now. Through clenched teeth, she said, "Darling, this is no time for one of your practical jokes." She looked back to Officer Nelson and said, "As you can see, my husband is quite the character."

We all looked. He did look like a character – the kind who hid pots of gold at the end of rainbows. Except in this case, the gold was mine, theoretically anyway.

Officer Nelson turned to me and said, "You pressing charges?"

I didn't know what to say. I wanted this to end. But I *so* didn't want the publicity. Plus, in a weird way, I actually liked my uncle.

When I'd been younger, he'd been the guy who dressed up as a pirate every Halloween. He'd taught me how to make mud pies and play the harmonica – badly. He'd attended every one of my school plays and all of my birthday parties, at least until Aunt Vivian had gotten her bony claws into him.

I was still considering the question when Bishop asked, "Care if I look around?"

Distracted, I murmured, "Yeah, sure. Go ahead." I turned back to Officer Nelson and asked, "Let's say I do press charges. What happens then?"

"What?" my aunt sputtered. "You're actually considering it?"

"Of course, I'm considering it," I told her. "What do you think? That you can stop by and rob me all the time, and that I'm never going to do anything?"

Her gaze narrowed. "Oh, you've done plenty."

If she was referring to the incidents with the hose and the safe, she was wrong. I hadn't done either one of those things. But I was glad someone had. The whole sorry situation made me want to scream. This definitely couldn't go on forever.

Next to me, Joel said, "I say we search them, see what they've got."

My aunt gave a dramatic gasp. "What?"

I was so tired of the theatrics. I looked to her and said, "Will you just stop it, already?"

Behind us, Jake said, "Hey Melody."

I turned toward him and asked, "What?"

"Got any rubber gloves?"

I stared at him. "Excuse me?"

"Rubber gloves," he repeated, flashing an ominous grin in my uncle's direction. "We'd better go full-cavity."

I was still staring. Did that mean what I thought it meant? I turned and gave Joel a questioning look.

Oh, my God. He was actually nodding.

"Good thinking," he said, glancing toward the center of the house. "You got a basement, right?"

As Joel obviously knew, I *did* have a basement, in the form of the wine cellar. But it's not like I had access to it, as he *also* knew. Reluctantly, I asked, "Why?"

"If they scream," Joel said, "it'll be less noise for the neighbors."

At this, my aunt gave a little shriek that might be considered a scream.

From a few feet away, Jake gave a low chuckle. "See?"

I looked from brother to brother. I didn't have any neighbors within screaming distance. But that was hardly relevant. Besides, they couldn't be serious.

Desperate for a dose of sanity, I gave Officer Nelson a pleading look. Shouldn't *he* be taking charge of this?

As if reading my frustration, he finally spoke up. "Let's you and me talk." He flicked his head toward the front door. "In private."

My aunt blurted out, "No!"

In unison, Officer Nelson and I turned to look.

Her eyes were wide, and her skin was flushed. "You're not leaving us alone?" She swallowed. "With *them?*"

I looked to the "them" in question. In truth, they did look kind of scary, not that *I* was afraid. But of course, they weren't threatening *me* with a full cavity search.

Over my aunt's objections, I ducked outside with Officer Nelson. Closing the front door behind us, I lowered my voice to ask, "What do you think?"

He shrugged. "Looks to me like a family problem."

It was. And it wasn't. I persisted. "But let's say I *wanted* to press charges. Could I?"

"Sure," he said. "Doubt it would stick though."

I felt a surge of new despair. "Why not?"

"You got a relative who swiped a soup ladle."

"Actually, it's not for soup. It's for the punch bowl." I waved away the distraction. "But never mind that. I'm just saying, they broke in. Past midnight." I turned and gave the house a worried glance. "And who knows what else my uncle has."

"So you *do* want to press charges?"

I sighed. "I don't know."

So far, the conversation hadn't been reassuring. I could just see it – a boatload of bad publicity, and all for nothing. Worse, if there were no real consequences, even after I pressed charges, it might even encourage them further. Who knows? They might rent a moving truck and load up the furniture.

I was still pondering all of this when Officer Nelson mentioned that without signs of a break-in, I might be fighting an uphill battle.

In the end, I told him that we'd try to work it out amongst ourselves, but asked if he wouldn't mind sticking around, just in case.

"Mind?" he said. "I want to see how this ends." He leaned closer and lowered his voice. "You *do* know, you can't *really* do a cavity search, right?"

I gave a vigorous nod. "Sure. We're just teasing." I summoned up a smile. "You know, family stuff, like you said."

Right. Because nothing says family fun like a rubber glove up the butt.

Officer Nelson gave me a dubious look. "Your friends *do* know that, right?"

"Sure. Totally."

The words had barely left my mouth when the sounds of yelling made both of us rush back inside. We burst in through the door just in time to hear my aunt screech, "He's *not* a leprechaun! He's a human being! What's the matter with you people?"

"Return the stuff," Joel said, "and you won't have to find out."

"There's nothing to return!" she yelled. And then, as if noticing for the first time that we'd returned, she visibly reeled in her temper. She gave Joel a stiff smile. "Because, as I've already explained, we haven't taken anything."

"Yeah?" Joel said. "You want us to take it up with Lucky?"

"Go ahead," she said. "He's not afraid of you."

The sound of a hard thud made all of us turn to look. It was my uncle, setting a crystal salt-shaker on a nearby side table. This was followed by the pepper shaker, three spoons, and a white dish cloth.

My aunt sighed. "Well, this is just lovely."

Ignoring her, I zoomed in on my uncle. I just *had* to ask, "Why the dish cloth?"

He glanced around. "What dish cloth?"

I didn't even know what to say.

Next to me, Joel said, "It was for the shakers. So they didn't break."

Of course. I knew that. Or at least, I should've. Obviously, the whole sorry scene was turning my brain to mush.

Across from us, my aunt was giving my uncle the look of death. Under her breath, she said, "*I'll* break something, alright."

Funny, I wanted to break something too. I gave her a hard look. "How about you?"

"What about me?" she said.

"Fork it over."

"Fork *what* over?"

I crossed my arms and waited.

"Oh, alright. Fine." She reached into her purse and pulled out a crystal candlestick. She marched to the side table and slammed the candlestick onto it, next to the shakers. She turned toward us and said, "There. You happy now?"

Why lie? "No."

"Why not?" she demanded.

I eyed her purse. "Because that purse is too big for one candlestick."

She lifted her chin. "I'll have you know, this is a Fendi."

I smiled. "And I'll have *you* know, I've got rubber gloves in the kitchen."

In the end, it didn't come to that. After a lot more haggling, along with my reluctant promise to not press charges if, and *only* if, she cooperated, she finally thrust her purse in my direction. By the time it was all over, I'd recovered the matching candlestick, along with a silver gravy boat and the matching ladle.

Two ladles – even for them, that had to be some kind of record.

My aunt looked to my uncle. "Are you getting the car or not?"

I spoke up. "Wait. You can't go yet."

Her gaze narrowed. "Why not?"

"Because you *still* haven't told me how you got in."

"Yes, I did," Aunt Vivian said. "Remember?"

I rolled my eyes. "Give me a break. The door *wasn't* open. I checked it before bed."

She smirked. "Well, maybe you didn't check it good enough."

We were still going back and forth when Bishop emerged from who-knows-where. He looked to me and said, "Hey Melody."

"What?"

"You should give it up."

My jaw dropped. "Give it up? Why?" I turned to give Joel a pleading look. "We can't give it up *now*."

But he only shrugged. "Eh, it's probably for the best."

The response seemed so out-of-character that I didn't know what to think. "But—"

He reached for my hand. "Just trust me, okay?"

I glanced around, hoping to see what I was missing. When I looked to Jake, he said, "I still say we go for the gloves."

My aunt gave a loud huff. "That's it! We're leaving!"

And then, she grabbed my uncle's elbow and practically dragged him past Officer Nelson and straight out of the house. From the open doorway, I stood ,watching with the others, as the two of them marched down my long driveway, heading to who-knows-where.

A couple of minutes later, the police car, with Officer Nelson behind the wheel, drove past them and disappeared down the lonely country road. My aunt and uncle paused for only a moment before, once again, resuming their march.

But where, exactly, were they going? I turned to Joel and asked, "You said you saw their car?"

"Yeah. Maybe a quarter-mile up the road."

I gave a weary sigh. "Well, at least they're working harder for it."

Now, in the aftermath of that whole sorry spectacle, it struck me that nearly nothing had been accomplished. True, I *had* gotten my stuff back, but that wouldn't solve the bigger problem.

Not only would they surely be back. They'd probably be back sooner than I dared to hope. There was a time, not too long ago, when they came by only once a month. Now, they were showing up every few days.

Things were getting worse, not better.

And worst of all, I had no way to stop them, because I *still* had no idea how they were getting in. Tonight, I might've finally found out, if it weren't for Bishop butting in at the worst possible time.

With another sigh, I turned and headed back into the house. Joel's brother or not, Bishop deserved a word or two about that, and I was determined to give it to him.

CHAPTER 48

I gave Bishop an annoyed look. "Why'd you do that?"

"Do what?" he asked.

"Tell me to give it up." I turned to Joel and said, "Now I'll never know."

He said, "You mean how they're getting in?"

I nodded. "That was one of the reasons I didn't press charges. I was hoping they'd tell me."

From somewhere behind me, Jake gave a derisive snort.

I whirled to face him. "What?"

He was now leaning against the inside of the front door. "They weren't gonna tell you jack."

"Oh yeah?" I crossed my arms. "Why not?"

"Because you called the police."

"What's wrong with calling the police?"

"Nothing," he said. "If you're a sucker."

I stared at him. *Talk about rude.*

Next to me, Joel said, "Hey dickweed. No one asked you."

"Wrong," Jake said. "*She* asked me. Didn't you hear?" He grinned. "Or were you too busy checking out her legs?"

On instinct, I looked down. My shorts were definitely on the skimpy side, which meant that a lot of leg was showing. Maybe even too much. But in my own defense, I hadn't been expecting a houseful of people.

And now, I was blushing. Of course.

I turned my nervous gaze to Joel. He was looking at Jake in a way that made me wonder if a fight might break out any minute now.

I looked back to Jake. The idiot was still grinning, even in the face of Joel's hostility. Was Jake goading him? It sure looked that way.

In frustration, I looked to Bishop. He was their brother, too. Shouldn't *he* be doing something to diffuse this?

My gaze narrowed. Apparently not. He wasn't even paying attention. Instead, he was scrolling through his cell phone, acting like everything was just fine.

I said, "What are you doing?"

"Waiting"

"For what?" I asked.

He looked up. "For them to finish."

"Finish what?" I said. "Fighting?"

He looked utterly unconcerned. "They're not gonna fight."

"Oh yeah? Why's that?"

"Because Joel wants you to think he's civilized."

I gave a little shake of my head. "What?"

Bishop looked back to his phone. "Hard to look civilized when you're beating the hell out of your own brother."

I snuck a quick glance at Joel and paused. He still had that same ominous look, except now, it was aimed at Bishop. "The question is," Joel said, "which brother first."

From the door, Jake gave a derisive laugh. "Take your pick. But no one's beating the hell out of *me*."

Joel said, "You sure about that?"

"Hell yeah," Jake said. He turned his attention back to Bishop. "And who says he'd win?"

Again, Bishop lifted his gaze from his phone. He looked from Jake to Joel, as if considering the question.

Unable to stop myself, I looked, too, trying to see what he saw. Both guys were both tall and muscular, with a certain attitude that I couldn't quite place. If I were a guy, I wouldn't want to face off with either one of them.

Finally, Bishop said. "My money?" He looked to Jake. "Sorry, it's on Joel."

"Your ass," Jake said, sounding almost insulted now. "Why him?"

Bishop only shrugged. "Because he's motivated."

"And me?" Jake said.

Bishop looked back to his phone. "You're just dicking around."

I looked back to Joel. He *did* look motivated – to kill *both* of his brothers and bury the bodies in the back yard.

I couldn't say I blamed him. In fact, I was feeling pretty motivated myself. And, I had a nice supply of shovels in the shed out back.

Bishop pushed away from the wall and shoved his phone back into his pocket. He looked to me and said, "As far as your visitors…"

"Which visitors?" I asked. "Officer Nelson? Or my aunt and uncle?"

He gave me a deadpan look. "You got the police breaking in, too?"

Just great. Sarcasm. My favorite. I looked to Joel.

In a tight voice, he said, "What my brother's *trying* to say, is that he knows how they're getting in."

CHAPTER 49

I looked from brother to brother. "Are you serious?" I zoomed in on Joel. "You really know?"

He shook his head. "Sorry. Not me." He flicked his head toward Bishop. "Him."

I looked to Bishop. "How would *you* know?"

"Because I looked."

The answer seemed woefully inadequate. I'd looked, too, several times, in fact. But there were so many things in play – the locks, the alarm system, the windows, the doors. Just last year, I'd had everything checked. I'd even changed the locks – not that it had done a bit of good.

"Wait a minute," I said. "Is *that* why you told me to give it up? Because you think you know?"

"I don't *think* I know," Bishop said. "I *know* I know."

Desperately, I wanted to believe him. And I was dying to hear his theory. But first, I had a different question. I turned to Joel and said, "Is *that* why you stopped me from pushing the issue?"

"What'd you think?" he said. "That we'd just shrug it off otherwise?"

Actually, I *did* think that, but I hated the idea of saying so. So instead, I asked, "But if you personally didn't know how they were getting in, how did you know that *he* knew?"

"Bishop?" Joel said. "I knew, because he told you to give it up."

Trying to make sense of everything, I looked again to Bishop. "But if you knew at the time, why didn't *you* just say so?"

"When you see it, you'll understand."

I had no idea what he meant. All *I* knew was that it would've been really nice to prove my aunt and uncle wrong, right there on the spot, and more importantly, in front of the police. But it was no use arguing about it now. My relatives were gone – thank goodness – and so was Officer Nelson.

So all I said was, "Alright. So tell me. What's your theory?"

"A theory, huh?" He looked to Joel. "You've got a cynical one on your hands."

"I'm not cynical," I told him. I turned to Joel and asked, "You don't think I'm cynical, do you?"

"If you ask me," he said, "you're not cynical enough."

I turned to Bishop. "See?"

Bishop looked unimpressed. "You think that's a compliment? Now c'mon, lemme show you."

He motioned me and Joel toward the kitchen while Jake waited near the front door, just in case company showed up, whatever that meant.

A few minutes later, I was staring at a door that I hadn't seen open in years. It was the door to the wine cellar. And it was open *now*.

How on Earth had *that* happened?

For the first time in forever, I peered down the cellar stairway. It looked the same as I remembered. Trying to make sense of this, I pulled back to give the cellar door a closer look. It didn't look damaged or anything – so that was good.

I gave Bishop a perplexed look. "How'd you do that?"

"Do what?" he asked.

I pointed to the open door. "That."

He followed my gaze. "The lock?" He shrugged. "That thing was a piece of junk."

I couldn't quite believe it. The lock was a big, steel deadbolt. It required a key, which I didn't even have. Wondering how the lock looked from the other side, I stepped through the open doorway to check it out.

From *inside* the cellar, the lock had just a regular twist mechanism, which meant that getting *out* of the cellar would be a lot easier than getting in.

No doubt, it was a safety measure, designed to prevent anyone from getting locked inside. But I still didn't know what this had to do with my aunt and uncle. Trying to make sense of it, I stepped back into the hall and said, "So what are you saying? They were hiding in the wine cellar?"

Bishop shook his head. "No. I'm saying they came *in* through the wine cellar."

"But they couldn't," I said. "It's just a cellar. It doesn't *go* anywhere."

He gave me a look. "You sure about that?"

I'd grown up in this house. Until the last few years, I'd been in that cellar plenty of times. There was no other exit.

My shoulders sagged in disappointment. So much for Bishop's theory. "Sorry," I said, "but I'm sure." Trying not to sound as deflated as I felt, I said, "But thanks for trying though."

Bishop made a scoffing sound. "And you say you're not cynical." He flicked his head toward the open cellar door. "You wanna go first?"

I moved forward, only to feel a hand on my elbow. It was Joel's hand, and I turned to give him a questioning look.

He smiled. "Sorry, but he was talking to me."

"But why you?" I asked. It was my cellar, after all.

"Because," Joel said, "if anyone comes in, they'll be facing me, not you."

The sentiment was so sweet and chivalrous that I couldn't help but smile. Still, I had to point out the obvious. "But no one's coming in."

"We'll see." Joel moved toward the cellar door and flicked on the lights. "C'mon. Humor me."

So I did. With Joel in the lead and Bishop following behind us, we took the steps downward until they ended in a decidedly upscale cellar.

I glanced around. It looked the same as I remembered, with its ornate tile flooring, rows of recessed ceiling lights, several burgundy armchairs, and a natural color scheme that made it look more like a fashionable smoking room than anyone's basement.

Surrounding the small sitting area, I spotted the familiar rows of big, wooden racks. Most of the racks were packed with bottles of wine, nestled into individual wooden cubbies. In passing, I had to wonder, how much was all of this worth?

No doubt, it had *some* value. But it couldn't be a fortune. After all, most of the bottles had come from a winery just a few counties away.

Still, it did look impressive. That had to count for something, right? Bishop said. "You see it?"

"See what?" I asked.

It was Joel who answered. "That." I looked to see him pointing at something on the far wall. I followed his gaze, but saw nothing out of the ordinary – just a regular wine rack, even if it *was* empty.

I gave him a confused look. "That's always been empty." I knew this for a fact, because when I'd been younger, I'd stored countless things in those empty wooden cubbies – dolls, markers, bananas.

"Forget the rack," Bishop said. "Look at the floor."

I moved forward to get a closer look. And then, I spotted them, faint footprints on the tile floor, like someone had recently come through with damp or dusty shoes.

I felt my eyebrows furrow. The footprints seemed to pass straight through the wine rack, as if it weren't even there. But that didn't make any sense. The rack was positioned against an external wall. There was nothing behind it, well, except for earth, anyway.

I turned and gave Bishop a questioning look.

"Step back," he said.

When I did, he moved forward and reached above the rack. Something clicked, and the whole rack swung inward, leaving us staring at a dark, mostly empty space. Squinting through the shadows, I saw cinderblock walls and a cylinder-shaped tank in the far corner.

I was utterly confused, until I heard it – the low sound of waves, lapping against an unseen shore. And then, I understood. I was looking at the inside of the old pump-house, which was located just down the bluff from my home.

I recalled how the pump-house looked from the outside. It was a small shed-like building with a cinderblock exterior, two small windows just below the roofline, and a thick, wooden door that was always locked.

I'd never been inside the pump-house, but I *had* seen my dad enter it a time or two. Now, I watched as Joel stepped into the darkened space and looked around.

A moment later, he motioned for me to join him. I did, and together, we studied the secret doorway from the external vantage point.

From the other side of the doorway, Bishop said, "Hang on." He dug into his pocket and pulled out a penlight. He clicked it on, and offered it to me through the opening. "I'm gonna shut this, so you can see how it works from that side."

A moment later, the rack swung forward, closing the gap and leaving us in near darkness. Together, Joel and I studied the closed passageway. From here, it didn't look like a wine-rack at all. Instead, it looked like a wide, wooden shelving unit, almost like a bookcase.

Some of the shelves even had things on them. Running the beam of light across its surface, I saw a couple of metal boxes and a few random tools. On the wall that surrounded the shelving unit, thick wooden trim made the illusion complete.

If I were unfamiliar with the setup, I'd see nothing out of the ordinary.

I looked to Joel. "What do you think?"

He smiled in the dim light. "I think it's cool as hell." He reached out and pulled me close. "But forget that." His voice was soft in my ear. "I missed you." His voice grew intense. "You have no idea."

Actually, I did. I smiled against his chest. "I missed you, too."

"If we were alone," he said, "I'd show you how much."

I couldn't resist teasing, "Actually, we *are* alone."

He squeezed me tighter. "Not alone enough."

I couldn't argue with that. As I stood there, in his arms, listening to the muted sounds of the unseen waves, everything felt a million times better than I ever would've dreamed. Joel was here, and somehow, we'd work everything out.

On top of that, I'd finally have a way to stop my aunt and uncle from popping in whenever they wanted. I could add some new locks or maybe, just move something heavy in front of the secret passage, to prevent the wine rack from swinging inward.

Either way, those annoying raids would finally be a thing of the past.

But that wasn't the primary reason I was happy. Holding me like he'd never let go, Joel felt warm and hard, and too wonderful for words. I burrowed closer and said, "So I'm curious. Did you get everything worked out?"

"Hell yeah."

I pulled back to gaze up at him. "Really?"

"Really." He leaned forward and brushed his lips against my forehead. "I've got a lot to tell you."

"Good news? Or bad?"

His hands caressed my back. "That depends."

It wasn't *quite* the answer I was hoping for. "On what?"

His voice was nearly a caress. "You."

"Why me?"

"Lemme back up," he said. "*Your* news? It's all good. So don't worry, okay?"

"What do you mean *my* news?"

"I love you." His eyes held the hint of mischief. "And if you don't love me back? Well, that's bad news for me, right?"

I had to laugh. "Oh stop it. You *know* I love you." I rolled my eyes. "I must, right?"

"That's what I'm counting on." His expression turned serious. "Just so you know, I'm not messing around. I do love you. And I'll always love you, no matter what you say."

I wasn't sure what that meant, but I really liked the sounds of it. When he once again pulled me close, I let my eyelids drift shut and simply savored the joy of being close to him.

In spite of all my questions, I couldn't bring myself to pull away – at least, not until Bishop's amused voice broke into my thoughts. "Should I come back later?"

My eyes flew open, and I pulled back. As I did, the penlight slipped from my grasp and clattered to the cement floor. Funny, I hadn't even realized that I was still holding it.

I looked down. The light was still on, thank goodness. In front of me, Joel bent down and picked it up, and then, slapped the penlight into Bishop's hand with more force than necessary.

Bishop gave a low laugh. "Hey, I was just asking."

CHAPTER 50

When the three of us returned upstairs, I was still reeling from the discovery. On our way back through the cellar, I'd grabbed a random bottle of wine, and was planning to get started on it right away.

All things considered, I definitely needed it.

I'd already mentioned what I knew of the house's history, focusing on the fact that it had been built by a Chicago bootlegger during the height of prohibition.

Afterward, we all agreed that the secret passage made a lot of sense. The narrow beach beyond the pump house would be the perfect place to launch a small boat – or to reach a larger one by dinghy.

From there, it would be a straight shot to Chicago, crossing over Lake Michigan.

As for my relatives, they wouldn't even need a boat. They'd just need a lack of scruples and knowledge of the secret entrance. I couldn't help but wonder, had my parents known about the entrance, too? And if so, why didn't they tell me?

But the more I thought about it, the more it made sense. The whole secret passageway would've been a huge temptation, especially to a kid. And just beyond that passageway were slippery rocks, a narrow beach, and endless water.

If that wasn't a safety hazard, I didn't know what was.

Now, standing in the kitchen, Joel and Bishop were discussing the mechanics of the passageway and how it might be secured. While they talked, I retrieved a corkscrew and some wine glasses from a far cupboard.

When I returned and began working at the wine bottle, Joel held out his hand. "Here. I'll get that."

Silently, I handed it over, along with the corkscrew, and then watched as he opened the bottle easily and set it down on the nearby counter.

I gave Joel and Bishop a hopeful look. "You're having some too, right?"

Bishop declined, saying that he wanted to – in his words – check the perimeter for more breaches.

It was a nice thought, but I wasn't sure that was a good idea. "But it's so late."

Bishop nodded. "Exactly."

"But—"

Joel spoke up. "Just let him, alright?" He reached for my hand and gave it a squeeze. "Besides, we need to talk."

Before I could protest further, Bishop turned away and started heading toward the back door. Unable to stop myself, I called out after him. "Be careful. The steps are probably slippery..." But he was already gone, so I let my words trail off. "…because it's been raining and all."

Next to me, Joel said, "He'll be fine."

"But—"

"Stop thinking about it."

But I couldn't stop, even as I poured two glasses of wine and took a long, steady drink from one of them. I still felt guilty. Outside, it was dark and muddy. And where was I? In a nice, warm kitchen, drinking wine.

When I returned my half-empty glass to the counter, Joel gave me a concerned look. "Don't worry. They won't be here long."

"Who? Your brothers? I'm not worried." I glanced toward the back door. "Well, I'm a little worried about Bishop being out there in the dark, but I'm not worried on my own behalf, if that's what you mean." I considered the time. "It's pretty late. Should we see if they want to spend the night?"

Joel stiffened. "No. Not gonna happen."

"Why not?"

"Because I don't trust him."

I didn't need to ask who. "You mean Jake?"

"Yeah. That's exactly who I mean."

"I don't get it," I said. "When you guys showed up, you seemed to be getting along just fine." Under my breath, I added, "Sort of."

"We were," Joel said. "But that doesn't mean I'm gonna trust him."

I bit my lip, thinking of what Luna had told me during her recent visit. She'd asked me to tell Joel a secret, something that Joel should've heard years ago.

I glanced around. Was *now* the time? After a long, jumbled moment, I decided that it probably wasn't. The plan was to tell Joel in private, not blab it while Jake could walk in at any time.

I tried to smile. "Let's talk about it later, okay?" I hadn't quite given up. It was more of a strategic retreat. In the back of my mind, I was still thinking. Maybe we talk upstairs for a few minutes?

Joel moved closer, and his expression softened. "Listen, forget my brothers, alright? There's something I want to ask you."

There were things that I wanted to ask him, too. But even though Joel and I were the only ones in the kitchen, it still didn't feel like we were alone. Reluctantly, I said, "Should we wait until later?"

"Probably," he said. "But I'm not gonna."

"Why not?"

"Because I've waited long enough." He leaned closer. "Fuck waiting."

I paused. "What?"

"I love you. You know that, right?"

Gazing up at him, a wonderful gooey glow settled over my heart. It wasn't the first time tonight that he'd told me that. But the way I saw it, he could tell me a million times over, and I'd never tire of it. I smiled. "I love you, too."

"That other night…" He glanced around. "…right here in this kitchen, come to think of it, I was an ass."

"You were not, at least not any more than I was."

Joel gave a slow shake of his head. "You weren't the one who messed up."

Now, I was shaking my head, too. "It was both of us." Even now, I was beyond embarrassed about the whole thing. "I guess I should've realized that you wouldn't just show up and propose out of the blue." I gave a nervous laugh. "I mean, who does that, right?"

Joel looked at me for a long intense moment. And then, he did something that I totally didn't see coming. He sank slowly to one knee.

I felt myself go very still. "What are you doing?"

He gazed up at me. "Funny, that's the same thing you said the last time."

My heart was pounding, but with what? Joy? Nervousness? Raw, unbridled fear? The last time, everything had ended so very badly, and the thought of a repeat performance was more than I could take. Suddenly, I could hardly breathe. "Seriously, get up, okay?"

"Sorry, not gonna happen." He reached into his pocket and pulled out a small, red velvet box. And then, he opened it to reveal a massive diamond engagement ring.

I felt my eyes widen. "What's that?"

"You know what it is."

I *did* know, but it looked well beyond anything that Joel could afford. And that wasn't even the point. For some reason, I thought of all that teasing from Steve. And before I could even process what I was saying, I said, "You know I'm not pregnant, right?"

"I know." His gaze locked onto mine. "But you're gonna be."

I sucked in a breath. "What?"

The corners of Joel's mouth lifted. "You told me you wanted ten kids."

"Well, yeah, but…"

His eyes filled with mischief. "What? You wanna wait?"

I tried to laugh. "Oh, stop it. You don't really want ten kids."

"Wanna bet?" His expression grew suddenly serious. "The night you told me that you weren't pregnant, wanna know what I was?"

"What?"

"Disappointed."

I blinked. "What? Why?"

"Because I don't wanna wait." He gave me a crooked smile that melted my heart. "And I don't think you want to either."

My head was swimming. "Wait for what?"

"For any of it," he said. "You. Us. A family." His voice softened. "Like the one you lost. And the one I never had."

I stared down at him. He was still on one knee, and the longer he was down there, the more surreal this all seemed. "Really," I said, "you should get up."

But again, he shook his head. "No way."

"Why?"

"Because I haven't even asked you yet."

Almost in a panic now, I blurted out, "Maybe you shouldn't."

I almost expected him to be angry. After all, this wasn't what the script called for. Yes, I wanted him. I wanted *this*, more than words could express. But what if he didn't? What if he was just telling me what he thought I wanted to hear? What if, once again, I'd be crying in the end?

My statement hung between us, like a bomb waiting to explode.

But it didn't.

Joel flashed me a sudden grin. "Or maybe, I *should* and see what you say." He reached for my hand. "Melody—"

Breathlessly, I said, "What?"

"Will you marry me?"

"I, um…" *Oh, my God.* I could hardly think. Desperately, I wanted to say yes. I loved him, and if he meant all those things he'd just told me, he and I wanted exactly the same things. But it all seemed so far-fetched.

I searched his gaze. He looked surprisingly unruffled in spite of my unconventional reaction. I said, "How can you be so calm? I mean, isn't this awkward for you?"

He grinned up at me. "Nope."

"Why not?"

"Because I know you're gonna say yes."

"But what if I don't?"

He gave something like a shrug. "Then I'll just ask you tomorrow."

I stifled a sudden laugh. "You wouldn't."

He was still grinning. "Try me."

But I didn't want to try him, and somehow, his smile was contagious.

Joel said, "See?"

"See what?"

"You're gonna say it."

"What?"

"Come on. You *know* what."

Damn it. He was right. Who was I kidding? I couldn't stop myself, even if I wanted to. And I *didn't* want to, because he was exactly what I wanted and exactly what I needed. And in my heart, I knew that I was perfect for him, just like he was perfect for me, in spite of all our differences.

When I said it, it came out in a breathless whisper. "Yes."

And then, right there on my kitchen floor, he slipped the ring onto my finger and said, "I'm gonna hold you to that." With that, he stood and pulled me into his arms. His lips found mine, and he kissed me like there was no tomorrow.

As his mouth claimed mine, I almost couldn't believe this was happening. Either this was a dream come true, or I was being stupid beyond belief. But I couldn't bring myself to care. All I knew was I was happy, and felt full and complete for the first time since he'd left.

And then, something was ringing.

The doorbell.

With obvious reluctance, Joel pulled away. He looked toward the front of the house and gave a low curse. "That was fast."

I didn't know what he meant, but I felt like cursing, too. I glanced at the kitchen clock. It was practically the middle of the night. I didn't care who was at the door. There was no way I'd be answering it.

Besides, there was only one person I wanted to see, and he was already here.

But then, Joel said something that made me pause. "It's your aunt and uncle."

I shook my head. "It can't be."

"Why not?"

"Because they just left."

"Yeah," he said. "And now they're back."

"How can you be sure?"

He smiled. "You'll see."

CHAPTER 51

By the time we reached the edge of the foyer, the front door was already open. I saw Jake standing in the open doorway, looking out at whoever had just rung the bell.

In a bored tone, he said, "Can I help you?"

Aunt Vivian's voice echoed off the walls. "Well, *someone's* gotta help us!"

"Yeah?" Jake said, looking oddly unconcerned. "Why's what?"

"Because," Aunt Vivian announced, "someone stole our car!"

"No kidding?" Jake said. "Wow, sucks to be you, huh?" And then, with a shrug, he began to shut the door, only to stop in mid-swing when the bottom of the door thudded against a stylish black pump, caked with mud.

Jake looked down at my aunt's foot. "Nice shoe. Where's the other one?"

"It's stuck in the mud!" Aunt Vivian yelled. "Not that *you* seem to care. So, are you gonna let us in or what?"

Jake stroked his chin, as if giving it some thought.

My aunt gave an exaggerated sigh. "Well?"

"I'm thinking," Jake said.

"About what?" she demanded.

"Breakfast."

After a long pause, she said, "What?"

"Yeah," he said. "You think it's too early?"

Aunt Vivian made a sound of frustration. "For what?"

"Waffles."

"Forget the waffles! Forget breakfast! Aren't you listening to me?"

"Not really."

"Oh, for God's sake," she muttered. "Where's my niece?"

I gave a resigned sigh. I guess that was my cue. I moved forward, only to stop in mid-step when I felt Joel's hand on my elbow. I turned and gave him a questioning look.

In a low voice, he said, "Wait."

"For what?" I whispered.

He smiled. "You ever see someone lose it before?"

I felt my brow wrinkle. "Lose it?"

He flicked his head toward the doorway. "I'll give it two minutes, three tops."

At the door, Aunt Vivian and Jake were still going back and forth. And with every exchange, my aunt was sounding more and more unhinged.

I looked back to Joel and whispered, "If you're talking about my aunt, she's *already* losing it."

The words had barely left my mouth when Aunt Vivian hollered out, "Forget the fucking waffles!"

I froze. I'd never heard my aunt curse before.

I gave Joel another questioning look. Did *that* qualify as losing it?

He made a low, scoffing sound. "That's nothing. You watch. In a minute, she'll be throwing things."

"How do you know?" I asked.

His gaze slid to Jake. "You gotta ask?"

I saw what he meant. The way it looked, Jake had a real knack for goading people. Even now, he was standing there, looking utterly unconcerned as my aunt raged and sputtered on the other side of the doorway.

I recalled what Jake had said earlier, about waiting for company. I edged closer to Joel and said, "Wait a minute. Did Jake *know* she was gonna show up?" I paused. "And did *you* know?"

Joel shrugged. "We figured the odds were good."

"Oh, my God," I said. "Did *you* steal their car?"

He looked ready to laugh. "No."

I closed my eyes and breathed a long sigh of relief.

And then he said, "Bishop did."

My eyes flew open. I stared up at Joel. He looked utterly serious. In a hushed voice, I said, "Let me get this straight. You're telling me, your brother stole their car?"

"Nah," Joel said. "He moved it. That's all."

Well, that was a relief.

I guess.

"To where?" I asked.

"Down the road." Joel smiled. "See? Not a big deal."

That's what *he* thought.

From the doorway, my aunt yelled, "Yeah? Well you can take those waffles and shove them up your ass!"

Jake said, "Sorry. Not my kink."

"What?" she sputtered.

Jake held up his hands, palms out. "Hey, I'm not judging."

"There's nothing to judge!"

"I'm just saying, what you and the leprechaun do is your own business."

"For the last time, he's *not* a leprechaun!"

Trying not to snicker, I leaned closer to Joel and asked, "How *far* down the road?"

"Not that far."

I gave a confused shake of my head. "But why?"

Joel looked to the door, and his voice hardened. "Because they had it coming."

I followed his gaze. My aunt's foot was *still* there, preventing the door from closing. If nothing else, I had to give her points for persistence.

Suddenly, my aunt hollered out, "Melody! I *know* you're in there!"

In front of her, Jake made a scoffing sound. "Dude, I'm not Melody."

Through gritted teeth, my aunt said, "I'm not a dude, and I *know* you're not Melody."

"Then why'd you call me that?"

"I didn't!"

"Yes, you did."

Her foot was still there. And then, it disappeared, pulled out of sight. A moment later, a familiar, muddy black pump flew through the partially open doorway, and splatted against the far wall before thudding to the floor in a messy clump.

I couldn't help it. I snickered.

Next to me, Joel said, "See?"

The sound of a car pulling into the driveway made all of us pause. Soon, I heard Officer Nelson's voice coming from just outside the front door, "We got a call about a stolen car?"

Aunt Vivian snapped, "Well, it sure took you long enough!"

I still couldn't see Officer Nelson, but I could hear him just fine. He told my aunt, "Sorry, I was on break."

She gave a derisive snort. "How nice for you."

"By the way," he said, "I found your car."

My aunt paused. "Really? Where?"

"A mile down the road. That way."

"But that's not where we parked."

"If you say so."

In a tight voice, she said, "I *know* so."

For the first time, I heard my uncle's voice. "*I* know so, too."

My aunt snapped, "Well goodie for you!"

Officer Nelson asked, "You want a ride?"

My aunt gave a loud sniff. "Well, we're certainly not going to *walk* there, are we?"

From inside the door, Jake said, "Hey, Officer."

"What?" Officer Nelson asked.

"You should probably hose 'em off first."

Aunt Vivian gasped. "What?"

Jake gave a loose shrug. "I'm just sayin'."

"Well, don't!" my aunt said. "I've had enough of hoses, thank you very much."

But outside the door, Officer Nelson said, "Hate to tell ya, but the guy's got a point."

Aunt Vivian paused. "What?"

"Sorry," Officer Nelson said. "City property and all."

My aunt gave a long-suffering sigh. "I don't believe this."

Officer Nelson asked, "So, you want the ride or not?"

"Oh, fine," my aunt muttered, "since this tattooed freak won't let us in."

Ignoring the insult, the freak-in-question pointed to something beside the porch. "There's the hose. Have at it."

A moment later, I heard stomping down the front steps, followed by the telltale sounds of water running, more bickering, and finally, car-doors slamming.

And then, at last, I heard the sound of a car – the police car, obviously – driving slowly away.

I felt myself smile. *Good riddance.*

CHAPTER 52

Standing in the entryway, I was still smiling. It was a funny thing, because in a way, I felt like I was exchanging one set of family members for another.

I was definitely trading up. I moved closer to Joel and whispered, "Oh c'mon, let's invite them to stay."

He stiffened, but said nothing.

From near the front door, Jake said, "Forget it."

Oh, crap. He *heard* that? I turned to face him. "But why?"

Jake's gaze shifted to Joel. "Don't worry," Jake said. "As soon as Bishop's back, we're outta here."

I spoke up. "But you can't leave."

"Oh yeah?" Jake said. "Why not?"

I gave him my sunniest smile. "Because we have news."

Jake's gaze strayed to my ring finger, where my new engagement ring sparkled in the foyer light. "It's not news to me," he said. "Good luck with that, by the way."

My smile wavered. "Shouldn't you be saying congratulations?"

"That depends," Jake said. "You really want to put up with him?"

"There's nothing to put up with," I said. "He's perfectly wonderful."

Almost in unison, both guys made a scoffing sound. And then, just as quickly, they both stopped to glower at each other.

I sighed. I would've killed for a brother. And what were they doing? Fighting over little stuff. It was time to end this. I said, "You know what? You guys don't know how lucky you are."

Joel reached out and pulled me close. "Me? I'm the luckiest guy around."

As sweet as that was, I forced myself to pull away. "I'm not talking about that." I looked from Jake to Joel and back again. "Like tonight, you guys backed each other up. Wasn't that nice?"

Joel's gaze shifted to his brother. "He wasn't being nice," Joel said. "He *likes* dicking with people."

I looked to Jake. He gave a loose shrug, and didn't deny it. And yet, under the surface, there was something there that I couldn't quite place. Somehow, I had the distinct impression that he cared more than he wanted to admit.

I looked to Joel and said, "Whether he likes it or not, it doesn't matter."

Joel's mouth tightened. "Is that so?"

"Definitely," I said. "He did me a huge favor, and not just tonight." I looked back to Jake and said, "I know I already thanked Luna, but seriously, thanks for the help with the sewer."

"I wasn't helping *you*," Jake said. "I was helping *me*. I had to send them *somewhere*." Under his breath, he added, "Better your place than mine."

I shook my head. "Sorry, but I don't believe that."

"Yeah? Why not?"

"Because," I said, "you could've sent them anywhere, like cripes, even on a vacation or something. And just so you know, they were really great." I felt a wistful smile cross my lips. "Luna's really lucky." I looked from Jake to Joel. "And you guys are, too."

Joel and Jake exchanged a look. I couldn't exactly read it, but it wasn't a look of brotherly love.

Switching gears, I turned back to Jake and said, "And about the sewer, I'll definitely pay you back." My face grew warm as I had to admit, "But it might take a while."

Joel spoke up. "No, it won't." He turned to me and said, "Tomorrow, we'll go to the bank and get that money."

I wasn't following. "What money?"

"From the safe deposit box."

Now, I knew which money he meant. He meant *his* money, in the form of all that cash that he'd been saving since who knows when.

I said, "But that's your money."

He shook his head. "It's *our* money. And I say we pay him back now, so we don't owe him anything."

"But we can't," I said.

"Why not?"

I smiled. "Because tomorrow's Sunday."

He didn't smile back. "So we'll write a check."

Jake's voice cut across the foyer. "Listen, dickweed. You don't *need* to write a check. I don't want your fucking money."

"Too bad," Joel told him, "because you're gonna get it. I'm not owing you anything." His jaw tightened. "And neither is she."

I made a sound of annoyance. "Oh, just stop it!"

Both guys turned to look. Joel said, "You mean him, right?"

"I mean both of you." Again, I heard myself sigh. This wasn't how I planned to do it, but if I didn't say something now, they'd probably be brawling in the entryway.

I looked to Joel and just blurted it out. "He didn't sleep with Sally."

Joel's eyebrows furrowed. "Who?"

"Sally," I repeated. "That whole thing was just a big lie to protect you." My voice softened. "To protect *all* of you."

Jake said, "Who's Sally?"

I turned to him and said, "Oh come on. You know who."

But the way it looked, he didn't. With something like a laugh, he said, "If I screwed someone named Sally, I think I'd remember."

I looked back to Joel. But from the look on his face, he didn't know who I meant either.

Feeling suddenly uncertain, I looked from brother to brother. They both shared a look, as if to say, *"Who the hell is she talking about?"*

I made a sound of frustration. "Oh, come on. *You* know. Your dad's girlfriend?"

For a long moment, neither one of them spoke. And then, Jake started to laugh.

I whirled to face him. "What's so funny?"

He was still laughing. "Oh, man. You're kidding, right?"

I felt my gaze narrow. Was he making fun of me? It sure felt like it. I looked back to Joel. To my extreme annoyance, he looked ready to laugh, too.

Well, this was just great. I was glaring now. "Whatever the joke is, could one of you *please* fill me in?"

Joel shoved a hand through his hair. "Well, the thing is, her name wasn't Sally."

I stared at him. That *was* the name he'd told me, right? I tried to think. Had Luna told me a different name? I couldn't be sure either way.

And then, it slowly dawned on me. "Oh." Already, my face was in flames. "So the Sally thing, that was just a word to go with—"

"Uh, yeah." Joel cleared his throat. "Sandpaper."

I lowered my voice. "So, what was her real name?"

Joel's mouth twitched at the corners. "Debbie."

"Oh." I tried to think. Sandpaper Debbie? Nope. Definitely not as catchy.

I looked back to Jake. He'd stopped laughing, but he still looked annoyingly amused.

I swallowed my embarrassment and gave him a stern look. "Go on, tell him."

Jake said, "Tell him what?"

"Tell him what really happened." I crossed my arms. "And why."

Jake's eyebrows lifted. "Shouldn't you wait 'til *after* you're married to give me grief?"

"I'm not giving you grief," I said. "I'm trying to clear up a misunderstanding."

Next to me, Joel said, "Sorry, but Jake admitted it. I *did* tell you that, right?"

"Yes," I said, using my overly patient voice, "but like I said, he was lying."

Joel shook his head. "He was not." He looked to Jake and said, "Go ahead. Tell her."

But Jake didn't. And the longer the silence stretched out, the less certainty I saw in Joel's eyes.

Finally, I broke the silence by saying, "He only said that to make your dad angry – and to get rid of Sally. I mean, Debbie."

Joel was still looking at Jake. In a careful voice, he said, "Why would he do that?"

"Because," I explained, "Debbie was always giving you grief, pushing you around and stuff. And Jake didn't like it."

Joel was staring now. As if thinking out loud, he said, "But dad was so pissed."

Jake shrugged. "Eh, big deal. He was always pissed."

Joel said, "At you."

I spoke up. "Right, because Jake, being the oldest, decided he'd rather have his dad, well I guess I mean your dad, too, beating on *him* rather than the rest of you."

Jake made a scoffing sound. "Beat on me? Get real. I could hold my own."

I gave Jake a look. He looked tough as nails now, but I couldn't help but wonder how he looked years ago. No doubt, he *had* to be tough.

I turned back to Joel. He was still looking at Jake. With a slow shake of his head, Joel asked, "And what about the other stuff?"

When Jake only shrugged, I said, "You mean the thing with that sports agent? It was like everything else. He was just looking out for you." Again, my voice softened. "Like a brother should."

After a long, intense moment, Joel asked Jake, "Is that true?"

Jake gave something like a shrug. "Hey, someone had to do it." He grinned. "Pussy."

I rolled my eyes. Neither one of them were pussies. And from the look on Joel's face, he took the remark the way it was intended – as a twisted sign of brotherly love.

Or maybe that was just wishful thinking on my part.

Behind Jake, the front door opened, and Bishop walked in. He looked to Jake. "You ready to go?"

Joel spoke up. "Hey, it's late. You guys wanna stay over?"

CHAPTER 53

Jake leaned back in his armchair. "Hey, I could make Gandhi hit me."

I couldn't help it. I laughed. I was sitting on the sofa in the front room, with Joel's arm draped over my shoulder. The arm felt nice, and I snuggled closer.

I felt nice, all warm and happy, in spite of all the previous drama.

A half-hour earlier, I'd retrieved another bottle of wine, along with two more glasses – one for Jake and one for Bishop, who was sitting in a neighboring armchair.

While filling their glasses, I'd also refilled mine and Joel's. My own wine had disappeared surprisingly quickly. But I couldn't blame *that* for the warm, happy sensation that had settled over me.

I was content for other reasons. It was the feel of Joel, pressed tight against me on the sofa. It was the sound of Jake, laughing at how insane he'd driven my aunt. It was the news from Bishop, that he'd already secured the pump house door, so no one would be breaking in – at least not in the near future.

He'd also mentioned that we'd need to rig up something more permanent, just to be safe.

It was the "we" that did me in. It made me feel misty all over again, especially when Joel told him, "I'll do it tomorrow." And then, he'd given my shoulders a comforting squeeze. "So don't worry, okay?"

It was funny. I wasn't worried. I felt like I had a family again.

I laughed with the three of them as Jake relayed a story about getting some sports star so angry that he beat up his own car. It was so insane that I had to wonder what, exactly, I was getting into.

Whatever it was, I couldn't help but love it. Did that make me crazy? Probably. But it was the best kind of crazy, because whatever came up, I wouldn't be facing it alone.

Across from us, Jake reached for his glass and took a long drink. He set it down on the side table and looked to Joel. "So, did you tell her yet?"

I looked to Joel. "Tell me what?"

Jake said, "He brought you a present."

I extended my hand and gazed at my ring, sparkling with the promise of an amazing future. It was one of the most beautiful things I'd ever seen. I gave a happy sigh. "I know. Isn't it wonderful?"

Jake made a scoffing sound. "Not that. Something else."

Confused, I looked back to Joel.

He gave me a crooked grin. "I was gonna tell you later, but—"

Jake said, "Screw later. I wanna see her reaction."

Now, I was dying to know. "My reaction to what?"

When neither one of them answered, I looked to Bishop and asked, "Do *you* know?"

He grinned. "I might."

I gave him a pleading look. "Well?"

It was Joel who finally answered. "We got a copy of the paperwork."

"What paperwork?" I asked.

"Everything," Joel said. "The will, the financials. You name it, we got it."

Was he saying what I thought he was saying? "You mean for the estate?"

Joel nodded. "Oh, yeah."

"Seriously? How'd *you* get that stuff? *I* don't even have it. Well, not most of it, anyway."

"I know," Joel said. "But you *should* have it."

No doubt, this was true. For months, I'd been asking for all of this. The only thing I ever received was the runaround. "But you didn't say, how'd you get it?"

"Trust me," Joel said, "you don't wanna know."

"Sure I do," I insisted.

He shook his head. "Better if you don't."

"Why?" I asked.

This time, it was Bishop who answered, "Because he didn't go through the normal channels to get it." Bishop glanced toward Joel and added, "He didn't want you involved. And he's right."

When I looked to Joel, he didn't dispute any of this. "If someone asks," he said, "you don't know a thing."

I felt my brow wrinkle. "But who would ask?"

His voice hardened. "Guess."

Oh. Of course. "Derek."

"*And* his dad," Joel said. "You know he's got a place in Bermuda, right?"

I shook my head. "Actually, I *didn't* know."

"Well, he does," Joel said, "And let's just say he had all kinds of interesting stuff there."

"Wait," I said. "So *that's* where you were? Bermuda?"

He shrugged. "That and other places."

"Like where?"

"Remember that lawyer I mentioned?"

I nodded. "The one from Troy? Did you see him?"

"Oh, yeah."

I leaned forward. "Did he look at the paperwork?"

Joel shook his head. "That's for you to decide. It is *your* stuff, right?" He grinned. "But the guy's chomping at the bit if you're interested."

I *was* interested, but I wasn't sure how we were going to manage it. I lowered my voice. "Can we afford him?"

"Probably not," Joel said. "But he's already been paid for the first look."

I felt my brow wrinkle. "What do you mean 'the first look'?"

"To go through the paperwork, see what's there."

"But how was he paid?" I asked. "I didn't pay him."

"Like I told you before," Joel said, "he owes me a favor."

I frowned. "It must've been *some* big favor."

Joel shrugged. "Nah, it was nothing."

Somehow, I wasn't so sure. But whatever the favor was, I didn't want it to be for nothing. I said, "And he's ready to get started?"

Joel nodded. "Don't you know it. And as far as the legal fees, if he sees a good case, we'll work something out."

I tensed. "Like another favor?"

"Sure, why not?"

"No." I tried to laugh. "No more favors, okay?"

"Alright, so we'll pay him," Joel said. "Not a big deal. We've got that money, right?"

"In the safe deposit box? But that's your money."

"No. It's *our* money, like I keep telling you."

In the end, we agreed that we'd give the lawyer the paperwork and take it from there.

Across from us, Jake said, "Hey Joel."

Joel turned to look. "Yeah?"

"Maybe you should marry her now. You know, like tonight."

I had to laugh. "Why tonight?"

"Because," Jake told me, "if you end up loaded, you won't want to slum it with a guy like him."

I rolled my eyes. "Oh, shut up."

Next me, Joel said, "You know. He *does* have a point."

When I turned to look, his eyes were filled with mischief. Still, I gave him a playful shove. "Oh, stop it," I told him. "Maybe *you're* the one who's slumming it."

At this, his brothers laughed. I turned and tried, unsuccessfully, to glare at them. "Hey, you never know."

When I turned back to Joel, something in his expression had softened. He leaned his head close to mine and said, "Hey, *I* know what I have. And if I could, I'd marry you tonight."

I felt a giant smile spread across my face. "Well, it's kind of late tonight, but I'm free next Saturday."

Now, Joel was grinning, too. "You serious?"

I gave it some thought. *Was I? Yes, definitely.* But I didn't want to push him into anything, especially if he was just kidding around. I said, "That depends. Are you?"

"Hell yeah." But then, his expression turned serious. "But if you want to do the big wedding thing, I'm up for that, too. Whatever you want."

I gave it some thought. Crazy or not, I didn't want a big wedding. All my life, I'd been the center of attention. A lot of that attention has been unwanted, especially where the media was concerned.

If I had *my* way, I'd get married in a private ceremony, right here on the estate, with Aunt Gina and only a few of my closest friends – and of course, anyone Joel wanted to invite.

In my own jumbled way, I tried to tell him this without sounding like a total babbling idiot.

When I finished, Joel was smiling again. He turned to his brothers and said, "Got any plans for next Saturday?"

CHAPTER 54

The room was dark and quiet, with tiny slivers of moonlight filtering in through the open blinds. "You know," Joel teased, "if I get you pregnant, you'll *have* to marry me."

Laughing, I rolled my eyes. "Not *this* again."

In the four days since his return, it had become a recurring a joke. But in spite of my feigned protest, I never grew tired of hearing it – or, of trying to make the joke a reality.

Who knows? Maybe it was already reality, given the fact that we'd been in and out of bed, along with other places, pretty much non-stop since his return.

Now, we'd just gotten out of a bath for two and were lying naked across my fresh sheets, with the ceiling fan, turned on low, wafting a nice, cool breeze across our warm, glistening skin.

The last few days had been a whirlwind of secret planning and getting the house ready for guests. In just three short days, we were going to be married out on the back patio, overlooking Lake Michigan.

Oh sure, it was December, and snow wasn't completely out of the question. But we'd splurged on a few patio heaters and were definitely planning to use them. And if we got a little chilly? So what? The way I saw it, it would make everything that much sweeter when we returned to the house and gathered around the main fireplace for cake and warm cider.

Unconventional? Probably. But it was what I wanted, and I couldn't regret a thing – especially the guy I'd be marrying.

Aunt Gina was flying in from France, and a few of my closest friends, Cassie in particular, had been sworn to secrecy, even as I frantically worked to finalize all the arrangements.

Two of the guests had already arrived – Steve and Anthony, who had shown up early to help repair the lawn – and to snag any pizza or beer that happened to cross their path.

This time, they weren't staying in the guest house, but rather in one of the guest rooms downstairs – a big one, where they'd have plenty of space to fling dirty laundry, hide beer, and argue over Kung fu.

I'd also been talking to the lawyer from Troy. From what he'd told me on the phone, he was still sifting through all of the details, but already, I knew a lot more than I'd ever known before.

Happily, the news was better than I dared to hope. All of my parents' money was still there, tied up in a trust that was practically unbreakable.

Oh sure, I wouldn't have access to the actual funds until I turned twenty-five, but in the meantime, there were plenty of things I could do to protect myself – starting with moving the estate-management away from Derek's dad.

Already, the new lawyer was working on the necessary paperwork. If things went smoothly – which he assured me they would – I'd soon have Derek and his dad out of my hair forever.

Still, I couldn't help but be at least a little nervous.

Even here, in my quiet bedroom, lying next to the guy I loved, I wasn't blind to the possibility of a long, nasty court battle. I turned to Joel and said, "About the estate thing, what do you think will happen if Derek's dad fights it?"

Joel reached out and pulled me close. "Don't worry. He won't."

"But how can you be so sure?"

"Just trust me, okay?"

It was the same thing he always said when I brought it up. "It's not that I don't trust you," I said. "It's just that I don't see him giving up without a fight."

Joel ran a soothing hand along my naked back. "Baby, the fight's already won, so stop worrying, alright?"

"Believe me, I *want* to," I said. "But you don't know them like I do."

"You think so, huh?"

I pulled back to ask, "What does *that* mean?"

After a long pause, Joel said, "Alright. Let's just say this. The dad? I met him in Bermuda."

"What?" I gave Joel a playful shove. "But you never told me."

"Yeah." He pulled me back into his arms. "And I wasn't gonna."

"Why not?"

"Because you had enough to worry about."

It was a sweet sentiment, even if I couldn't quite agree with it. "So why are you telling me now?"

"Because I want you to *stop* worrying. So let it go, okay?"

"But just tell me. What happened?"

"Nothing big," Joel said. "We had a talk. That's all."

I wasn't quite sure I believed him. "What *kind* of talk?"

"The guy's a bully," Joel said. "So we bullied him back. Not a big deal."

Not a big deal, huh? I asked, "What'd you do?"

"Nothing he didn't deserve."

I couldn't decide if I felt concerned or relieved. Pushing *that* question aside, I said, "But aren't you worried you'll get in trouble?"

"Hell no," Joel said. "With all *he's* done? He got off light, and he damn well knows it."

I wasn't so sure. "But what if he stops knowing it?"

"Then we'll remind him."

"But—"

Joel laughed. "Forget it." He pulled me closer and planted a kiss on my forehead. "It's gonna be alright. You'll see."

Desperately, I wanted to believe him. He sounded so sure. And yet, I wasn't blind to the fact that my twenty-fifth birthday was still nearly four years away. A lot could happen in that timeframe. And the estate needed a ton of repairs. Somehow, I'd have to find the money – and soon.

Even with Joel's help, it would be a huge financial challenge.

On a more positive note, I'd finalized all of the paperwork for

Joel's art endowment, and after an initial period of disbelief, he seemed to finally accept that he'd won on his own merit. After the wedding, we were going to finish setting up the studio above the garage, so Joel could paint whenever inspiration struck.

Based on what I'd seen so far, inspiration would never be in short supply. Somehow, I just knew that Joel would follow in my dad's footsteps and take the art world by storm.

I smiled in the near darkness. It felt like a circle of life, completed in a happier way than I'd ever thought possible.

Joel's voice, quiet in the darkened room, interrupted my thoughts. "Maybe I should try again."

"Try what?"

"To get you pregnant."

And just like that, any remaining worries faded into the background. I felt my lips curve into a smile. "So *that's* what you've been doing?"

"Well, that and other things." His tone grew teasing. "I mean, it can't be *all* work."

I had to laugh. "Oh, stop it."

"You think I'm kidding?"

"I don't know," I said. "Are you?"

"Hang on," he said.

"For what?"

"This."

CHAPTER 55

Almost before I knew it, I was flipped on my back with him on top of me. I stifled a giggle. "Hey! What was that?"

"Wrestling move," he said.

I was still laughing. "You wrestle?"

"I do *now*," he said. "So what do you want? A boy or a girl?"

I smiled against his bare shoulder. "Both."

The sheets were twisted around us, but I wasn't going to let *that* stop anything. With a quiet laugh, I kicked the sheets aside, sending them falling away to who-knows-where.

Already, I could feel his hardness pressing against my hip, hinting at the promise of what I wanted.

He shifted slightly to the side and reached between us, grazing the intersection of my thighs. Almost on instinct, I felt my legs part, opening myself to more of whatever he was thinking.

And what *I* was thinking, too.

With a smile in his voice, he said, "You're beautiful, you know that?"

Everything – his words, his touch, and just the fact that he was here at all – had me wondering, and for the first time, how I'd gotten so very lucky.

He was beautiful, too – not just on the outside, but every inch of him. With this thought in mind, I reached out, taking his hardness into my hand. "I know lots of things," I said, giving his length a long, smooth stroke.

With a muffled moan, he said, "Yeah? Like what?"

Already, his fingers had zeroed in on my favorite spot, and I let my eyelids flutter shut. "I know that I love you."

"I love you, too," he said, touching me in that special way of his. "I did almost from the start, you know."

I *didn't* know. I was still stroking him, loving the feel of him, hard and ready, in my grip. And yet, I *had* to tease him, just a little. With my eyes still shut, I asked, "Are you sure? Because I'm pretty sure it was *me* chasing after *you*."

He was still touching me. I was still touching him. In a teasing tone, he replied, "You think so, huh?"

Did I? In truth, I was finding it hard to think at all. I could feel my slickness, welcoming his touch more urgently now. Breathlessly, I admitted, "I'm not sure I *can* think."

"Yeah?" His fingers moved in a slow leisurely circle, making my breath catch and mind go fuzzy. In a tone filled with sin, he asked, "Why not?"

I felt my hips rise, seeking more of whatever he was offering. I confessed, "Because I want you inside me."

His fingertips drifted back and forth, making my hips move and my pulse jump. In a tone that was almost teasing, he said, "Now?"

A whimper of need escaped my lips. "Yes."

He slipped a finger inside me, even as his thumb continued to entice that special spot. "How's that?"

It was absolutely wonderful, but it wasn't the thing I'd been desperately craving. And yet, I had to smile. "You *know* what I meant."

"Oh yeah?" Another finger joined the first. "What?"

I was still stroking him. I knew beyond a single doubt that he wanted *me* just as much as I wanted *him*. His hardness throbbed against my fingers, making me long to feel his hardness somewhere else.

I just had to ask, "How can you wait?"

"I love watching you." As he talked, he moved his fingers in a way that soon, had my hips surging upward, seeking more of his touch. "And," he whispered, "I want you good and ready."

I almost whimpered, "I'm ready *now*." I gave him another smooth stroke and felt myself smile when a sound of pleasure escaped his lips.

"And you're ready, too."

"Yeah, I am," he said. "But admit it. You love this."

He was right. I did. But the urge to have him, *really* have him, was growing so strong, that the idea of waiting was impossible to consider.

My breath was coming faster now. I said, "Maybe I'll flip *you* over, so I'm on top."

"Yeah? Just try it."

I did. Sort of.

Nothing happened. But it really wasn't my fault. His touch was magic, and the idea of moving away from it, even for an instant, was making it hard to do much of anything.

I was such a goner.

He gave a low chuckle. "See?"

I opened my eyes, and I *did* see – the guy I loved, looking at me like I was everything he'd ever wanted.

I had to smile. The way it looked, he was a goner, too.

With our gazes locked, he finally gave in and moved closer, covering my body with his own. Soon, it wasn't his fingers teasing me to distraction, but the tip of his hardness, poised to give me what I'd been craving.

And then, a moment later, he was surging into me, just as I was rising up to meet *him*. As we moved together, I felt full and happy in a way I might've considered impossible just a few months earlier.

I reached up and ran my hands along his back, loving the feel of his muscles shifting and moving as he drove into me, harder and faster as I rose up to meet him again and again.

And then, with a kiss so intense, it felt out of this world, we reached our peak together and practically collapsed in a breathless, happy heap.

I didn't want to move, and the way it looked, neither did he, so we held each other for a long, blissful moment, letting the night settle around us as our breathing slowed and something like sanity returned.

A few minutes later, we were still lying there when his lips brushed my ear, and he whispered, "Don't move."

I wasn't *planning* on moving. Still, I whispered back, "Why?"

"You *know* why."

At this, I had to smile. I *did* know why. A moment later, I felt his hand brush across my cheek. He said, "I hope they take after you."

I was still smiling. "They?"

"You said you wanted both." His tone grew teasing. "So I was going for twins."

And of course, I had to tease him right back. "Only twins? Not triplets? Or quadruplets?" I might've gone on, but for the life of me, I couldn't recall the next in the series.

"Quadruplets, huh? Well, you *do* have a big house."

I shook my head against his shoulder. "No. *We* have a big house."

This felt like a dream. But it wasn't. I lifted my hand from his back and gazed at the engagement ring, barely visible in the shadows.

But I didn't have to see it to know. It really *was* beautiful. And yet, I couldn't help but wonder how Joel had managed it. I couldn't stop myself from saying, "If I ask you something, will you promise to not be offended?"

He pulled back to smile down at me. "Now?" he said. "I don't think you could offend me if you tried."

Deciding to take him at his word, I asked the question that had been drifting in and out of my brain for the last few days. "How could you afford this? The ring, I mean." Quickly, I added, "I really, *really* love it. But I know I had all your money…" I gave a shaky laugh. "… so I'm wondering if you had to sell a kidney or something."

Sounding not offended at all, he said, "You didn't have *all* the money."

Now, *that* surprised me. In my sleepy, blissful state, I couldn't recall the exact amount in the safe deposit box, but I *did* know that it was over fifty thousand dollars. I said, "So there was more?"

"Oh, yeah."

"How much more?"

"The other half."

"Wait a minute," I said, feeling almost awake now. "Are you telling me you had *another* fifty thousand dollars?"

"Give or take. But there was no way I was turning *that* over."

"Why not?"

"Because I didn't want you telling me that I was spending too much."

I considered the timetable. He'd given me that cash before Derek's threat had driven us apart, before the moving truck, before the parking lot, before all of that.

In a tone of utter disbelief, I said, "Wait a minute. Does that mean you were planning this before that whole moving truck fiasco?"

"I wasn't just planning it," he said, "I'd already picked out some rings."

"Some rings?"

"Well, I figured you might want to pick your favorite."

It was so crazy that I couldn't help but smile. "Actually, I didn't *have* to, because *you* did. I absolutely love it." My voice softened. "And you know what?"

"What?"

"I would've married you, even without a ring."

Now, he sounded insulted, sort of. "The hell you would've."

"I'm serious."

"Yeah? Me, too."

I wasn't going to argue. I loved him. He loved me. So there, in the moonlit room, I drifted off to sleep with love in my heart and a smile on my face.

Somehow, everything was going to work out perfectly. I just knew it.

CHAPTER 56

The next morning, I was still asleep in Joel's arms when the pounding on the bedroom door started. I burrowed closer to him and mumbled, "If we ignore it, will they go away?"

"Those guys?" Joel sounded ready to laugh. "What do *you* think?"

The door-pounders were Steve and Anthony, who had just informed us through the locked bedroom door that someone was here to see us.

Who it was, I had no idea. But I *did* know that being naked in the arms of my future husband was a million times sweeter than anything outside this bed.

Again, the knocking sounded, followed by Steve's voice. "Hey! You're not still asleep in there, are you?"

I turned my face into Joel's chest and groaned, "I think I'm gonna kill him."

A moment later, Anthony's voice called, "Hey! If you don't come out, we're coming in!"

With a sigh, I flopped onto my back and yelled, "Oh, for God's sake, we're still asleep!"

"You're not asleep," Steve said. "I can hear you yelling."

I turned to Joel. "You've known them longer. Shouldn't *you* be dealing with this?"

He grinned. "Hell no."

"Why not?"

"Because I'd toss 'em down the stairs. And you'd be mad at me."

"I would not."

He was still grinning. "Liar."

"Oh, alright," I muttered. With a sigh, I sat up and called out, "Who is it?"

"It's Steve!"

"And Anthony!" In a lower voice, Anthony said, "Damn. You think she'd know our voices by now."

"Well," Steve said, "pregnancy *will* do that to ya."

"No kidding?"

"Eh, I dunno."

I hollered out, "I didn't mean at the *bedroom* door. I meant at the *front* door."

Steve called back, "Then you should've said so!"

Anthony called out, "It's some lawyer. He says it's important."

Suddenly, I was wide awake. And so was Joel.

Fifteen minutes later, we were dressed in casual clothes and sitting in the den, across from the lawyer. He was a big, dark-haired guy wearing a flashy business suit that probably cost more than Joel and I were spending on our entire wedding.

Then again, that wasn't saying much.

I looked to the lawyer and confessed, "I've got to admit, I'm a little surprised to see you." I smiled. "Not that I'm complaining or anything."

"Oh, trust me," he said with a smile that dwarfed my own. "When I'm done, you're not gonna be complaining about anything."

"Why?" I asked.

"I've been pouring through all the particulars, and it turns out, you won't have to wait 'til you're twenty-five to fully inherit."

"Really?" I said. "Why not?"

"Well, once I got digging, I found all kinds of interesting sub-clauses. You said you're what, a year away from getting your degree?"

I nodded. "Yeah, but I had to drop out to take care of estate stuff."

And, because I had no money.

"Well, if I were you," the lawyer said, "I'd get back to school pronto."

I gave a confused shake of my head. "Why?"

"Because once you graduate, you get full control."

No way. Joel and I exchanged a look. Under his breath, Joel said, "Those pricks."

I knew which pricks he meant – Derek and his dad. I was almost too stunned for words. "So *that's* why they made it impossible for me to go."

I turned back to the lawyer and explained how several months earlier, all of my college funds had suddenly dried up, forcing me to drop out.

The lawyer nodded. "Eh, gotta hand it to 'em. It was a good plan."

"It was not," I said. "It was horrible."

The lawyer reached up to tug at his tie. "Yeah, well, I meant in the professional sense."

Yup, he was ruthless, alright. And horrified or not, I was glad to have him on my side. I looked to Joel and said, "Well, it looks like I'm going back to school."

The lawyer laughed. "Or, you could always get married."

In unison, Joel and I both turned to look. At the exact same time, we said, "What?"

"Married," the lawyer repeated. "Didn't I mention?"

I was staring at him now. "No."

"Oh. Sorry. That was the other thing. Lemme back up. There are three ways you can get control of the money." He held up a single finger. "One, you can turn twenty-five." He shrugged. "You gotta wait for that one."

He held up a second finger. "Two. You can graduate from college. If you need a quickie degree, lemme know. I've got a few contacts."

He held up a third finger. "Or, you can get married." With a chuckle, he looked to Joel and said, "You seem to like her. You up for the job?"

From the look on Joel's face, he didn't know whether to kiss the guy or toss him out the front door. All this time, we'd been holding hands. I looked down. Joel's hand was closed over mine, hiding the ring from view.

With a laugh, I pulled my hand from Joel's and waggled my fingers for the lawyer to see. His gaze zoomed in on the ring. "Nice rock." He looked to Joel. "That from you?"

I spoke up. "Yes, in fact. It's a really big secret, but we're, uh, actually getting married this Saturday."

"Damn," the lawyer said, getting to his feet. "I guess I'd better get to work."

I had to laugh. "I guess you'd better."

On his way out the door, the lawyer promised to have a bunch of paperwork for me to sign on Monday.

I said, "But wait, won't Derek's dad have to sign everything over?"

The lawyer frowned. "Who's Derek's dad?"

"Sorry," I said, "I meant Mister Mitchell."

"Oh, don't worry about him," the lawyer said. "He's been signing anything I put in front of him."

I almost couldn't imagine. "Really?"

"Yeah," the lawyer said. "Gotta give the guy credit, too."

I wasn't sure what he meant. "Why?" I asked.

"You know, because of the broken arm."

I *didn't* know. I gave a confused shake of my head. "He broke his arm?"

"Yeah. Some accident in Bermuda." The lawyer grinned. "A damn shame, huh?"

When I gave Joel a sideways glance, he reached up to rub the back of his neck. "Uh. Yeah," he said. "A shame."

The lawyer was still grinning. "Not just a shame. A *damn* shame." And then, whistling a happy tune, he was soon gone.

CHAPTER 57

The day of the wedding dawned clear and bright, with sunny skies and almost no breeze at all. Around me, the house was bustling with activity, minus the one person I was most longing to see.

I hadn't seen Joel in almost two whole days – not since he'd left to stay in the guest house with his brothers and a few of his friends, including Cal. The arrangement had been my idea – something to honor the age-old tradition of not seeing each other until the actual wedding. But already, I was going crazy missing him.

Happily, I wasn't lonely in the least. The house was bursting with family of the old *and* new variety. Aunt Gina had arrived two days earlier, followed by Luna and her sister, and finally, Cassie, along with my closest friends from high school.

Throughout all of this, Luna's brothers roamed the house freely, in search of – in their words – cake and free beer. Oh sure, they could *claim* that was their motivation for sticking around the house, but in my heart, I knew it was more than that. A blossoming family relationship? Yes. *And* Steve's determination to tease me about being pregnant.

Was I pregnant? Maybe. I hoped so with all my heart. The house was huge, and now that I felt more certain of keeping it, I wanted to fill it with everything that I'd lost – the sounds of laughter, the aroma of pie, and the knowledge that no matter what, Joel and I would weather whatever storms came our way.

To everyone's surprise except my own, Joel had asked Jake to be his best man, and although Cassie was my maid of honor, I invited Luna to be a bridesmaid – partly to keep Jake focused on the actual wedding and also because I had a sneaky suspicion that Luna – and maybe her sister, too – would be part of the big family that I'd been longing to have.

Speaking of family, a better person might've invited my Uncle Ernie and Vivian to share in the festivities. But I didn't, and not only because they'd surely be unpleasant. I mean, seriously, who wants to spend their own wedding day keeping a watchful eye on the good china?

Not me. That was for sure.

I had something better to keep my eye on, and his name was Joel, the guy who made my life complete in too many ways to count.

Just after noon, with me in my mom's wedding dress and Joel in a borrowed tux, we said "I do" overlooking the endless waters of Lake Michigan, surrounded by everyone we loved best – even if all of them were a little crazy.

But that was family, right?

EPILOGUE
One Year Later

I couldn't be sure of the *exact* moment it happened, but just over nine months later, all of that so-called work paid off, when Joel and I welcomed into this world Braydon Joel Bishop – the first of what we both hoped would be a whole houseful of kids.

Shortly after our marriage, the lawyer had made all of his happy predictions come true by transferring estate-management, not to another law firm, but directly to me and Joel.

As far as the money itself, except for what was needed for critical home repairs, most of it was still in the trust, where it kept growing under the watchful eye of a new, and extremely good, financial manager.

And even if that weren't the case, Joel and I wouldn't have been hurting for money. At Joel's premiere art show, demand for his paintings was so high, the gallery owners practically had to sell tickets.

His most popular painting? A new mother who looked an awful lot like me. And yes, I *did* buy that one, even if I did have to bid like crazy to get it.

Between a new marriage, a new baby, and a new outlook on life, I was busy in the best possible way. Already, the house was in a lot better shape, which was a very good thing, because our family – which included our crazy extended family – was filling the house with everything that had been missing.

I never did finish my art history degree. Who knows? Maybe I would someday, but for now, I was happy *making* art history with the guy I loved.

THE END

Other Books by Sabrina Stark
(Listed by Couple)

Lawton & Chloe
Unbelonging (Unbelonging, Book 1)

Rebelonging (Unbelonging, Book 2)

Lawton (Lawton Rastor, Book 1)

Rastor (Lawton Rastor, Book 2)

Bishop & Selena
Illegal Fortunes

Jake & Luna
Jaked (Jaked Book 1)

Jake Me (Jaked, Book 2)

Jake Forever (Jaked, Book 3)

ABOUT THE AUTHOR

Sabrina Stark writes edgy romances featuring plucky girls and the bad boys who capture their hearts.

She's worked as a fortune-teller, barista, and media writer in the aerospace industry. She has a journalism degree from Central Michigan University and is married with one son and a pack of obnoxiously spoiled kittens. She currently makes her home in Northern Alabama.

ON THE WEB

Printed in Great Britain
by Amazon